CRISIS ZERO

CRISIS ZER

WALDEN POND PRESS

An Imprint of HarperCollinsPublishers

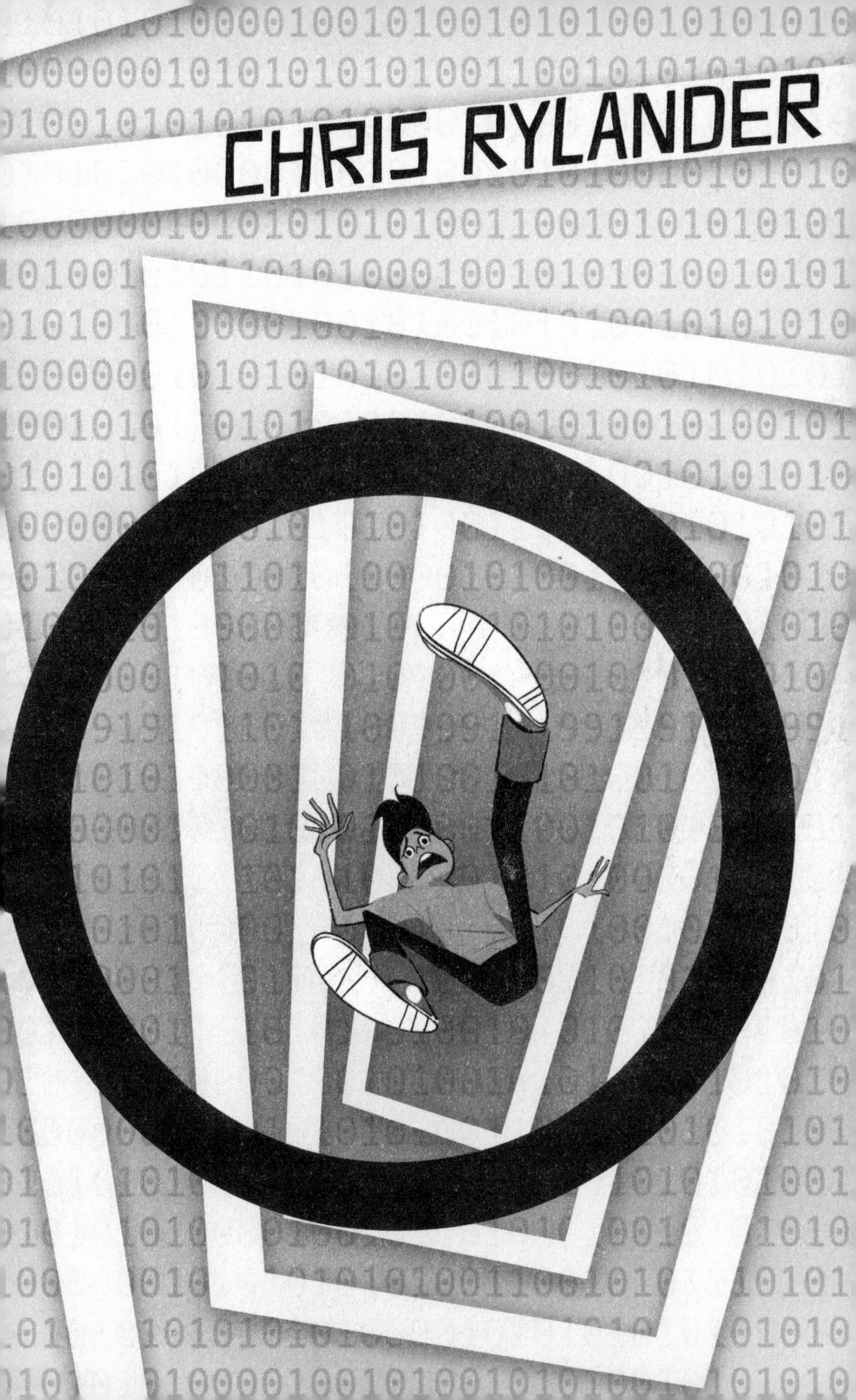
CHRIS RYLANDER

Walden Pond Press is an imprint of HarperCollins Publishers.
Walden Pond Press and the skipping stone logo are trademarks and registered
trademarks of Walden Media, LLC.

Crisis Zero

Library of Congress Control Number: 2015943573
ISBN 978-0-06-232747-5

Typography by Michelle Gengaro-Kokmen
15 16 17 18 19   CG/RRDH   10 9 8 7 6 5 4 3 2 1
❖
First Edition

For my mom

0001010101010101010011001010101010101010101
1010101010100001010010101010010101010
0101000010010100101010010101010101010
0001010101010101001100   10101
0101011010100010010   0100
0101000010010100101   CHAPTER 1   010
0001010101010101011   101

PRINCIPAL STREET-FIGHTING TOURNAMENTS

"**W**HAT IS THE MEANING OF THIS?" PRINCIPAL GOMEZ shouted at the men who had just barged into his office.

I had been four seconds away from getting expelled from middle school, and so I can't say this interruption was an unwelcome one. But I still wasn't sure if I should be happy or scared to see four dudes who looked like secret agents surrounding me. After all, I was something of a secret agent myself (codename: Zero). It's a long story, but the point is, it takes one to know one—and these guys definitely weren't just members of the school board or a group of angry rival principals here to partake in a Principal Street-Fighting Tournament.

One of the men held out a badge.

"Mr. Gomez, I'm Agent Loften, National Security Bureau," he said. "You're under arrest on suspicion of treason, terrorism, espionage, and activities deemed dangerous to the United States of America."

My jaw swung open and I looked at Mr. Gomez in shock. He met my stare but said nothing. Was his lack of a reaction an admission of guilt? Or was he simply as confused as I was? I couldn't be sure. But I did know I was pretty relieved knowing that the agents weren't there for me.

"Son," another NSB agent said, putting his hand on my shoulder, "we're going to have to ask you to go back to class now."

I nodded without saying anything and stood up. Mr. Gomez's wide, unblinking eyes never left me as I backed out of his office in a daze.

"But he's expelled," Mr. Gomez mumbled. "He's finally getting expelled."

The NSB agents ignored him as if he wasn't even speaking at all.

Just as I was leaving the office, I saw Agent Loften

placing handcuffs on Mr. Gomez. Then I was out in the hallway, still too stunned to do anything but just stand there and stare at the now closed administration office door.

Could my bungling principal, Mr. Gomez, really have been an enemy agent all this time? That didn't seem possible. But then again, me becoming a secret agent and saving the world twice in less than a few months wouldn't have seemed possible at the start of seventh grade, either. Yet that's exactly what had happened, so I really couldn't rule out anything.

The one thing I did know was that the sudden arrest of my principal by the National Security Bureau had to somehow be related to the government agency I worked for, the one so top secret that its name was classified even to its own operatives. The agency with headquarters miles underground, right below my school. The very one who I'd now helped thwart the plans of an evil psychopath and former agent named Mule Medlock twice. Most recently by preventing him from getting a deadly virus called Romero that could have ushered in a near apocalyptic outbreak.

Either way, I knew I'd find out eventually. And I also suspected I'd once again find myself mixed up with whatever was going on. That just seemed to be how things worked for me.

I'm Carson Fender, aka the retired Prank Master, aka Agent Zero, aka both the World's Greatest Hero and Screw-up, all in one, and I always seem to find myself smack-dab in the middle of trouble one way or another.

I couldn't see why this would turn out any differently.

010010101010101010100110010101010101010101010
1010101010100000101001010101001010101010
0101000010010100101010010101010101010101
000101010101010100110001010101010101010101010
010101101010001001010101010101011001
01010000100101001010101010101010101

CHAPTER 2

THE ARBY'S INTERROGATION

I WASN'T QUITE SURE WHAT TO DO AT FIRST. MR. GOMEZ HAD brought me down to his office to expel me from school. He'd made that much very clear. Was I still expelled now that he'd been arrested? Should I go back to class? Or just keep standing there in the hallway until I got trampled during the period break?

Going back to class ultimately seemed like the best option. Maybe if I just went to social studies class like normal and pretended nothing was wrong, it would be like nothing at all unusual had happened that morning.

Nobody would even know I was technically supposed to be expelled.

So that's what I did. I simply went back to class.

But acting normal was harder than I expected. I didn't remember a single word anybody said to me the rest of the morning. I was too busy thinking about Principal Gomez. About the possibility that he was actually a secret agent. That he had been the entire time I had been working for the Agency. Could it be a coincidence?

By lunchtime, the news had gotten out. Several classrooms had gotten a front row view out their windows of the NSB putting a handcuffed Mr. Gomez into the back of a black sedan that morning. Though nobody seemed to quite have all of the facts right. Take my best friend, Dillon, for instance. He greeted me at our usual table with his own theory on why Mr. Gomez had been taken away in handcuffs.

"I knew he'd get caught eventually!" Dillon said excitedly as I sat down in between him and his twin sister, Danielle.

She gave me a look that said she also suspected this was related to the Agency somehow. During my last mission, she had intervened and saved me and my mentor, Agent Nineteen (and in doing so, the world). As a result, the Agency also brought her in to work for them. Her codename was Atlas. Given the fact that we had known each other our entire lives and the fact that we were the only ones each of us could really trust, I couldn't think of a better partner to have.

"Get caught doing what?" I asked.

"Mr. Gomez was an alien in hiding," Dillon said, his voice lowering to show he was serious. "And those men in black suits were the Men in Black."

"Like from the Will Smith movies?" our friend Ethan asked. "That's not very original."

"No, not like in the movies," Dillon said as if this was the most obvious fact in the world. "Well, I mean, sort of like the movies. Hollywood has to get inspiration from somewhere. But that movie is not at all what the *real* Men in Black are like!"

Most kids would think Dillon was just joking around, but we all knew better. That was the thing about Dillon; he had a crazy conspiracy theory for everything. To him, the world was never as it seemed. Everyone we met had a hidden agenda, everything we saw was hiding something. An apple falling from a tree on a summer day wasn't just an apple falling from a tree. To him, that was surely the start of the Great Apple Rebellion. The beginning of a war in which genetically altered apples finally rise up against their human slavers and take over the world. Yes, this is actually something he said once when we saw an apple fall to the ground in a park last summer.

"An alien, huh?" I said. "Isn't that a little cliché? My principal is an alien. I think there's already, like, fourteen books, movies, and TV shows out with that same plot."

"Well, see, that's the thing," Dillon said, his voice rising again as he got more excited about his theory. "That's the point! That's what they *want* you to believe."

"So he's not an alien, then?" Danielle asked.

All of Dillon's friends, his sister especially, knew it was just better to humor him and let him get it all out rather than try to argue logically or reason with him.

"Of course not!" Dillon nearly shouted, getting so worked up he was standing now. "That'd be ridiculous. In reality, Principal Gomez is a Galaxy Ranger, and the men in suits were enemy aliens just *disguised* as Men in Black. Right now, as we speak, old Gomez is probably being tortured in some secret alien lair. I bet it's the Arby's. I always knew there was something off about the Arby's on Buchanan Street. You know what I mean."

Normally I'd have laughed at Dillon's theory. Usually I found them funny. But this time, since I actually suspected that I sort of knew the truth behind Gomez getting arrested, or at least part of the truth, I was too worried about what it all might mean to play along.

But I forced a laugh anyway, so Dillon wouldn't suspect that I knew more than I did.

"You know, most kids just think he was arrested by the FBI for drug smuggling or something," Danielle said.

"Most kids are wrong," Dillon said quietly, sitting down again. "As usual."

"I agree with Dillon," our friend Katie chimed in. "I kind of like the idea of Mr. Gomez getting his face sliced off by an Arby's roast beef machine."

"I heard it was just unpaid parking tickets," our friend Adie said. "Hundreds of them."

"Secret agent–looking dudes don't show up in black SUVs to arrest people for unpaid parking tickets," Zack countered.

"Yeah, if there are, like, a thousand of them, they do," Adie shot back.

And so started our table's debate over what had happened to Mr. Gomez—very likely mirroring what was happening at every single table in the school cafeteria at that moment. But the truth was that I wasn't really listening to them. Instead, I was focused on my school lunch.

Not on actually eating it of course, that'd be gross. I was more interested in searching for a secret message. That's how the Agency contacted me at school: secret messages from Agent Chum Bucket snuck into my school lunch. And I'd say our own principal getting arrested for being some sort of secret agent merited some sort of message. Was Gomez really an enemy agent? Can we be sure those guys in suits were even with the NSB? Had the Agency framed Gomez to keep me from getting expelled?

I focused on my lasagna, sure there was going to be a message inside it from the Agency. The other kids at the table were probably wondering what the heck I was doing with my lunch, but I didn't care. I needed answers.

After completely dismantling it, I found nothing but thick, gooey noodles, orange sauce, and a white paste that somehow passed for cheese. No information from the Agency whatsoever. And there was no way I could just go ask either of my two mentors, Agent Nineteen or Agent Blue, who normally doubled as teachers at the school for their covers. They hadn't been back to school since my last mission had spiraled out of control and resulted in Agent Nineteen getting shot a few times and Agent Blue bitten by a poisonous snake. They were still recovering from their injuries.

I was seconds away from picking up my tray and throwing it across the cafeteria in a fit of frustration when Danielle suddenly grabbed my arm underneath the table.

I looked at her and she motioned with her eyes for me to look down. In her other hand, on her lap, she held a small marinara-covered slip of paper.

AGENT ZERO AND AGENT ATLAS: COME TO THE SHED. IMMEDIATELY.

0000101010101010101010100110010101010101010
0101010101010000101001010101001010101010
1010100001001010010101010010101010101010
00001   9011001010101010101010
0010   0010101010010101010100
101   101010010101010101010
000   1100101010101010101010

CHAPTER 3

PERMANENT
NEUTRAL FACE

NORMALLY WHEN I NEEDED TO SNEAK AWAY FROM OUR LUNCH table for secret agent business, I'd have to make up some crazy excuse. Partly because Dillon was always so suspicious of everything that everybody did, and partly because it wasn't like me to suddenly bail on lunch with friends. But that day it was easy. Our table, and the cafeteria in general, were so consumed with arguments speculating about Mr. Gomez that Danielle and I simply stood up and left.

"Do they always contact you that way?" Danielle asked

as we walked quickly down the sledding hill adjacent to the practice football field.

"In school lunches, yeah," I said, a little offended they'd sent her the message and not me. "Agent Chum Bucket is one of the cafeteria workers."

"So that's why you've been suddenly leaving during lunch so much lately!" she said.

I grinned and shrugged. This was technically Danielle's first school day as an official secret agent. It felt kind of nice not being the new kid anymore.

When we got to the school's maintenance shed, which hid the entrance to Agency headquarters, I was shocked to see that none of our usual contacts were there to meet us. Not Agent Blue, Agent Nineteen, or Director Isadoris. Instead, it was some woman I'd never seen before.

She was young—younger than my mom, anyway, but still an adult. Maybe as old as a college student, or perhaps just a little older, it was hard to tell, especially since her expression was completely blank. If she hadn't been standing on her feet and moving, she probably could have passed for a corpse. She had long blond hair and dark eyes, and wore a gray business suit that matched her unflinching face.

"I'm Agent Smiley," she said as we approached.

I almost laughed at her codename. But decided it might come off as kind of rude if it wasn't meant to be a joke.

"Uh, hi," I said.

Danielle said nothing. I could tell how nervous she was without even glancing at her. Danielle liked to help me with my pranks and was pretty cool under pressure. But at the same time, she'd always been the most responsible of the three of us, the one with enough sense to talk Dillon and me out of our craziest ideas. So all of this risky secret agent business was still likely hard for her to take in.

"Director Isadoris sent me here with an assignment for you two," Agent Smiley said, getting right down to business.

"Where are Agents Blue and Nineteen?" I asked.

Her expression didn't change. She gave away nothing. Her mouth barely even moved when she spoke. And her voice was more monotone and robotic than Betsy's voice. (In case you don't remember, Betsy was the talking, self-destructing data device that had gotten me mixed up in this mess to begin with.)

"They are both still in the medical bay," Agent Smiley explained. "It's going to be two more days, at the very least, before they're ready to return to action, so to speak."

That seemed reasonable enough to me.

"Are we going, uh, to your headquarters?" Danielle asked, speaking for the first time.

"No," Agent Smiley said. "There isn't time. This mission requires immediate action."

I didn't like the sound of that. But I said nothing, having learned it was best to just keep quiet and let Agent Smiley explain. Asking questions Agent Smiley was going to answer anyway would only waste what little time Danielle and I had to complete whatever crazy mission they had lined up for us.

"As you know, Principal Gomez has been arrested in connection with suspected traitorous activity," she continued. "We need you to retrieve Principal Gomez's computer hard drive from his office as soon as possible."

"So he really *was* some sort of enemy agent?" I asked. "Or do you need his files because he was one of our agents, and you don't want all of his top secret data to get into the wrong hands?"

"No, he has no affiliation with any agency whatsoever," Agent Smiley said. "The truth is, we really don't know yet why he was detained by the NSB. That's why we need you to retrieve his files. We'd like to find out what he's being brought in for. The Agency and the NSB don't exactly . . . Well, let's just say there is very little cooperation between the two agencies, even at the highest levels."

I gave her a quizzical look. It was hard to believe that two agencies on the same side, working for the same government, couldn't manage to work together from time to time.

"Over ninety-nine percent of NSB personnel don't even know the Agency exists," Agent Smiley said. "Regardless: Principal Gomez's arrest by the NSB as an enemy combatant in our jurisdiction, even if it is erroneous, is something we cannot consider a coincidence. We need to know everything we can. As I said, we simply can't walk into Mr. Gomez's office and ask the NSB to hand over the files. At present, two NSB agents are guarding the data while it awaits proper extraction and transport. One agent is stationed inside Mr. Gomez's office and one just outside. We need you two to get inside and retrieve his hard drive."

"Why us?" I asked, even though I suspected I already knew the answer.

"You can get close to the area in question without arousing suspicion, being students."

"What about the other teacher agents?" I asked,

remembering that Agent Nineteen had told me once that he and Agent Blue weren't the only secret agent school employees. "Surely they're better equipped for this sort of mission."

"There are no other agents posing as teachers," Agent Smiley said. "As for Agent Chum Bucket, what looks more suspicious—a school cafeteria worker loitering outside the administration office after lunch or a known trouble-making student getting himself into more trouble?"

She made a good point. But my mind was still reeling from her casual revelation that there were no other agents at the school until Agents Nineteen and Blue came back. It was now just Danielle, Chum Bucket, and me.

"Remember, all we need is his computer's hard drive," Agent Smiley said, checking her watch. "And don't get caught."

I nodded. Danielle had been pretty quiet, and I glanced her way, just to see how she was taking this in. Her face was pale, almost white. She was either seconds from barfing or keeling over dead. Or both. I didn't want her to feel like she was being forced into this.

"What if we say we're out, that we don't want to be a part of this anymore?" I asked, more to give Danielle a way out than for myself.

Agent Smiley's face remained an unmovable wax mold. It revealed nothing.

"Then you're out," she said coldly.

"Just like that?" I asked.

Agent Smiley nodded. "How effective can an agent be if he or she is unwilling? If he or she isn't completing assignments with real *purpose*? But I've read your files, Agent Zero. You have more natural talent as a spy than most we've seen—and we've seen plenty. And I don't think you, or Agent Atlas, would turn your backs on this Agency or this country. Not now, not with Medlock still operating somewhere nearby. That has become our lone acting directive: eliminating Mule Medlock before he completely compromises the Agency and our national security. But even still, if you do want out, then we will turn to our secondary plan, which is simply to take out the NSB agents guarding the office and go in by force to get what we need."

If I had ever considered walking away, I certainly wasn't going to now. She was right. I had tried to go back to a normal life a few months before—going to class, taking tests, pulling the occasional prank. It hadn't worked. This was the only thing I wanted to do. But did Danielle feel the same way?

She swallowed. "I'm in," she said.

"Yeah," I agreed. "Me, too."

"So, we obviously need a prank, right?" Danielle asked me as we walked back toward the school. "A diversion."

We both knew we had just a few hours before school let out. A few hours before it would be too late to successfully complete our mission.

"Yeah," I agreed. "The more important question, though, is what sort of prank would be big enough to distract two highly trained NSB agents whose sole purpose is to watch the one room we need to get into? Not to mention, how will we be able to get out of English class to execute it?"

We had the same class fifth period, which would make it even harder for us both to get out. Most teachers had a policy that only one student was allowed out of class at a time.

"Well, Mrs. Hutchison *loves* me," Danielle said. "So *I* can get out easily. No problem there."

That was no surprise. All of the teachers loved Danielle. In their eyes she was the perfect student. She was never late, always did her homework, participated in class, and was smart and opinionated enough to challenge them intellectually in a way that few students probably could. Danielle made their jobs both easy and fun all at once. A whole classroom full of Danielles was probably what most teachers dreamed about at night.

Me, on the other hand, well, I was most definitely every teacher's worst nightmare. Which meant that I usually couldn't just ask to leave class politely and be allowed to go. In fact, Mrs. Hutchison regarded me uneasily, as if I were plotting horrible deeds 100 percent of the time. Which, to be honest, used to be mostly true. Back before I became a secret agent and had more important things to worry about.

"Back to the prank," I said. "We need to figure that out before even worrying about getting out of class. What's so insane it could practically clear an entire building?"

"There's always the fire alarm?" she suggested.

A classic. Its reliability and success rate were unparalleled. But somehow I doubted that even a fire alarm would have two NSB agents abandoning their post.

"What about an actual fire?" I suggested.

"No way," Danielle said immediately. "I'm not starting our school on fire. I don't care what the reason is."

I sighed and shook my head. She was right; starting the school on fire could result in someone getting hurt.

Besides, it might not even work. It was hard to imagine two NSB agents running from their jobs, screaming in terror at the simple sight of a few flames.

"Hey, Carson," Danielle said as a grin spread across her face. "A minute or two is all we need to get in, grab the hard drive, and get out. Right?"

"Yeah, so?"

"So, I think I need to give my cousin Brad a call."

010101010101000010100101010010101010
1010100001001010010101010101010101010
000010   00110010101010101010101
0010   0010101010010101010100
101   1010100101010101010101
000   1001010101010101010

CHAPTER 4

THE CLASSICS

I SAT IN MY FIFTH-PERIOD CLASS AND SQUIRMED NERVOUSLY IN my seat. I checked my phone discreetly for probably the 342nd time since class had started fifteen minutes ago. If Dillon and Danielle's cousin Brad didn't come through for us, the mission was screwed. And, of course, it didn't help that I couldn't tell him the real reason we needed this to happen today.

But apparently the importance didn't matter. Brad must have really hated Gomez, because the text showed up even as I was sitting there staring at my phone. It just appeared in the notification banner right in front of my eyes:

eta 10 minutes gomez going to freak way better than last time lololol

Brad didn't know Principal Gomez had gotten arrested that morning. I'd once again told him we needed him for an awesome prank on Gomez. Brad had a history with our ex-principal, one that apparently ran deep enough for him to go to such lengths to get even this many years later.

I texted a quick reply as discreetly as possible, telling him that the east door would be propped open.

Now, I just had to get out of class somehow so I could get to Principal Gomez's office window.

Danielle had already been excused from class, as we'd predicted. She'd asked if she could spend the entire class in the library doing research for her term paper on the history of British literature at the turn of the century. Or something like that. Danielle had a thing for old books, the sort that I found excruciating to read. If books like *Great Expectations* really were classics, then I didn't want any part of anything else people liked from that time. I'd rather stab out my own eyes with fish bones than read another chapter from that book. And I don't hate reading or anything. I love a good book. I don't know. Maybe I'll understand when I'm old and boring, like everybody else.

But all that was beside the point. The point was, Danielle was already out of class. Now I needed to find a way to get out as well.

I glanced up at Mrs. Hutchison.

Several crazy plans flashed through my head. One involved army crawling across the floor and knocking her out with a karate chop. Others were even crazier, like the one that called for me starting an all-out revolution complete with a declaration of independence and rulers fashioned into crossbows. There was even one that required two dozen eggs, a box of staplers, and three small turtles.

But then it dawned on me that I could simply ask to use the restroom. As much as Mrs. Hutchison didn't like me, she wasn't completely barbaric. She'd still give me a bathroom pass if I needed it.

Sometimes the best solutions are so simple you look right past them.

Once I was out in the hallway with my ten-minute bathroom pass in hand, I headed toward the east door, the one nearest the administration offices (besides the front door). The east door also offered the advantage of being right next to a large chunk of parking lot that was rarely full, and so there'd be plenty of room for Brad to park his truck.

I exited the school, propping the door open a few inches using the wooden doorstop. After a quick text message to Danielle telling her to get into position, I headed toward the outside of Principal Gomez's office window, staying low as I moved around to the other side of the school.

The window was pretty easy to find since it still hadn't been repaired after I crashed through it a few weeks before. Instead of fixing it, the school had merely duct-taped a double layer of cardboard over the jagged hole in the window. I sat below it and waited, checking the time on my phone.

We had just nineteen minutes left to execute the plan before fifth period ended. As I waited for Brad, I had enough time to wonder if this could possibly work. We'd come up with it so quickly. Then again, it wouldn't be the first time we'd run this prank. And it's not exactly the sort of thing you can plan for, even if you have a week to work out the details. Either way, though, it didn't matter now; it was too late to back out, as evidenced by a new text message from Brad.

pulling in now will release in three minutes

I texted back a thumbs-up emoji and then called Danielle.

"Is it happening?" she answered in a whisper.

She was currently hiding in the girls' bathroom across from the administration offices. Her job was simple: Tell me as soon as the NSB guys stepped out of the office. We knew that if this worked, they'd only allow themselves to be distracted for a few minutes at most, so we couldn't waste any time.

"Yeah," I said, "he's pulling up now, supposedly."

"This is going to work," she said.

We waited on the phone in silence. Waited for something to happen. Because when it did, we'd know.

And then, it did.

"I can see the goats, Carson," Danielle said, her voice shaking.

Danielle and Darren's cousin Brad owned a farm north of our town of Minnow, and his most popular livestock was goats. But not just any goats. Fainting goats. Which, if you've been listening to my story of being a secret agent from the beginning, you might have already known.

I hate to repeat myself when it comes to pranks. But,

like I said about the fire alarm, classics are classics for a reason. And if there is one word to describe two herds of Brad's prized fainters running loose inside a school in the middle of an otherwise normal day, it's *classic*.

"It's happening," Danielle continued. "And . . . it's beautiful."

"Wish I could see it," I said.

"You really do!" she said excitedly. "There are so many of them! Oh no, the secretary just noticed and came out into the hallway and screamed. Then a bunch of goats fainted."

In between her words, in the background, I could hear the baaing of goats and the shrieking screams of the school's attendance secretary. Then more chaos erupted on the other end of the line. I heard a few kids shouting now and a lot more screaming.

"Kids are coming out of nearby classrooms," Danielle reported, clearly trying to hold back giggles. "It's insane! The goats are going crazy."

"No, not again!" some teacher screamed in the background.

"Have the agents come out?"

"Nope," Danielle said, openly laughing hysterically now.

"If this plan is going to go up in flames, I at least wish I could see them," I whined.

"I have an idea—call you right back," Danielle said, and the call was disconnected.

I stared at the phone in shock. Was she crazy? Without her telling me when the coast was clear, how would I know when to enter Gomez's office? But a few seconds later, an incoming video call from Danielle showed up on my phone.

She was a genius! Her laughing face appeared on my screen.

"Check this out," she said.

Then the view on my screen spun as she pointed her camera at the action in the hallway. It was chaos, the hallway was packed full of goats. Some were standing around, others were rigid and passed out like giant plastic figurines. There were kids everywhere, having come out from surrounding classrooms. Several teachers were in the middle of the herd, trying to calm everyone and assess the situation. I practically saw steam shooting from their ears as their brains attempted to make sense of the mess.

Danielle wasn't even trying to stay concealed anymore. And why should she? Through her video feed, I saw several other kids, and even a few teachers, holding up their phones, filming the insane action. Likely all of them were envisioning their videos becoming the next viral smash success on YouTube.

But we were getting sidetracked; we needed to stay focused on the mission at hand.

"Danielle, point it toward the office doors," I said into my phone.

She complied, tilting the phone toward the left. The administration office area was now fully in view on my screen. The attendance secretary had retreated back inside and the other three secretaries were on their feet, staring at the Goat Siege with open mouths. Two of them were trying to stifle laughs.

Then I saw him: one of the NSB agents standing next to Principal Gomez's door. He was alternating between staring in shock, shaking his head, and laughing. He opened the door behind him and motioned for the inside guard to come over and take a look.

On my phone, via Danielle's video feed from the inside, I saw them both step out of Gomez's office and into the administration office doorway several feet away. They laughed and gaped at the ongoing mess of goats. Brad hadn't been kidding—he'd really upped the goat factor on this one. But there was no time to sit there and admire the chaos that herds of fainting goats could cause; it was time for me to execute my end of the mission.

I took stood up, took a deep breath, and then jumped shoulder first into the cardboard- and tape-covered window.

CHAPTER 5

THE GHOSTS
OF TV GAME SHOWS

THE CARDBOARD GAVE WAY MUCH EASIER THAN I EXPECTED—certainly easier than the glass windowpane had when I'd crashed through it a few weeks before. The tape and cardboard helped break my fall as I landed next to Gomez's desk.

I peeked at the doorway. The two NSB agents stood twenty feet away, just outside the office. They were still facing away from me as they took in all of the goat insanity in the hallway. I knew they'd probably glance back this way at least once or twice, so I needed to stay out of sight and work quickly.

I moved toward the ancient computer tower under Gomez's desk, so I could snag the hard drive. During fifth period, I'd watched a quick video on my phone explaining how to remove a hard drive from an old tower desktop. After quietly removing the housing, it was easy to spot the drive and slide it out. I quickly shoved it into my backpack.

I glanced at my phone, which was still displaying the scene from the other side of the hallway. The two NSB agents continued to watch the goats, completely transfixed. Danielle had been right: the two out-of-town agents had no idea what to make of herds of fainting goats running through a school.

Still, the goats would only distract them for so long. And so I zipped up my bag, quickly pivoted, and dived back out the window.

As I walked calmly around the side of the school toward the east entrance, a thought occurred to me: Who was going to help round up all the goats? And wasn't Brad going to be pissed at us when he found out Gomez wasn't even at school anymore? And with Gomez gone, who would be laying down any sort of punishment for this one? Could they even tie it back to me?

Reentering the building through the east door, though, I shook off those questions. In the grand scheme of global terrorism and the threat Medlock posed, all of those things were as insignificant as an old game show rerun. One so old that the corny TV host was now dead and so were all of the contestants, and any of the money that had been won was long gone, and nobody even remembered what lame jokes were told or what prizes were won and lost.

All of those questions that had flooded my brain were nothing but ghosts.

0000101010101010100110010101010101010101
010101010101000010100101010010101010101010
1010100001001010010101010010101010101010
0000100011001010101010101010101
0010   001010101001010101010100
101   101010010101010101010
000   1100101010101010101

CHAPTER 6

KLEEN(EX) GETAWAYS

THE SCHOOL SEEMED SOMEWHAT CALM BY THE MIDDLE OF SEV-
enth period. I still wasn't sure how they'd eventually
gotten everyone to go back to class, or what they'd done
with all of the goats, but by the time the seventh-period
bell rang, it was almost as if nothing unusual at all had
happened.

Almost.

There was still the matter of the goat poop stinking
up the main hallway, of course. Someone had cleaned
it all out, but the smell wouldn't be gone for days. But

besides that, everyone was back in class, ready to learn. Or, more accurately, back in class buzzing wildly about the goat incident and how it might be related to the wild and insane rumors surrounding Mr. Gomez's sudden absence. Several of my classmates tried to give me credit for both incidents, but I deflected them emphatically.

"No, no," I said. "It must have been a copycat prankster."

They seemed to buy it because my denials were followed by heated speculation as to who actually might have pulled it off. The debate lasted until our algebra teacher, Mr. Kittson, strode into the room and silenced us by raising his hand.

"There will be no more talk of goats," Mr. Kittson said. "I assure you that whoever instigated that mess is going to be severely punished. But beyond that, it seems we have an even more urgent matter on our hands."

The classroom was so quiet you could practically hear all of our hearts pounding inside our chests as we waited anxiously to find out what could possibly be more urgent than herds of goats running free through the school hallways.

"As some of you may or may not already know," Mr. Kittson continued, "it appears that Principal Gomez is involved in an ongoing investigation by the National Security Bureau. And they have reason to believe that a student broke into his office today and stole items related to this investigation."

Many of the kids in my class gasped. I flung open my jaw and made scoffing noises at the audacity of some kids to think they could interfere with an official national security matter. I tried not to let my eyes betray me and show my panic. I tried not to think about my backpack sitting inside my locker, still stuffed with the stolen hard drive. I sat there and tried not to puke as Mr. Kittson kept spilling out even more bad news.

"Nobody is going into or out of the school building until the NSB agents have searched every last classroom, locker, and backpack."

"But they can't do that," one of my classmates shouted. "What about, like, our human rights and stuff?"

As other kids made similar protests, I stared at the back of Danielle's head, several rows in front of me. She did not turn around, which was smart. But I desperately wanted to ask her what we were going to do. Because as I thought of my backpack, sitting in my locker with the fugitive hard drive inside, I realized that I certainly had no idea. I'd almost broken down into tears by the time I decided that I had no choice but to act. I had to do *something*.

I stood up and started walking calmly toward the front of the classroom, passing Danielle without looking at her. I was afraid she'd try to stop me if I did.

"Carson, back in your seat," Mr. Kittson said.

"I'm just getting a Kleenex," I said, pointing at the box of tissue on top of the marker tray near the door.

Mr. Kittson hesitated and then turned his attention back to the questions still flying at him from the stunned, excited, and nervous students.

I reached the door and pulled a Kleenex from the box. I pretended to blow my nose and then dropped the tissue next to the trash can, missing on purpose. As I bent down to pick up the Kleenex with my left hand, my right hand reached up and grabbed the doorknob. I opened the door and tipped over the trash can in front of it, all in one motion. Then I ran from the room, leaving behind a stunned Mr. Kittson with a minor obstacle in his way. His few seconds of shock and a few more untangling the door from the trash can would hopefully be just enough time for me to get to my locker.

After that . . . I had no idea what I'd do. I obviously hadn't had much time to lay this plan out in my head. But it didn't matter either way.

I didn't even get close to my locker.

9001010101010101010011001010101010101010101c
1010101010100000101001010101001010101010c
9101000010010100101010010101010101010101
9001010101010101001100101010101010101c
9101011010100010010101010101010101001
9101000010010100101010101010101c
9001010101010101001100101010101c

CHAPTER 7

URINE—A SPY'S
BEST KEPT SECRET WEAPON

AFTER RUNNING DOWN JUST ONE SHORT HALLWAY, I TURNED the corner and crashed right into Agent Chum Bucket's stained and smelly white T-shirt. I bounced off his deceptively muscular gut and landed on the floor with a grunt.

He looked down at me in surprise and then threw a small slip of paper onto my lap right before two NSB agents tackled him from behind.

All three of them went sprawling to the floor beside me. I scooted back against the lockers, subtly closing my hand around the small message Agent Chum Bucket had passed along. I quickly slid it behind the tag on the underside of the tongue of my shoe and then planted a shocked and scared expression on my face.

A backpack Agent Chum Bucket had been carrying had flown off his shoulder during the takedown. The contents were now spilled out across the hallway floor as he struggled with the two agents detaining him. The backpack wasn't mine, but among the contents was the hard drive I had just stolen from Principal Gomez's office.

My stomach dropped. Agent Chum Bucket must have been trying to sneak it out of the school before the NSB could search my locker. Now his cover would be compromised *and* the mission would fail. My head fell onto my knees, and when I looked up, there was a large hand in front of my face.

I recognized the guy in the suit standing above me as NSB Special Agent Loften, one of the men who had arrested Mr. Gomez earlier that morning. He was tall and skinny, yet still looked like he could wrestle a grizzly bear and win. But at the same time, there was something strangely comforting about the concerned look on his face.

"Come on, up you go," he said as I grabbed his hand and he helped me to my feet.

The two agents who had tackled Agent Chum Bucket were putting him in handcuffs now as two more collected everything that had fallen out of the backpack and placed it in a black duffel bag with the letters *NSB* stenciled onto the side.

"Do I know you?" Agent Loften asked me.

"Yeah, well, no," I stammered nervously, trying my best to sound like a normal kid who was face-to-face with an NSB agent. "I mean, I was in Mr. Gomez's office this morning when . . . you know, when you arrested him, or whatever."

"That's right," he said, eyeing me from head to toe. "We meet again."

I shrugged just as Mr. Kittson rounded the corner. He was about to start yelling at me when the scene before him diverted his attention. He looked at the school cafeteria worker in handcuffs and the presence of several NSB agents and then locked eyes with me.

"What . . . ?" is all he managed to say aloud, even though it looked like he wanted to say so much more.

"And you are?" Agent Loften asked him.

"I'm Mr. Kittson. A teacher." He pointed at me. "His teacher. He just ran from my classroom."

"Did he?" Agent Loften said, squinting at me. "Well, we'll escort him back to your room after we're finished asking him a few questions. If you don't mind?"

Mr. Kittson blinked. It was pretty obvious that Agent Loften wasn't really asking his permission.

"Umm . . . sure," Mr. Kittson finally managed. "Room two fourteen."

"Thank you," Agent Loften said, placing his hand on my shoulder and steering me down the hall away from the action. He stopped halfway down, once we were out of earshot of the other agents and Chum Bucket.

"What did he say to you?" Agent Loften asked, nodding back down the hallway.

"Mr. Kittson?" I said. "Nothing . . . you were right there."

"No, the cafeteria employee."

"I don't know . . . something about lettuce, I think," I said. "He's always seemed a little crazy. Loves lettuce. Is he, like, a terrorist or something?"

Agent Loften smiled. It didn't seem to properly fit his face. Like sunglasses that were too small or a black toupee on a guy with a red beard.

The smile faded a second later.

"He didn't give you anything?" he asked.

I shook my head.

"You're sure?"

I nodded.

"So you would allow us to search your person to verify that?" he asked.

I nodded again. I was too busy working on an answer to a question I knew was coming eventually. Coming up with that answer was hard work—I hadn't had much to eat or drink that day.

"How can you explain your sudden departure from class?" Agent Loften asked, as he gestured for me to empty my pockets.

I pointed down at my pants, having finally gotten my answer ready.

He looked down and then took a quick step back.

"I didn't make it," I said, probably looking as uncomfortable as I felt in my freshly peed pants.

"Go get yourself cleaned up," Agent Loften said, trying to hide his disgust. "And then get back to class, okay? Here, take my card, call me anytime day or night if you remember anything more, okay?"

I nodded and then headed toward the locker room.

This was now the second time I'd peed my pants on purpose to get out of a jam as a secret agent. Who knew that peeing your pants and fainting goats were such great secret weapons for a spy?

CHAPTER 8

THE SECRET SAUCE

ONCE I WAS SAFELY INSIDE THE BOYS' LOCKER ROOM AND HAD changed into the spare pair of jeans I always kept in my gym locker, I sat on the bench and tried to wrap my head around what I'd just witnessed.

For one thing, the mission had been an utter failure. The NSB now had the hard drive. Whatever was on it was probably already on its way to Washington, DC.

Secondly, Agent Chum Bucket was now officially compromised. Or maybe he'd keep his cover and instead get pegged as a terrorist and sent to some secret prison on a deserted island out in the middle of the Pacific Ocean. After all, rule number one as a secret agent was never, ever break your cover, not even to other government agencies. Either way, though, this was bad.

I stared down at the floor with my face in my hands and then my eyes passed over my shoes. I'd almost forgotten about the message! I quickly pulled out the slip of paper from behind the tongue of my shoe and unfolded it.

It looked the same as all the other messages he'd slip into my school lunches. Except those messages were usually pretty clear and straightforward. This one seemed like gibberish.

THE SCHOOL BURGER'S SECRET SAUCE IS REALLY JUST BARBECUE SAUCE AND KETCHUP MIXED.

What in the world did that mean? And why would he give it to me? Agent Chum Bucket couldn't have just lost his mind in the last few hours. Which meant the message had to mean *something*. But what? And what was I supposed to do with it? I checked my phone; school was out in twenty-one minutes. Not only that, but I likely needed to get back to class soon before Mr. Kittson started wondering what happened to me.

So I needed to figure it out fast.

I thought back to every encounter I'd had with Agent Chum Bucket. The first time I'd met him was when he'd given me my spy gadgets for my first assignment at the beginning of the school year. We'd met in what he'd called his office, which was really just a pantry. He'd even blown a hole into a giant tub of mayo in order to demonstrate how to use the fruit roll-up explosive.

That's it!

Now it seemed so obvious I was a little embarrassed I hadn't figured it out right away. I jumped up from the locker room bench and ran out into the hallway, quickly making my way toward the school cafeteria pantry. I just hoped I would get there before the NSB decided to search it. Now that they thought Chum Bucket was involved in whatever sort of insanity Mr. Gomez was mixed up in, it likely wouldn't be too long before they started confiscating his stuff.

I made a quick pit stop at my locker to get my backpack. The door was closed and locked; yet the hard drive I had taken from Mr. Gomez's office was no longer inside my bag. Which meant that Agent Chum Bucket had indeed removed it somehow.

I slung the empty bag over my shoulder and continued on toward the cafeteria, passing a few other kids and a teacher. They didn't pay any attention to me. The school must not have been on lockdown anymore now that the NSB had retrieved the stolen drive.

The door to Agent Chum Bucket's pantry room was slightly ajar. Which meant he'd either left it open for me or I was going to find NSB agents already inside, searching through the school's food supplies. I held my breath as I pushed the door open.

The pantry was chock-full of giant drums of salad dressings, sauces, and condiments, as well as fifty-pound boxes of crackers, bread, noodles, and other typical school lunch ingredients. About the only thing I didn't see inside the huge pantry room were NSB agents or any fresh and healthy lunch ingredients.

It didn't take as long as I expected to find a couple massive drums of secret sauce. I considered for a moment how gross it was that all of the condiments we ate in school lunches came from giant plastic barrels.

After pushing the thought aside, I unscrewed the lid on the closest barrel. The strong odor of vinegar and sugar and tomatoes quickly filled the confined pantry. I looked around and spotted a box of plastic gloves on a nearby shelf. I pulled on a pair and then slowly dipped my hand into the reddish-brown sludge.

Even at room temperature, it felt surprisingly cold through the glove. I swished my hand around for a few seconds, feeling nothing. Sauce sloshed over the sides of the jug onto the floor and my pants. I was ready to give up, but decided to plunge my arm in a little bit deeper. That's when my fingers grazed something solid. Either there were rat carcasses inside our secret sauce, or I had been right about what the message from Agent Chum Bucket meant.

I grabbed the object and pulled it from the drum. It was a freezer bag dripping with red goop. Inside was a computer hard drive.

This had to be the one from my locker! The drive Agent Chum Bucket got caught with must have been a decoy. I had to admit it was pretty ingenious that the Agency had such a contingency plan ready to go. Although it was also a little annoying they hadn't told me about Chum Bucket's assignment. So much could have gone wrong.

So much still could.

If the stuff he'd been caught with weren't the real files and hard drive, it meant the NSB was going to figure that out eventually. Which meant that I needed to get the real one out of the school as soon as possible. I couldn't even waste time cleaning the condiments off the freezer bag.

I made a face as I shoved the secret sauce–covered freezer bag into my backpack. It was probably going to smell like McDonald's for the rest of its existence. But that didn't matter—getting this stuff to Director Isadoris was way more important than how my backpack smelled.

Before I left, I checked the other tubs of secret sauce. I didn't find more material from Gomez's office, but I did find several sealed packages of spy gadgets that Chum Bucket must have kept hidden there for emergencies. I recognized some of the equipment, but other items looked completely new. I stuffed all of it into my bag as well, then zipped it up, pulled off the plastic gloves, and exited the pantry faced with a significant decision. I had two options:

Take a right: exit the school, risking expulsion, and head directly toward Agency HQ with the hard drive.

Take a left: head back to seventh-period class, risking

another run-in with Agent Loften and his NSB goons and the reconfiscation of the hard drive, as well as the task of explaining to Mr. Kittson why I was covered in greasy red gunk.

I turned right, pushed open the door underneath the glowing green exit sign, and was out of the building about fifteen minutes before the end of seventh period.

0000101010101010101001100101010101010101010
0101010101010100001010010101001010101
101010000100101001010100101010101010101
00001   0011001010101010101010
0010   0010101010010101010
101   1010100101010101010101
000   110010101010101010

CHAPTER 9

A TICKER TAPE PARADE
IN GHOSTOWN

TO AN OUTSIDE OBSERVER, I WOULD HAVE LOOKED LIKE A CRAZY person. Just some kid, half covered in gloopy condiments, jumping around in a snowbank without a coat like a lunatic. But what a passerby wouldn't have known, of course, was that there were secret cameras hidden inside the swallows' nests adjacent to the small snowbank I was frolicking in.

Hidden cameras planted there by a government agency so secret that its very name was classified and unknown by its own employees.

But I knew the cameras were there and so I jumped up and down in front of the swallows' nests, waving my arms like a madman. All I wanted was to get the evidence in my bag down to Agency personnel before the school bell rang and the odds of getting caught with the stolen hard drive would increase exponentially. After all, everybody, NSB agent or otherwise, would take a second and third look at a kid dripping with greasy barbecue sauce. Besides, it really was freezing without a coat—I was right in the middle of an infamous North Dakota winter, after all.

Luckily, I didn't have to wait very long before I heard the maintenance shed door open behind me.

Agent Smiley poked her head out and motioned for me to join her. I ran inside, where the secret elevator was already waiting. We stepped onto the platform.

"You have the hard drive?" she asked before pressing any buttons.

"Yep."

Then we were shooting down into the earth, leaving our stomachs up at the surface. During the ride down into Agency headquarters, Agent Smiley held a hand over her normally unflinching face and tried to hide her crinkled nose.

"Sorry," I said, looking down at the secret sauce stains on my pants and shirt. "Things got a bit, uh, messy."

She didn't say anything back. Then we hit the bottom and the elevator doors opened. I'd been down to Agency HQ before, and each time it looked completely different. Sometimes it was bustling with activity, people in suits everywhere working hard to thwart whatever rogue threats faced the country. A few of the times I'd been greeted by armed guards pointing huge machine guns at my face. This time, however, I was stunned to find a virtual ghost town.

The place was empty. Deserted. The normally busy atrium was quiet and still. Half the lights were off, the dimness giving it an even darker vibe, as if it had been converted into an evil lair in my absence.

"Where is everyone?" I asked, suddenly worried that perhaps the base had been compromised and everyone I knew was dead or captured.

"Director Isadoris will explain," Agent Smiley said. "Come on, follow me."

I trailed her up the glass staircase and along the secret hallway at the end of the balcony that led to the director's office. He was seated behind his desk. Two other agents I didn't recognize were working on laptops at a small folding table behind him. His hair was frazzled as if he hadn't showered in days, and his face was covered in dark stubble. It made the massive man look even more like a giant grizzly bear than he usually did.

"Agent Zero," he said, not standing or smiling. "Have a seat."

I took a chair across from him while Agent Smiley crossed the room and joined the other two agents at the small card table.

"You succeeded?" Director Isadoris asked.

I unzipped my backpack and looked down into the splattered interior. I debated giving him the whole bag, but then decided he didn't really need to know that I had snagged a few spare gadgets from the pantry. After all, he was the one who thought it wasn't worth telling me about the Chum Bucket contingency plan.

I plucked out the bag containing Gomez's hard drive and plopped it onto the desk.

"There it is," I said.

He nodded and shoved the messy heap into a duffel bag.

"Agent Scion," Director Isadoris said, "take this to the tech lab and see what you can find."

One of the agents working behind him stood and

walked over to retrieve the bag. Then he slung it over his shoulder and left the office without saying a word. Director Isadoris treated the entire transaction as if he were asking a friend to get him a soda from the fridge. Then he turned back to me with a blank look.

I tried to suppress my annoyance. Did he have any idea what I'd gone through to get that? How close I had come to getting myself kicked out of school? How I'd risked being arrested by the NSB? How Agent Chum Bucket actually had been arrested? If it wasn't that important, then why ask CB and me to do it at all?

Director Isadoris must have noticed my glare.

"What?" he snapped. "You want a medal every time you complete an assignment?"

I was stunned by his words. And even more stunned to see one of the agents behind him smirking. I just sat there and failed to come up with any sort of a reply.

"That's what this job is, *Agent* Zero," Director Isadoris continued. "You're given a dangerous mission, and if you can complete it without being captured or killed, you are given another. This was just another day at the office. You don't see florists getting a ticker tape parade each time they pick a flower, do you?"

I shook my head, despite not really knowing what a

ticker tape parade was. He had a point either way, but that still didn't quite take the sting out of his words.

"I'm sorry, sir," I said, not able to look him in the eyes.

Then he sighed and leaned back in his chair.

"No, I'm sorry, Agent Zero," he said. "My words still stand, but they should have been expressed more tactfully. I'm used to dealing with adults, after all."

Even his apology felt like a backhanded slap to my face. But I nodded and accepted it. Once again, I couldn't really argue with his logic.

"As I'm sure you've noticed," he continued, "things are a little different around here at the moment. First, we diverted a healthy chunk of agents to a new initiative, one that could be a real game changer. But even more drastic has been the need to scale back to essential personnel only. We simply don't know who we can trust anymore. The fact is, we've never had a security breach of this severity in the seventy-year history of the Agency. A former agent, systematically taking down every aspect of our operation . . . Medlock has all but destroyed us from the inside out."

I nodded slowly, the true gravity of the threat starting to sink in.

"Which is why capturing him has become our sole

objective at the moment. Every other resource—outside the new initiative that we have—is now aimed entirely at finding, detaining, or eliminating Medlock. In the pursuit of this task, everything—even an agent—is considered expendable."

I could only assume that was his way of confirming that Agent Chum Bucket was now on his own. I wanted to ask the director if he counted himself as expendable, too, but I stayed quiet. I didn't want to make him even angrier than he already was.

"And in line with that," Director Isadoris said, "we have another immediate assignment for you. One that relates back to our primary subdirective, which is to figure out what exactly Medlock is up to. That is, if you feel you're up to the challenge."

Director Isadoris might have been a little sarcastic with that last bit. But it didn't matter: I was in too deep to back out now.

"Yeah, I'm in," I said.

"Good. As you know, we believe Medlock has yet another operative inside the school. Someone who likely framed Principal Gomez, set him up to get caught by the NSB. And it could be an adult, but it's just as likely another student."

"What makes you think that?" I asked.

"Jake, Medlock's son," Director Isadoris said. "Children are easier to manipulate than adults, and generally appear less suspicious. And, as you and Jake have both demonstrated, can be just as effective. While Medlock could have planted adult agents at the school, it's equally possible that Jake recruited other agents himself among the student populace."

It made sense, but it was hard to imagine who else might be working for the bad guys. What kid would get on board with a plot for world domination, or whatever Medlock's endgame was, besides his own kid?

"Let me guess," I said. "You want me to find out who this inside agent is?"

"Indeed," Director Isadoris confirmed. "It could be anyone, so suspect everyone, and discount no one."

"One thing I still don't get," I speculated aloud, "is why Medlock would go to the trouble of framing Gomez if he wasn't working with the Agency."

"Well, that's another thing we're hoping you can help us find out," Director Isadoris said. "It must have something to do with the base, the Agency, and our ties to the school. As we speak, a new principal, Ms. Pullman, is being brought in to take over for Mr. Gomez.

Her background checks out: she has a family, a complete educational record; it's hard to imagine that she could be under Medlock's thumb. But circumstances dictate that we consider her a suspect for the time being."

"So, what's next?" I asked.

"Well, that's hard to answer completely until we know what Medlock is up to. Once we figure that out, we can come up with a definitive way to stop him. So, *next* is simply doing everything we can to uncover his plans, starting with a thorough search through the files on the hard drive you brought in. Hopefully to confirm that it was a frame job and also look for clues as to who executed it and how and why," Director Isadoris said. "In the meantime, the new direct assignment for you and Agent Atlas is twofold. One: Discover who, if anyone, framed Gomez and continues to execute small acts of sabotage that are interfering with Agency operations. Two: Look for evidence inside the school regarding why Gomez may have been framed, and ascertain Ms. Pullman's possible involvement. I'm going to level with you, Agent Zero: With Agent Chum Bucket in NSB custody, our other agents working on the new initiative, and Agents Nineteen and Blue still not ready for fieldwork, you and Agent Atlas are our best chance at finding out anything from inside the school."

I nodded. It was pretty simple, though I didn't really have any idea how I was going to start. Not yet, anyway.

"Speaking of Agents Nineteen and Blue . . . would it be possible for me to visit them?" I asked.

Director Isadoris sighed and said, "Yes, but I must warn you that you may not like what you see."

0000101010101010101010100110010101010101010101010
010101010101010000010100010101010010101010101
101010000100101010010101010010101010101010101
000010   0011001010101010101010
0010   0010101010010101010
101   1010100101010101010
000   110010101010101010

CHAPTER 10

LUKE SKYWALKER
AND THE BIONIC WOMAN

AGENT SMILEY ESCORTED ME TO THE MEDICAL UNIT. WE DIDN'T pass a single person along the way. The emptiness of Agency headquarters somehow made me feel empty as well. It made me question why any of us were still trying, even though the answer was pretty obvious and undeniable.

The med unit was very much like a hospital, just with fewer people. It consisted of a few wide, bright, and generically tiled hallways with rooms branching off on both sides. As we entered, I saw a few men and women in white coats and green scrubs, holding clipboards and discussing something just down the hallway to our left.

Agent Smiley asked me to follow her into a large room with several huge pieces of machinery that looked straight out of a science fiction movie. In fact, one machine, which was basically just a huge glass tank filled with clear liquid, looked almost identical to a bacta tank. A bacta tank is the thing that they put Luke Skywalker in after Han Solo rescues him on the ice planet of Hoth at the beginning of *The Empire Strikes Back*. I'm not a Star Wars geek, but Dillon definitely was and he made me watch the whole series at least once a year, complete with his thorough breakdowns, commentaries, behind-the-scenes trivia, and explanations of various set pieces.

"It's like a bacta tank," I said as we entered the room.

Agent Smiley gave me a look. Then she motioned for me to follow her around to the other side, and pointed at the top of the machine.

Affixed to the top of the metal seal was a long piece of white tape. On it, someone had written these words in thick black marker: *Bacta Tank I.*

"One of our lab technicians is a science fiction nerd," she said humorlessly.

I resisted the urge to laugh and shook my head as a young guy in a white coat and scrubs entered the room. He walked over to a small desk in the corner and opened a folder. He leafed through the papers for a few moments, jotted something down, and then came over to us.

"Can I help you?" he asked.

"We're here to see Agents Blue and Nineteen," Agent Smiley said.

"Of course," the doctor said. "This way."

He led us into an adjacent room. It was nearly identical to the one we'd just come from. This room also had a bacta tank, except this tank wasn't empty. Floating inside it, just like Luke Skywalker, was Agent Nineteen. A breathing mask was affixed to his face, and his eyes were closed. I saw several nasty bullet wounds in his torso, as well as several older scars scattered about his abdomen, back, arms, and legs.

"He suffered the more severe injuries of the two agents," the doctor said behind me. "He's currently in a medically induced coma while the tank does its thing, so to speak."

"A coma?" I said, frowning.

"Don't worry," the doctor assured me. "It's standard procedure. We find that being submerged in the tank while conscious can cause claustrophobia, disorientation, and other undesirable side effects. Agent Nineteen is in stable condition, and should make a full recovery. He has been through far worse in his career."

I looked at my wounded mentor. It was hard to imagine him looking any worse. I tried to reassure myself that the doctor knew what he was doing. If he said Agent Nineteen would be fine, then he would be. I took a deep breath and forced myself to look away.

"What about Agent Blue?" I asked.

"I'm right here, Carson."

I spun around, startled to hear his voice. He was lying in a hospital bed at the other end of the room. The sight of the occupied bacta tank had distracted me from noticing anything else when I'd entered.

"Mr. Jensen," I said, rushing over to him.

Giving him a hug seemed awkward and unprofessional, so instead I reached out to shake his hand. But he had raised his hand for a high five, and so we ended up doing a kind of awkward hybrid where I grabbed and shook his raised palm. I looked down, embarrassed, and that's when I noticed the void under the sheets where his leg should have been. There was nothing there.

"Your leg!" I gasped before I could stop myself.

"It's okay, Carson," he said. "They had to take it off, but it's okay."

"How is that okay?"

"Well, when you put it that way, I guess it is pretty horrible," Agent Blue said, looking as if he was about to cry.

I panicked for a moment before realizing he was just having some fun with me.

"Sorry," I mumbled.

"I said, it's okay. I'll be getting a replacement artificial limb. Pretty high-tech stuff, as you can imagine. I'll be like the Bionic Woman."

I had no idea what he meant by that, but I was happy to see that he was staying so positive. I bet he was probably just feeling happy and lucky to be alive at all. The last time I saw him, sitting in the Ford Fusion we'd stolen from Snaketown, rambling deliriously and his venom-filled leg bloated and swollen, he looked just a few seconds from death.

And so instead of focusing on his leg, I filled him in on my new assignment, after Agent Smiley said it was all right. She had yet to crack half a smile since I'd met her. She hadn't even so much as sneezed, or coughed. She was like a robot or something. Maybe she *was* a robot? With the Agency's funding and technology, anything was possible.

"When will you be back?" I asked Agent Blue.

"The doctor says a few weeks. But I suspect I can get back sooner."

"Awesome," I said. "I don't like not having you guys there."

"You can handle the assignment just fine on your own," he said. "You're among the best agents I've ever worked with. Well, you still have a lot to learn, but you get what I'm saying. . . ."

He trailed off, clearly embarrassed. They must have had him drugged up on some good stuff. He had never been so jokey and smiley and complimentary before. Agent Blue was usually surly, not so different from Agent Smiley. I sort of liked the painkiller version of Agent Blue.

"Uh, thanks," I said. "Still, I can't wait for you to get back. I'm nervous, there's so much resting on my shoulders. I'm still just a kid, after all."

Agent Blue shook his head.

"No. You're not *just* a kid. You're Agent Zero."

0000101010101010101001100101010101010101010
010101010101000010100101010100101010101
1010100001001010010101010010101010101010
0001   0011001010101010101010101
010   0010101010100101010100
01   1010100101010101010
                        1100101010101010101

CHAPTER 11

RADIOACTIVE MUSHROOM RAMPAGES AND CHICKEN FEET RAIN

BEFORE DANIELLE AND I HAD BECOME SECRET AGENTS, I CAN'T think of one time when the two of us hung out without Dillon. He was my best friend and her twin brother, after all. Turns out, though, that this is necessary when plotting missions as secret agents. Dillon still had no idea that we were working with the Agency, with codenames and everything. Even with all of his crazy conspiracy theories, he still hadn't guessed that one.

But meeting up without him later that night ended up being easier than expected.

"He's distracted by this new master theory of his," Danielle explained, as I closed the door to my room behind her. "It has something to do with all of the fungus growing around town. He's convinced that nuclear missile silos surrounding Minnow have created radioactive mushrooms that will one day sprout legs and go on some sort of nationwide rampage, inducing black-and-white, slow-motion hallucinations that will involve talking buildings and pickled chicken feet falling from the sky."

"Wait, the radioactive . . . What?"

Danielle grinned and shook her head.

"Carson, I have no idea. He didn't give me much of an explanation. But he's really into this one; I've never seen him so preoccupied before. Right now, he's spending the night out in the coulee behind our house, extracting and carefully cataloging fungus samples."

I laughed. "That sounds like Dillon."

"So what happened this afternoon?"

I explained how I'd managed to get away with the evidence, and how Agent Chum Bucket had taken the fall for the success of the mission. I told her about how I'd met up with Director Isadoris and how eerie and deserted Agency headquarters had been. She was shocked, horrified, relieved all in one. Then I told her about our new mission.

"Pretty straightforward," I said. "Find the enemy agent and figure out why they framed Gomez. Of course, this is assuming they let me back into school tomorrow. I mean, I did ditch out on seventh period. And I'm sure someone is going to want to punish me for the goats, even if it's not Mr. Gomez. And that's not even mentioning what Ms. Pullman will do once she arrives and reads the files Gomez kept on my pranks. *And*, that's all aside from the possible scenario in which she is in fact an enemy secret agent sent to eliminate the Agency's people inside the school."

"Wait a second," Danielle said, stemming my nervous rambling. "You're getting way ahead of yourself."

"What do you mean?"

"You can't control any of that stuff," she said calmly. "Let's just focus on our mission. If you get expelled, or whatever, then we'll deal with it. But we'd be wasting time and energy worrying about it now."

This was why Danielle was the perfect partner. She was way more logical and reasonable. After all, she'd figured out how to get inside the secret Mount Rushmore base to save Agent Nineteen and me all by herself. I guess if you really stepped back and looked at it, she was probably a better secret agent than I was. All I had going for me was being stupid enough to attempt the impossible and lucky enough to have succeeded a few times.

But all that is beside the point. What mattered was that Danielle was right; we needed to break down and make a plan for how to complete our two-pronged mission.

And so that's what we did for the next hour.

We started by making a list of teachers and students who could have possibly been enemy spies. Here's what we came up with:

1. **Mr. Lepsing**: seventh- and eighth-grade social studies teacher. He made the list simply by being a straight-up supersecretive weirdo. Mr. Lepsing had something strange hidden away in his supply closet. Everybody knew it. Rumors had swirled ever since I'd started school here about what it was that he kept in there. Some of the best theories were:
   - A leopard that he was secretly feeding a mixture of steroids and school lunches, which was creating a master race of muscular leopard mutants (courtesy of Dillon)
   - A colony of Venus flytraps that had evolved to

devour small animals, and which Mr. Lepsing was training to eventually eat students (also courtesy of Dillon)

- An earwax collection that he had molded into various members of early-00s-era boy bands (Dillon)
- A giant box of all the chewed-up pens and pencils he'd confiscated from students over the years, which he was saving in order to clone his best students to create an army of hyperintelligent and obedient slaves (this is what most students believed—he was a bit of a freak about taking away writing implements if he saw you chewing on them—except the last part about cloning, which came from—you guessed it—Dillon)
- A lobster man that he was secretly keeping just alive enough to have a never-ending supply of lobster to feed on (Dillon again, much to Danielle's horror and gagging)
- Seventeen twenty-three-year-old Whoppers from Burger King that he was using to grow an army of preservative-laced (and thus indestructible) super bacteria that would eventually incite the

apocalypse (take a wild guess)

- Special diet lunches and/or a stockpile of vitamins (another popular theory with the general student body, given that Mr. Lepsing was an unabashed health freak)
- A stash of gold bars and other valuables that he'd recovered while treasure hunting across the US (Mr. Lepsing was a proud amateur treasure hunter, but Dillon was really the only one who believed this)

Okay, so clearly most of the theories came from Dillon. But the point was, Mr. Lepsing definitely kept *something* locked inside that supply closet that he didn't want any students to see or find. He kept the key on a chain around his neck, after all. Who does that? Answer: someone hiding something very valuable—or very sinister.

2. **Gus Agriopoulas**: eighth-grade student. He made the list primarily for being the sort of kid who would probably be first in line to sign on for a plot of total world domination. If our middle school voted on awards at the end of each year, like Most Likely to be Famous or Most Likely to Succeed, Gus Agriopoulas

would have definitely won for Most Likely to Become an Evil Villain Planning to Blow up the Sun. It wasn't just that he was a bully; our school, like any other, had plenty of kids who were mean to other kids from time to time. It was the *way* Gus bullied kids that made him such a threat. He went after kids with reckless abandon—nothing was off-limits. Gus was the sort of kid who'd make fun of a kid whose parents had just died in car accident. In fact, he did that once when I was in third grade and he was in fourth. I wish I were exaggerating. One time, Gus lit a girl's ponytail on fire at recess. And the thing was, he almost always got away with it. He was the best athlete at every sport, he got straight As, his dad was one of the best orthopedic surgeons in the world, and all of these things generally gave Gus a free pass. No one wanted to believe that Mr. Small Town Superstar Rich Kid could be such a completely evil psychopathic jerk. That, and if Gus got expelled or sent away to juvie or something, the hopes for our town ever winning the state high school football championship would have been dashed. And that stuff is pretty important to people from small towns with nothing else to worry about.

3. **Ophelia Perkins**: fifth-grade student. She had made the list by being cousins with Jake Tyson-Gulley, and so was also Medlock's niece. That was pretty strong evidence for sure. But at the same time, it was the *only* reason she made the list. Nothing else about her seemed even remotely suspicious. In fact, everything else about her made her the least likely person, on or off the list, to be an enemy spy. She always followed all the rules, and she was always making a spectacle of herself, which aren't exactly the best traits for a secret evil spy. She would tattle on other kids for just about anything; she once tried to tell on a kid for dropping a green bean on the floor in the cafeteria at lunch and not picking it up. She almost cried once when she accidentally sneezed in class during a test, because she was so upset she broke the silence rule. The teacher had to reassure her four or five times that it was okay. But, even considering all of that, we simply couldn't ignore her bloodline connection to Medlock.

4. **Mrs. Food**: gym teacher. She made the list because of her alleged past connections and experiences. I'll explain more about that in a bit, but first I should

clarify that her name really isn't Mrs. Food, it's Mrs. Canterbury. Mrs. Food is just what people call her, going way back to when my dad went to school there. That's how long Mrs. Food has been teaching. Apparently there was this old TV host called Mr. Food, and she looks a lot like him. The funny thing is, Mr. Food is most famous for his big gray beard. Mrs. Food doesn't have a beard, but somehow the resemblance is there. It's hard to explain. But that's beside the point. She didn't make the list for being a seventy-year-old woman with a passing resemblance to a famous TV chef. Mrs. Food made the list because she *claimed* to be a former special ops double agent. She said her assignment was so top secret that even Presidents Kennedy, Johnson, and Nixon didn't know she existed. She supposedly served as a KGB double agent in Russia and across Eastern Europe. Mrs. Food always had all these crazy spy stories that she told while making kids do army crawls and insane military training stuff instead of normal calisthenics. For instance, she once claimed that she had been given the green light to assassinate Leonid Brezhnev, who was apparently a Russian president or something. She said she had slipped poison into his drink and then had to run back across the room and slap the glass from his hand at the last second when the hit was suddenly called off. Anyway, I was pretty sure she was just a weird, harmless old lady who loved telling stories to kids, since everyone knows that real double agents can never give up their identity, even after retirement. But just the same, we'd have been stupid to overlook her as a possible target, given her alleged past.

5. **Peter Nilsson, aka Junior**: seventh-grade student. He made the list for hating Mr. Gomez even more than I did, and thus likely to agree to a plan in which Gomez would be framed and extracted from the school in such an embarrassing and extreme manner. Other than that, I didn't think he was really capable of being a spy. In fact, I didn't think he should make the list at all; it was only at Danielle's insistence that I added him. For one thing, Junior was not the smartest cookie in the jar, or whatever. He was mostly known for being the school's biggest class clown, a goof-off of epic proportions. Whereas I had a reputation for carrying out elaborate, precise, well-planned pranks, Junior was known more as the kid making fart noises in class, usually by actually farting for real as loudly as he

could. Or for picking his nose and wiping the boogers on the kids around him. He also invited kids to dare him to drink entire bottles of glue, which he always did even when they insisted that he shouldn't. Other stunts of his included sticking pushpins into his ears, sucking the ink out of those multiflavored scented markers, making suicide school lunches (where you mix together everything on your lunch tray into one massive blob of food and eat it), and doing cartwheels down the school hallways in between classes. See what I mean? How could that kid possibly be an enemy spy? But Danielle insisted that we not overlook any student with a connection to Gomez, and it was true that he was in the principal's office almost as much as I was. And so here he is on the list.

6. **Tyrell Alishouse**: eighth-grade student. He made the list because he was pretty much a spy already. He'd transferred here after getting expelled from his old school, and had already developed a reputation for being an amateur sleuth. According to kids around school, he was a master of disguise and sneaking around and doing covert surveillance. He'd supposedly already gotten one teacher in trouble when he

caught her on camera smoking behind the school Dumpsters. He once told a kid in my homeroom that he's only seen when wants to be seen. I mean, any kid who says that sends off immediate red flags for being a possible spy. He seemed like the most obvious name on the list, especially since he was a new kid and could have easily been planted there by Medlock directly. But something inside my gut told me I was wrong. I could tell that he had a strong moral code, even if he was a bit shady.

Danielle and I split up the list. We each took three names.

"Now, what about investigating Ms. Pullman?" I asked.

"Why don't we wait to make a plan until she's officially started working at school," Danielle suggested.

I agreed. Besides, Director Isadoris had made one thing very clear before I'd left Agency HQ that afternoon: The primary objective was tracking down the unknown enemy agent. And so that's where we'd start, beginning first thing in the morning.

As long as the morning didn't start with me getting expelled.

0100010101010101010100110010101010101010
0101010101010001010010101010101010101
1010100001001010010101010010101010101
00001 001100101010101010101010
0010 00101010100101010101
101 101010010101010101
000 100010101010101010

CHAPTER 12

IT'S NEVER THE SWISS

DIDN'T GET EXPELLED THE NEXT MORNING.

At least, not right away—I still had no idea what the rest of the day would bring. First and second period came and went and nobody got called down to the office. The school was still abuzz from the bizarre and exciting events of the day before. But by the start of third period, things had begun feeling normal again. Middle school kind of had a way of sapping the energy and fun out of even the craziest events pretty quickly.

Third period also brought along the start of my investigation. It made it easy that the first name on my list also just happened to be my third-period social studies teacher, Mr. Lepsing.

I should probably mention that at one point during our sixth-grade year, Dillon had been entirely convinced that Mr. Lepsing was a Swiss spy.

"Swiss?" I had said at the time. "Why would Switzerland have a spy in our school? It makes no sense."

"Exactly!" Dillon had said. "Nobody ever suspects the Swiss! Which is precisely how they're getting away with taking over our government from the inside using brain-control fine chocolates, expensive watches, and rogue sentient bank accounts!"

I obviously didn't believe any of that for a second. But since becoming a secret agent I found out that Dillon had been right about way more stuff than I ever would have imagined. And so I figured there was a chance that he had been right about Mr. Lepsing being a spy, even if he wasn't a Swiss spy.

I thought I'd start my investigation by showing up to class as early as I could and trying to catch him coming into or out of his supply closet. But he was already seated behind his desk when I arrived.

Mr. Lepsing was tall and thin. Not just thin, but thin in a way that made you suspect he was really a giant praying mantis wearing a human skin for a disguise. He was mostly bald, except on the sides where long, brown stringy hair dangled down from his shiny scalp like tentacles. He wore glasses so thick that when he looked right at you, his eyes practically filled his entire face. He always wore skinny ties; sweat-stained button-up shirts; and old, thick pants with heavy textures from the 1970s.

Mr. Lepsing was generally a nice guy and a good teacher, despite being one of the weirdest people at the school. Most of the students really liked him, since his oddities at least made his class slightly more interesting than other classes. Even if the entertainment was mostly unintentional.

But his likability meant I needed to tread lightly. The rest of the class was already filing in, and if they thought I was making fun of Mr. Lepsing in some way, they'd turn on me. Being allowed to get away with somewhat obnoxious behavior was an advantage I didn't want to lose. And the best way to lose such a thing was to annoy your classmates.

"Mr. Lepsing." I raised my hand just after he'd handed out a reading assignment. "Can I come up and ask you a question?"

"You can't ask me from there?"

"Not really."

"Okay, come on up," Mr. Lepsing said.

I went to his desk, bringing my textbook with me so the class would think my question was related to social studies. Of course it wasn't. Or, well, I guess technically it *was*, but you'll see what I mean.

"I was wondering . . . where were you this past weekend?" I plopped my book onto his desk.

"I don't really see how that's pertinent to the downfall of the Roman Empire, Carson," Mr. Lepsing said, motioning at my textbook.

"Well, it's not, it's for another class," I said, words just tumbling out of my mouth without any thought or planning. "I'm investigating a crime that occurred here sometime between Friday evening and Monday morning. You know anything about that?"

His expression shifted from mild curiosity to something much closer to surprise, and perhaps even suspicion. He sat upright.

"Why would you ask *me* such a question?" he said. "What crime are you talking about? If this is more of your infamous trickery, I'm not finding it very amusing. Besides, what I do on my own time is no one's business but my own."

I pressed on. "You wouldn't happen to know anything about framing, would you?"

"You are treading on some thin ice now, young man," he said.

His eyes flickered wildly, as if he were looking for a way out. Maybe I was making him uncomfortable? Perhaps I was getting closer to the truth than I suspected. Even still, it was probably best to back off a bit. After all, even if I did get him to admit something here and now, what could I do about it in the middle of class?

"Mr. Lepsing," I said, smiling, "you've got the wrong idea. I'm talking about framing a portrait. You know, like of a person? I got a print of a portrait of my favorite aunt, and I was wondering if you knew where I could get a custom frame job. Since you got all these history posters hanging all over your room." I motioned to all the maps and historical posters on the walls.

Mr. Lepsing stared at me, trying to decide if I was joking or not. Or maybe he was wondering if I knew more than he thought I did. Or maybe he was trying to figure out if it'd be better to just kill me right then and there and be done with me, even if it meant breaking his cover.

"What did you think I meant?" I asked with a laugh. "Framing a person for a crime? That's funny."

"Carson, please take your seat before you end up with a detention," Mr. Lepsing said calmly. "Something of which I'm quite sure you already have an ample supply."

I nodded, conceding that the charade was over and returned to my seat. But the efforts had not been entirely fruitless. Not by a long shot. He'd acted suspiciously enough that I knew I had to investigate further. After that conversation, I wasn't entirely convinced that Mr. Lepsing was nothing more than an extremely odd, yet mostly harmless, weirdo. There was only one way to tell for sure.

The question was: When and how would I actually get inside his supply closet?

0000101010101010101010100110010101010101010101010
010101010101010000101001010101010001010101
101010000100101001010101001010101010101
00001   001100101010101010101010
0010   001010101001010101010
101   1010100101010101010101

CHAPTER 13   101010010101010101
000   11001010101010101010

CARSON-FACED SANDWICH

ONE THING WAS FOR SURE: I WASN'T GOING TO BE ABLE TO sneak into Mr. Lepsing's supply closet during morning classes. So I turned my attention to the next name on my list: Gus Agriopoulas, aka the Untouchable Mega-Bully. His reputation for fits of extreme violence meant I'd need to tread very carefully while investigating him.

Up to that point, I'd had nothing more than a few minor run-ins with Gus. I suspect this was because I think he saw me as a kindred spirit due to all my pranks over the years. He obviously couldn't differentiate between harmless pranks and outright brutal violence committed against innocent kids, but just the same, I wasn't complaining since it had mostly saved me from his cruelty.

That could change in an instant, though, if he suspected I was following him. Or spying on him. Or found out I thought he was an enemy agent, regardless of whether he actually was or wasn't. If any of those things happened, he'd probably be eating a Carson-faced sandwich later that day for lunch, using my guts as the meat, my skin for the bread, and my brains as mayo.

I knew where Gus's locker was. Everyone did. It's one of the first things every kid mapped out on the first day of school every year, so they'd know which part of which hallway to avoid every day for the entire school year.

After third period, I rushed out of Mr. Lepsing's class and directly toward Gus's locker. I might have been the first kid in school history to make such a move. Even most of Gus's "friends" tried to avoid him in the halls. School seemed to bring out his cruelty the most.

Gus was at his locker when I got there, but he wasn't alone. He was trying to stuff some poor sixth grader inside it. There was no way the kid was going to fit, but Gus just kept cramming limbs into his tiny locker as the kid squirmed and groaned in pain.

Gus laughed like a seven-year-old frolicking through a sprinkler on a hot summer day as he continued to jam.

"Come on, man, we'll be late," said Cade, Gus's best friend.

Strictly speaking, Cade wasn't Gus's best friend. But he pretended to be because being best friends with the star athlete and richest kid in school had its benefits. Avoiding the worst of Gus's torturous sense of humor was not the least of them. Getting playfully slugged in the arm or casually derided from time to time wasn't nearly as bad as having the palms of your hands forcibly super glued to your cheeks. Which is something Gus had done to countless kids over the years. It was his signature move. He called it the *phaf,* or Permanent *Home Alone* Face.

"Let's go, man." Cade pulled at Gus, trying to hide his concern for the sixth grader who was folded up like a pretzel, half inside Gus's locker.

"Whatever—keep your panties on," Gus said, finally allowing the sixth grader to clamber out and run away.

He slammed his locker shut and walked with Cade toward where I was standing and gawking at them just fifteen feet away. I diverted my gaze quickly, trying to pretend that I was looking for something on the floor nearby.

"What are you staring at?" Gus asked me. "Want to give it a try yourself? See if you'll actually fit?" He motioned back toward his locker.

"I'm good," I said.

Gus snickered and kept walking past me. Then he stopped and pivoted on his heels, as if he suddenly remembered that he did want to at least snap my vertebrae in half, if nothing else.

He grinned. "Nice job with the goats yesterday, bro," he said. "That was hilarious."

"Thanks," I said.

I finally remembered to breathe as Gus and Cade walked away, laughing.

How about that? Saved by fainting goats twice in two days. Not many kids could say that. I was starting to think that fainting goats might be my own personal guardian angels or something.

CHAPTER 14

THE ERIK HILL
MIDDLE SCHOOL TRAILBLAZER

AFTER TEMPTING FATE AND FOLLOWING GUS AND CADE TO their next class, I came to the conclusion that Gus was perhaps even more likely than Mr. Lepsing to be in cahoots with Medlock. The kid clearly wanted to cause as much destruction as possible, every moment of his life. He wouldn't think twice about getting behind a plan that ruined Principal Gomez's life or released a deadly virus out into the world or whatever other horrors Medlock was planning.

During their short walk to class, Gus and Cade spent

much of it laughing about what had happened to Gomez. Laughing the way that people did after witnessing the aftermath of a successful prank. Not only that, but he showed even further evidence of sadism by taking one kid's math notebook, tearing the whole thing in half, and tossing it into the hallway garbage can just to show off to Cade how well his new weight-lifting regimen had been working.

I knew I'd need to make Gus a priority for the time being. Of course, eventually breaking into Mr. Lepsing's supply closet was still on my radar, but at the moment I had more suspicions surrounding Gus than Mr. Lepsing. Mr. Lepsing ultimately just seemed like he didn't have it in him to work on a plan for mass chaos.

During my fourth-period gym class, I tried to map out a strategy while avoiding a barrage of dodge balls. I devised a way to make sure I could follow Gus around between every single class, during lunch, and then also to basketball practice, keeping my eyes open the whole time for anything suspicious. And if all of that produced no evidence, then I'd even follow him home. Whatever it took.

And so right after gym class, I tracked down Cade and Gus by heading in the direction of the classroom I'd seen them enter at the start of fourth period.

I ended up walking right by them. Gus definitely saw me, but had been too busy telling a story about this third-grade girl he stole an iPad from that weekend at the mall to acknowledge me.

As soon as they passed, I wheeled around and started to tail them. At a safe distance, of course. Eventually, they bumped knuckles and Cade split off down a different hallway, presumably to a different fifth-period class than Gus's.

Gus bobbed his head while he walked in time to some song apparently stuck in there. A few times he made a threatening gesture toward a passing kid. They all flinched, and Gus snickered each time as if the joke never got old.

One poor kid even got tripped, not realizing it was Gus who did it as he face-planted into the hard tiled floor. I had to resist helping him to his feet. Gus stopped just long enough to admire the pain he'd inflicted on the poor kid, and he would have seen me had I not quickly ducked behind a trash can. When he was finally satisfied that the kid had not enjoyed being tripped, Gus resumed his path of terror down the hallway. I stepped out from behind the trash can and resumed my pursuit. Gus took his phone from his pocket a few moments later, glanced at it, and then veered off suddenly into a bathroom.

Two kids hurried out a few seconds later, one of them still trying to hastily zip up his fly. As soon as Gus entered a bathroom, you got the heck out.

I knew this was my chance.

Judging by the way he'd changed his course upon checking his phone, Gus must have gotten a secret text message he wanted to read in private. And so I waited a few seconds and then entered the bathroom myself.

I had just become the first kid in the history of the school insane enough to knowingly follow Gus Agrio-poulas into a bathroom.

9000101010101010101010100110010101010101010.
910101010101010000101001010101001010101010
101010000100101010010101010010101010101010
90001   00110010101010101010101.
9010   0010101010010101010100
101   10101001010101010101010
900   110010101010101010

CHAPTER 15

LITTLE CHICAGO

THE BATHROOM WAS EMPTY.

All four urinals were unoccupied. I looked under the walls of the two stalls and saw no feet. Gus had come in here a second ago and now he was gone.

There were rumors that many of the town's oldest buildings had secret passageways that were used back in the days of Prohibition. They didn't call Minnow "Little Chicago" back then because it looked like a miniature version of the huge city or anything like that. It was called Little Chicago because it was one of the most important hubs of alcohol smuggling outside of Chicago itself.

Why would a kid be using a secret passageway in a school, if not to sneak around, committing acts of sabotage and framing principals as a part of some grand scheme to infiltrate and destroy the clandestine government agency located underneath the school itself?

But that's when one of the stall doors slowly creaked open.

Gus was standing on top of the toilet seat, which is why I hadn't seen his feet. He glared at me as he hopped down and took four impossibly quick strides, closing the distance between us in a fraction of a second.

Gus grabbed my shirt and lifted me several feet off the ground as if I were filled with helium instead of bones and blood and organs. He slammed me against the wall and put his face very close to mine.

"Listen," he said, his minty-fresh breath smelling surprisingly pleasant, "I don't know why you're following me around, but I don't like it."

"I'm sorry," I gasped, the collar of my shirt starting to dig into my neck. "I just think . . . you're cool."

"I don't care," he said. "But you're going to stop, got it? You're creeping me out."

I nodded. Or tried to. I didn't have much feeling left in my head or neck.

"Now, just as a fee for wasting my precious time, I'm going to dunk your head into that toilet a few times. You're lucky I like you, or else I would have taken a dump in it first."

He put me down, but only for a second. Before I could really react, he had lifted me up again. But this time he wrapped his arms around my waist and promptly tipped me upside down. He carried me over to the (thankfully) empty toilet and dunked my head into the water a few times. Then he set me down, not gently exactly, but he didn't drop me onto my head at least.

Gus crouched on one knee and looked down at my dripping face. I gagged. Just because the toilet had been empty didn't erase the cold fact that it was still toilet water. And the bowl had contained *contents* at some point in time. Maybe even that same day.

"Leave me alone," he said. "Or next time I'll tear your head off and use it to clog up the whole school's plumbing. Later, bud."

He walked toward the door, but then stopped. He turned back toward me, smiling.

"Again, though, dude," he said, "the goats were hilarious."

With that, he left me there, gagging on the water

running from my hair down into my eyes and mouth.

That hadn't necessarily gone well. Especially since I was still far from convinced that I could cross Gus's name off my list.

CHAPTER 16

MISSION PHASE ONE—
ELIMINATE ALL STEAK SAUCE

"**M**AKE ANY PROGRESS?" DANIELLE ASKED ME AS WE stood in line for lunch.

"Uh, sort of," I said.

I was reminded of Agent Chum Bucket's arrest when we saw his replacement, an old woman with a pouf of curly gray hair under a plastic net. I wondered how the Agency would contact us now if they needed to during school.

"What do you mean 'sort of'?" Danielle asked.

I explained my day as quickly and quietly as I could.

She seemed pretty horrified when I got to the swirly part. Which was fitting since it was actually pretty horrifying. In fact, I still hadn't recuperated enough to work up an appetite. I couldn't get the taste of the toilet water out of my mouth.

"So your top two names are 'maybes'?" she said.

I nodded as the old lady who'd replaced Chum Bucket scooped a blob of brown goo with chunks of some sort of "meat" in it onto my tray.

"What about you?" I asked.

"I think I can officially cross off Mrs. Food and Tyrell from my list," Danielle said. "Tyrell definitely isn't our guy. He has a solid alibi. Turns out he and his family were all away on vacation the past two weeks, visiting some spy museum in Washington, DC. I even saw the date-stamped pictures of them in front of the White House and Lincoln Memorial and at the museum."

"What about Mrs. Food?" I said.

"I asked her about some of her old CIA–KGB double agent missions at gym today."

"Really?" I asked.

"It's no big deal," she said. "Kids do it all the time. She loves telling those stories. I'd never really paid attention to them, of course, since I never had a reason to and always figured they were totally made up. Anyway, she spun off a few, one that I'd heard before about fighting off a twenty-seven-foot anaconda while snooping around inside the State Kremlin Palace in Moscow looking for a secret borscht soup recipe that doubled as the blueprints for creating a fusion bomb."

"Uhghghg." I shuddered. I hated snakes. Even more than swirlies.

"Yeah, well, that's the thing," Danielle said. "She said this was back in nineteen fifty-eight, but the State Palace at Moscow's Kremlin wasn't even built until 1961."

"Please tell me you had to look that up?" I said.

Danielle grinned at me and then shrugged.

"Hey, I like Cold War history, so sue me," she said. "But the point is none of the facts in her stories hold up. A bunch of other things she's said in the past don't add up either, like how Khrushchev was supposedly training a platoon of ferocious timber wolves to parachute into the US to wreak havoc."

"Hey, that could technically be true," I said. "You can't verify that it isn't as ridiculous as it sounds."

"Maybe not, except that she said Khrushchev got the idea from the opening scene of an old movie called *Red*

Dawn, but that movie didn't even come out until nineteen eighty-four."

"So?"

Danielle sighed as if she were talking to a wolf instead of a person.

"So, Khrushchev died in seventy-one! She's making it all up—she just likes to have fun with the kids, make them gasp and ooh and ah and all that."

"Okay," I said, as we headed toward our usual table. "But that doesn't prove much, does it?"

"Well," Danielle said, "it means she probably never was a spy, for one. And even more telling was when I snuck into her office during her off period. I saw her talking on the phone and she was talking to her granddaughter in, like, baby talk and telling her how she would make her cookies that weekend. Which proves she's lying about her whole backstory—she always tells us she never had kids. But she does—I saw pictures on her desk of her with a big family. And old pictures of her wearing a college cheerleading outfit and wedding photos and pictures of her with all of her kids when they were babies. She's just a strange old lady who likes to make kids do military drills in gym class while telling outlandish stories. Nothing more. At least, not as far as Medlock is concerned."

I nodded, impressed with her work so far. It made me feel sort of bad. I had two maybes and one complete unknown. She was definitely down to one name.

"What are you guys whispering about?" Dillon asked as we sat down at the table. "You guys plotting against me? Are you going to try and steal my brain during the night and use it to power your new PlayStations?"

Dillon was convinced that his brain generated its own powerful electricity and could be used as an everlasting battery should it ever be removed from his head. Well, that is, if you could keep it "entertained and hydrated," or so he said.

"Yeah, Dillon," I said. "We were just discussing where to buy the saw. I heard Home Depot's got a great deal on skull saws right now. Just forty-nine ninety-nine. Plus tax."

Danielle reached over and pretended to measure Dillon's skull with her hands.

"Come on, get off me." Dillon laughed, swatting at her hands.

Danielle and I laughed as well, almost like old times. I was again reminded that at some point we'd probably have to tell Dillon the truth. We both couldn't hide being a secret agent from him for much longer. Especially with how bad things were getting between Medlock and the Agency. For all we knew, the whole town could find out about the Agency soon, if Medlock's plan was carried out.

"What's up with you?" I asked him. "I haven't seen you much lately. Danielle says you're busy with researching some new theory."

"Oh, yeah!" he said getting that excited look on his face. "This is the Big One, man. In fact, I could really use your help with it. Want to help me collect samples Wednesday morning before school?"

"Before school?" I said. "As in, like, five or six?"

"Yeah, man," Dillon said excitedly. "That's the best time to catch the fungus unaware—that or late at night. But I need more morning samples. Come on, we haven't hung out in a while. It will be like old times. . . . Remember that summer when we went out every morning at six to see if we could amass the world's largest collection of living earthworms?"

To tell the truth, I didn't really want to get up that early to help Dillon with one of his ridiculous and pointless theories. But, honestly, I also felt really bad about how much I'd been blowing him off lately. Besides, it's not like I was really going to do any spy work at five in the morning.

"Okay, sure, let's do that," I said. "Tell me about the theory so I have some background."

"Awesome, you're the best!" he said, his eyes practically sparkling. "Well, I made some great progress just last night. Get this: I collected fourteen samples of fungus from the snowy fields north of our house. My early testing shows that they're just a few years from being able to pull themselves from the dirt on their own, having survived two winters now somehow. A few of them were even starting to form legs! I sent them off for more testing, lab testing, you see, but the preliminary results are good. Or, well, not so good when considering what the fungus is planning. Because I also uncovered evidence that their first-phase goals will be to eliminate all steak sauce—don't ask me why. But after that it gets even worse. . . ."

I was sort of listening to him ramble on about his new theory, but mostly I was trying to keep an eye on Gus. I'd spotted him in line shortly after sitting down. He sat at the same table he normally did with a few of his friends and hangers-on. He seemed to be acting relatively normal. He laughed and joked and made fun of several kids passing by. Typical Gus. Maybe he was just a sociopathic jerk and nothing more? Just because he was capable of supporting Medlock's insane plans didn't necessarily mean that he was actually the inside guy. That was pretty loose reasoning.

As I sat there, thinking it all over, I suddenly realized that I had been staring at Gus the entire time. And now he was staring directly back at me. With a scowl on his face.

A scowl that was now approaching me quickly from across the cafeteria.

0000101010101010101010100110010101010101010101010
0101010101010100001010010101010010101010101
1010100001001010010101010010101010101
000011010010011001101010101010101010
001001010101010010101010
101010100101010101010101
0011001010101010101010

CHAPTER 17

TRY MY RASPBERRY
TOE JAM

"**O**H, NO," I SAID.

"I know, right?" Dillon said excitedly. "If the strawberry jam didn't make the fungi samples recoil in pain, then why would apricot? It makes no sense at all, and yet it makes perfect sense!"

But Danielle noticed right away what I was talking about. Several of our other friends had, too. It was hard to miss a guy like Gus Agriopoulas charging across a school cafeteria with an expression like that on his face.

His expression could best be described as Grim Reaper.

I stood up quickly, accidentally knocking over my chair, drawing even more attention to the whole mess. For a moment, running seemed like the best option. But, then again, I was dealing with one of the fastest kids in the entire state. He'd probably be winning varsity high school track meets as an eighth grader later in the school year, breaking records set by kids four years older than him. I held up my hands.

"What did I tell you?" Gus shouted, only a few feet away from me now.

At this point, I had two options:

Cower and get the snot literally beaten out of my nasal cavity.

Try to figure out if Gus was working with Medlock, *and then* get the snot literally beaten out of my nasal cavity.

The way I figured it, if I was going to get pummeled in front of the whole school, I might as well accomplish something important while it happened.

"Wait, wait," I said, sounding desperate enough to make Gus pause right as he got to my table. I took a step back and spoke quickly, while I still had a fully operational mouth. "Did Medlock tell you to do this? Was it you who framed Gomez?"

I tried to speak softly, so that only he would hear me, since basically the entire cafeteria was watching us now.

My words stopped Gus dead in his tracks. His eyebrows furrowed up into a scrunchy mess on his forehead. Then he tilted his head like a dog seeing himself in the mirror for the first time.

"What are you talking about, Fender?" he asked.

He looked so utterly baffled that he might even have been reconsidering getting into a fight with me. What I had said must have sounded crazy, and crazy kids were unpredictable. Now that I was pretty sure Gus had no connection to Medlock (no one was that good an actor, not even Meryl Streep), I decided to play it up, try and use that angle to my advantage, now that I had it.

"I'm talking about jam!" I shouted, trying to sound like a lunatic, channeling my inner Dillon. "Raspberry jam! Gus-Putin, you've got to try my raspberry toe jam!"

I started flapping my arms like a bird. Gus took a step back. It was working! I was actually scaring him away from—

And that's when Gus's fist connected with my sternum. I have no idea why he went for a torso punch instead of caving in my face, but I suppose either way it was definitely a sign that he had tired of my antics rather quickly.

I flew back about five feet and landed hard. My chest felt like it had shattered into a million pieces. I gasped once and started climbing back to my feet. With a guy like Gus, you couldn't ever let your defenses down, no matter how bad you were hurt. Gus didn't feel remorse or empathy. He wouldn't stop a beating out of pity or satisfaction. Once he decided to destroy you, he wouldn't stop until someone made him stop.

I figured I had at least a small chance; after all, I was a secret agent who had taken down fully grown men with huge machine guns before.

But I never even got the chance to fight back against Gus, because the lunchroom aides were closing in on us now. Which, to be honest, I was pretty happy about. Three teachers swooped in and grabbed both Gus and me and then marched us out of the cafeteria while the fourth teacher tried to calm the cheering students and herd them back to their lunch tables.

Gus and I were taken to Mr. Gomez's office. Or, his

former office—it wasn't his office anymore. The name-plate on the door had been replaced with a new one:

Ms. Jayne Pullman

Ms. Pullman was behind the desk beyond the open door as we were led to the two chairs just outside the office. She sat there calmly and smiled at me as we passed. There was something about that smile that rattled my bones. I tried to shake it off as I took a seat outside. Gus was led directly into her office.

As I sat there and waited for my turn, all I could think about was that smile. It was a smile that told me all at once that she knew everything about me, had some sort of evil plan already in place, and that there was nothing I could do to get in her way.

It was the exact same smile I'd seen on Medlock's face.

0010101010101010100110010101010101010101010
1010101010100000101001010101010010101010100
010100001001010010101010010101010101010101
0010101010101010011001   101010
01010110101000100101   1001
010100001001010010101   0101
                CHAPTER 18

A FRESH START

I DIDN'T HEAR ANY SCREAMING OR SHOUTING AS I SAT OUTSIDE Ms. Pullman's office. In fact, I heard nothing at all coming from behind the wooden door. If it had still been Mr. Gomez's office, I'd have heard plenty of sputtering and shouting. Gomez was a classic screamer.

The attendance secretary looked at me as I fidgeted nervously. "Back again already, Carson?"

I shrugged. I had gotten to know Mrs. Bradshaw pretty well over the past year and a half. After all, I had probably spent a good third of my time at this school in this office. She was a nice lady, and I don't think she disliked me as much as most of the other adults at the school did.

"Well, don't worry." She smiled. "Ms. Pullman is real nice. I think you'll find her to be quite . . . *different*. She's even already approved a plan to get us a heated parking lot that Mr. Gomez had been rejecting for years. How neat is that?"

"Oh, yeah, sounds cool," I said, trying to sound sincere. "Thanks, Mrs. Bradshaw."

What she couldn't possibly know was that I wasn't nervous about whatever punishment was headed my way. I was nervous because it was a distinct possibility that Ms. Pullman was a diabolical secret agent working for one of the most evil criminal masterminds the world had ever known.

But there wasn't really enough time to explain that properly to the attendance secretary.

A short time later, the door opened and Gus walked out, and I saw something I never thought I ever would. Gus was crying. Tears ran down his cheeks and he wiped at them sheepishly. How in the world had Ms. Pullman managed that?

He looked at me and then looked away quickly. He turned back to Ms. Pullman.

"Thank you again," he said.

She just smiled and waved and then he bolted out of the administration office area before I could say anything to him. I was almost too stunned to notice that Ms. Pullman was beckoning for me to head inside her office now. Slowly, I stood up and followed her in.

"Close the door please," she said.

Her voice was soft and soothing. Like, you could listen to a recording of her reading aloud at night and it'd lull you into the most peaceful sleep of your life. It also made you want to obey every word without question.

I closed the door and then sat down across from her.

She'd already made a few decorative changes. It seemed brighter and somehow larger than the tiny death trap that had been Mr. Gomez's office. She'd even gotten the broken window fixed. For several weeks under Mr. Gomez, it had been covered by cardboard and duct tape. And now after less than a day in charge, she already had it replaced with a real new window. A pot of white lilies sat on the corner of the desk, enjoying the sunshine. I tried to focus on the flowers rather than look into the face of my new enemy.

Ms. Pullman was probably around my mom's age. She was pretty and had large eyes and never seemed to blink.

She smiled at me patiently. I attempted to smile back.

"So," she began, "Gus tells me you two had a sort of misunderstanding today?"

I nodded.

"Why don't you tell me what happened."

It was such an unusual thing to hear from the person sitting across from me in this office that I almost didn't understand her words at all. Mr. Gomez had never, ever asked for my side of the story first. He usually started things out with shouting and wild, paranoid accusations.

After taking a few breaths to calm my nerves, I explained to Ms. Pullman that I had been following Gus. I told her I was convinced that he had stolen a textbook of mine but was too afraid to confront him. Then later, I found it in the messy depths of my locker. At lunch, I had merely been daydreaming and was looking the wrong way and he thought I was staring at him. A small skirmish had ensued.

"Well, that more or less matches the account he gave me," she said. "Do you wish to add anything else before I officially close this matter?"

I froze for a moment. Was this over? Just like that? What was her game? I was baffled. I just shook my head.

"Great!" she said brightly, as if we were discussing cute

puppies instead of a school fight. "Well, I see no need to issue any detention in this matter. At least for you—Gus will be serving some detention, of course. Punching another student will not go unpunished. But, ultimately, Gus assured me that the whole thing is over now. Unless you feel otherwise?"

"Uh, no, ma'am," I said.

"Wonderful! Now, you and I have another matter to address."

My mind reeled. Was she going to tell me she knew who I was and then pull out a silenced pistol and plant a bullet in my forehead? I grabbed the arms of the chair and tensed, waiting for the possible arrival of a bullet. Would I feel it, even for a second? Or would there just suddenly be nothing?

"I've reviewed Mr. Gomez's file on you," she said. "It's quite extensive. Impressive, almost. The sheer size of it, and also the detail with which he documented your activities. That said, I'm not entirely certain that it was very fair or healthy or warranted for Mr. Gomez to obsess over you the way he did."

"Ms. Pullman, you don't underst— Wait, what?" I said.

"That's right," she said, smiling. "I think he had you pegged as a bad apple from the get-go. But there isn't much in the way of hard evidence linking you to any of the incidents he discusses. It reads more like the ramblings of a conspiracy theorist, to be honest with you. It appears as if he never really treated you fairly. Do you not agree?"

"No . . . I mean, yes," I said, not sure what to say. The fact was, I did agree . . . somewhat. He never had any evidence, but to his credit, I usually was the guilty party. Somehow I suspected Ms. Pullman knew that as well, in spite of what she was telling me. Not that I was going to admit to any of that. "Yeah, I suppose it wasn't fair."

Ms. Pullman nodded. Then she picked up my massive file from her desk, it was at least five inches thick. She dropped it into the trash can next to her. It landed inside the metal bin with a thump that almost sounded like a gunshot. I flinched.

"I want you to know that as of this moment, you have a clean slate," she said. "I want to give you a fair chance. Trust can be a very powerful and empowering thing. But, in order for it to work, it has to go both ways completely. I will always be honest and straight with you, and give you the benefit of the doubt in any future run-ins you and I might have. But I need the same in return. It's vital if we're going to make this work. You strike me as a good person, Carson, and I have a feeling you mean well. But if any evidence comes to my attention that you, say, let goats loose inside this school, and you lie about it, then whatever trust we have built will be destroyed, and you will find me much more unpleasant to deal with than Mr. Gomez. Do I make myself clear?"

Her tone was still mostly pleasant, but I got the sense that Ms. Pullman didn't deal in lies and empty threats. Once again, I'd been struck dumb.

"Yes, it's clear," I said. "Thank you for the second chance."

"It's not a second chance," she said. "In my eyes, you've yet to do anything wrong. But let's not ever get to second and third chances, right?"

I nodded.

"Okay, dismissed, Carson," she said.

I got up to leave, more confused than ever. She didn't seem at all like an evil enemy secret agent. Maybe Director Isadoris's hunch was completely off? Maybe her background check was squeaky clean because she actually was squeaky clean? But if that were the case, then why would Medlock go through all the trouble to have Mr. Gomez removed from school?

As I walked to my next class, I realized that the only

way I would get an answer to that question was to find out who had framed Gomez. And so I turned my focus back to my first mission objective: locating the enemy spy.

Gus Agriopoulas was officially crossed off. And so it was probably time to go back to the first name on my list, Mr. Lepsing. I had to find a way to get inside his supply closet and see what he was really hiding in there.

CHAPTER 19

GOOD LOCKS HIDE
GOOD TREASURES
IN THE VALLEY OF THE FOLD

I KNEW MR. LEPSING WOULDN'T BE IN HIS CLASSROOM AFTER school. He was an odd guy, sure, but he was also somewhat predictable. Every kid knew he had a routine that he always stuck to: Every day after school, he went out to his small car parked across the street, off school property, and smoked a pipe. He smoked a really long pipe with a small bowl at the end, kind of like the one Gandalf uses. It looked kind of ridiculous. Once the first kid in school saw him out there years ago, the word spread quickly. Now every kid in the school had taken the time to go see him smoking his wizard pipe by the end of their sixth-grade year—it was sort of like a rite of passage at Erik Hill Middle School.

Then he'd come back in and grade papers or do other work until 5:00 p.m. All teachers pretty much stayed at school until 5:00 p.m. It might have been some sort of rule. Not that all of the teachers followed it all the time. But, either way, I knew that from 3:16 p.m. to around 3:39 p.m., Mr. Lepsing would be in his car, smoking his weird pipe.

Danielle had agreed to help me make sure the hallway stayed clear by causing some sort of commotion around the corner. As I lurked near Mr. Lepsing's classroom, I heard a few kids talking to each other as they hurried her way.

"Dude, some girl is giving away prewritten essay papers and book reports."

"Hurry up," the other kid said as they rushed past. "I got one due in a few days."

And then I was alone in the hallway. For now. Her distraction probably had an expiration date. Most things did.

Mr. Lepsing's classroom was locked, but my skills picking standard locks were getting pretty sharp. It didn't take very long to get inside. I closed the door behind me and kept the lights off.

I moved toward his supply closet. Up until this point, picking a school lock had never been a problem. Every interior door in the school had the same type of lock: a simple four-pin tumbler lock, which is both common and easy to pick.

But Mr. Lepsing had installed a custom lock on his supply closet door to help conceal whatever was hidden inside. It looked slightly different from all the other standard school doorknobs. I inspected it. Just because it was a different model didn't mean it would be any harder to pick.

I got to work and quickly identified that one of the pins was a spool pin, which can make picking it a lot harder, especially for a relative beginner like me. Agent Nineteen had given me a little bit of spool-pin training, but not nearly as much as with standard tumbler pins.

I cursed even though nobody was around to hear me.

The trick was to release all tension on the lock in order to get the spool pin past the shear line. I gave it a few tries. They were unsuccessful. I silently wished that I had an Agency fruit roll-up with me. Not for a snack, of course, but for blowing this lock up. But that wasn't going to happen now. They'd made those things specifically for me and I didn't even know if they had any left, let alone how I could get my hands on one. There weren't any in the stash of other gadgets I'd gotten from Chum Bucket's storeroom the day before either.

I closed my eyes and tried to envision the inside of the lock. It was pickable. I knew that because I'd seen Agent Nineteen do it a few times back during my initial training. I'd also watched YouTube videos of people doing it. If some yokel who had time to post videos on the internet could do it, then so could I—I was a secret agent, with a codename and everything.

A few deep breaths later, I was back at work. I tried it again and again with varying levels of tension and angles, but just couldn't get the pin to move. If only I had some graphite powder to loosen everything up . . . sometimes that's all a tricky lock needed.

That's when it hit me.

Everything Mr. Lepsing had was old. Which mean he likely still had good old-fashioned graphite pencils in his desk. I dug around in the top drawer and found a few ancient, yellow number two pencils.

I scraped one rapidly across the wood grain of his desk for five or six seconds until two parallel lines of graphite powder developed. I used a piece of paper to gently scrape them onto a notecard. Then I made a single crease in the notecard down the center, creating an upside-down tent so all the graphite powder collected in the valley of the fold.

I slowly moved back toward the door, cradling the notecard in front of me like a tiny cup of radioactive waste. I steadied my hands as I positioned the front of the crease right next to the lock opening.

A very slight inhale was followed by a gentle exhale into the notecard's valley. I watched as most of the graphite powder disappeared into the key slot. I was still shocked it had worked, when, a short time later, I heard a click as I got all of the pins to finally slide into place. I grabbed the doorknob, careful not to move my equipment inside the lock, and turned. My heart leaped at the unlikely success of my makeshift lock lubricant.

Mr. Lepsing's supply closet door swung open in front of me, and then I was face-to-face with darkness.

0000101010101010100110010101010101010101010
010101010101010000101001010101001010101
1010100001001010010101010010101010101
00001 0011001010101010101010
0010 0010101010010101010
101 1010100101010101010101
000 110010101010101010101

CHAPTER 20

LARGER THAN LIFE

I WAS ALMOST AFRAID TO SWITCH ON THE LIGHT, AFRAID OF WHAT I might find. So many rumors, so much speculation. What if one of them ended up being true? I knew there was only one way I would find out.

After feeling around on the wall for a few seconds, I located the light switch and flipped it up.

As it turned out, one of Dillon's theories had been right yet again. I found myself staring at a small table covered in little sculptures. They appeared to be made of wax, and right away I had a feeling that they were earwax, as evidenced by the little wispy gray hairs sticking out of some of the figures.

The wax sculptures were mostly unidentifiable, but several of them appeared to be people dancing in groups of five, each a few inches tall. Even at that size, it was hard to mistake the tiny wax microphones in their hands. How in the world could Dillon have possibly guessed that? Earwax sculptures of boy bands?

I stood there and stared, completely dumbfounded. I didn't know whether to be amazed, disgusted, relieved, or disappointed—disappointed that Mr. Lepsing wasn't the spy, putting me right back to square one. Then again, I was now able to cross another name off the list, which was progress at least.

Turns out, Mr. Lepsing was so secretive because he was a legitimate weirdo with legitimately weird habits to hide. I switched off the light and closed the supply closet door behind me, and snuck back out into the hallway.

Just as I was turning to head toward the nearest school exit, I saw a dark figure running from a room at the end of the hall. It was someone in a black hooded sweatshirt, just a dark blur as they ran out the emergency exit.

The room they had just come from was Agent Nineteen's music room.

It took me a few seconds to act, but eventually I unplanted my feet and ran toward the room. Whoever the figure had been hadn't even bothered to cover their tracks. They'd left both the music room door and Agent Nineteen's office door wide open.

The office was completely trashed. Papers were scattered everywhere, all the equipment broken and smashed. The piano was even partially dismantled. I knew right away that the dark, hooded figure was my enemy spy. And I also suspected that I knew exactly what they'd been doing in there. They'd been looking for the entrance into Agent Nineteen's secret back office. Thankfully, the intruder had clearly failed. I turned to leave, to go running out the same emergency exit to see if I could pick up the trail.

But when I spun around, I found myself looking directly into Ms. Pullman's unsmiling face.

0010101010101010101001100101010101010101010101010
1010101010101000010100101010100101010100
0101000010010100101010100101010101010101
0001010101010101001100...............101010
0101011010100010010...............01001
0101000010010100101...............0101
0010101010101010100110...............1010

CHAPTER 21

GROWING GILLS

"**I** KNOW IT LOOKS BAD, BUT IT WASN'T ME," I PLEADED.

We were back in Ms. Pullman's office. Neither of us had spoken during the long walk there from Agent Nineteen's music room.

"Why were you even in that area of the school at all?" Ms. Pullman asked.

Her demeanor was different from the way it had been after the fight at lunch, but it was still calm. Controlled. Not at all the sputtering, shouting mess that Gomez always turned into when dealing with a disciplinary situation. It was sort of unnerving in an odd way. Like when your mom, instead of getting mad over something you did, just told you she was disappointed in you.

I wasn't sure how to answer Ms. Pullman's question. So I shook my head. Like an amateur. Sitting there shaking my head, opening and closing my mouth like a dying fish, was basically as good as an admission of guilt. That was me right then: Carson with gills and beady unblinking eyes, struggling to breathe.

The ultimate question was: If she actually was in cahoots with Medlock, then she knew darn well it wasn't me who had ransacked the office, and if that were the case, then why had she gone down there at all, considering that a spy was trying to complete a mission there? More and more, the signs pointed toward Ms. Pullman being innocent, which raised the possibility that Mr. Gomez hadn't been framed at all.

"Carson," she said.

I snapped out of my daze.

"We're not leaving until I get an answer," she said firmly. "Why were you in that area of the school?"

"I—I," I stammered. "I was walking through the halls, just on my way to meet up with my friend. And then I saw the craziest thing; it was this giant, like, rat. And its ears were human ears, or something, and then this tall guy with rat ears showed up and—"

"Let me stop you, Carson," Ms. Pullman interrupted. "If the next words out of your mouth are anything but the truth, then we're going to have a major problem. *Trust*, Carson, remember? You're giving me very little reason to ever trust you again right now. Think carefully before you speak."

I exhaled. Maybe she was right. And so I did the only thing I could do, something I'd never done before inside that office. I told the truth.

Not the whole truth, of course, about me being a spy and everything. But I told her that I had been breaking into Mr. Lepsing's supply closet on a dare. I explained the years of rumors among the kids, and that I had drawn the short straw on being the guy who had to finally find out what he kept in there. I even told her about what I found inside his supply closet, wondering if that part might actually make her think I was lying again. Those wax figures were hardly any less weird or disturbing than a rat with human ears. Then I explained how when I came out of the classroom I saw a dark figure running from Mr. Jensen's room and walked down there to investigate. And that's when she found me there, looking guilty, and rightfully so, but for totally different reasons than she suspected.

When I was done, she nodded slowly. "That's quite a story," she said.

"I know," I said.

"But I believe you. I appreciate your coming clean about breaking into Mr. Lepsing's supply closet. That takes guts, Carson. And intelligence, too. Don't you think?"

I shrugged. I seriously doubted I was that smart, not after finding a way to botch pretty much everything somehow.

"I'm proud of you," she said. "Truly."

"Um, thank you?" I said, shocked that the gamble seemed like it would actually pay off.

"That said," Ms. Pullman finished, "you're still getting one week of detention, an hour each day. And a stern warning, Carson. I'll admit I'm a bit disappointed that you've gotten yourself into trouble so quickly, considering what I thought was a very nice meeting we had today."

"I know," I said, looking down. "I'm disappointed, too."

And I really meant it. I *liked* Ms. Pullman. It was such an odd feeling, actually liking one of my principals. If it wasn't for the whole secret agent thing, I think I really would have been trying to be on my best behavior. But, as it was, I was a secret agent now and I couldn't change that. And so odds were that I'd find my way in here again before too long.

But unlike Mr. Gomez, Ms. Pullman wasn't going to let me keep getting away with it all. She was a woman of her word. She knew it, and I knew it. If I wasn't careful, I really would get myself expelled, whether or not I was able to save the world.

CHAPTER 22

ALWAYS PUT MONEY
ON FAMILY

ONE GOOD THING ABOUT WHAT HAD HAPPENED THAT DAY WAS that it allowed Danielle and me to cross off more names from our list of suspects. We were down to just one each. Which meant that by the end of the next day, we would either know who the enemy agent was, or we'd be back at square one with virtually no clues and no leads at all as to who might have framed Mr. Gomez and why.

Danielle's last suspect was Ophelia Perkins, Jake's cousin. My last name was Peter "Junior" Nilsson. I couldn't be sure whether either of them was the right size to be the hooded figure I'd seen running from Agent Nineteen's office. Which meant we still needed to thoroughly vet both the remaining suspects.

But my money was on Ophelia. She had the family connection, after all. Just like Jake, who, outside of that, also seemed an unlikely candidate to be an enemy spy. And so we couldn't let Ophelia's do-gooder status and high grades deter our investigation. I quietly reminded Danielle of that several times during lunch the following day.

After lunch, I had one goal in mind: finding Junior and verifying that I could cross him off the list. But as soon as I saw him later that afternoon, between sixth and seventh periods, I knew that it might not be that simple after all.

At first, when I spotted him heading to his locker, everything seemed normal. I caught up to him and said hi. We weren't friends technically, but as two of the school's more notorious troublemakers, we still crossed paths from time to time. And there was a sort of mutual respect there, in spite of our different styles.

"Hey, Carson," Junior said with a grin as he spun his locker dial. "Nice job with the goats the other day. Hilarious! Especially all the goat poo."

"Yeah, thanks," I said, not surprised that goat poo in the hallway was his favorite part. "So what have you been up to lately?"

"Me?" he said. "Nothing, why? Got something planned?"

"Maybe," I said. "So your schedule is totally clear if I needed your help with another prank?"

He finally got the correct combination entered and pulled open his locker. And that's when things started to get more suspicious. There was a black hoodie hanging inside it. There were a lot of black hooded sweatshirts out there, of course, but it was too much of a coincidence to ignore.

As was his eventual response.

"Uh, well, yeah, sort of," he said, suddenly seeming to be nervous. "I mean, I've got some stuff after school a lot lately. But I mean, yeah, I should be free."

He saw me eyeballing the hoodie and quickly slammed his locker shut.

"Hey, Junior, where were you yesterday at—" I started to ask, but he didn't let me finish.

"Look, man, I'd love to chat, but I gotta go," he said, turning away. "I'm running late."

I stood there and watched him scamper nervously down the hall, suddenly realizing that I now had a lot more work ahead of me.

But I also finally had a solid lead.

0000101010101010101010011001010101010101010
0101010101010000101001010101001010101
1010100001001010010101010010101010101
00001   001100101010101010101010
0010   001010101010010101010
101   1010100101010101010101
000   110010101010101010101

CHAPTER 23

HANDCUFFED IN DETENTION

THE WORST PART ABOUT THE DETENTION I'D GOTTEN FROM Ms. Pullman was that it kept me from being able to follow Junior to investigate his activities. Instead, I was stuck in a room with a few other kids, just sitting there and staring out the window into one of the school's parking lots.

A few minutes after I got there, two construction trucks rolled up and guys in overalls and hard hats began setting up orange cones. Moments later, one of them was hammering away at the pavement with a jackhammer.

"I wonder what's going on," I muttered, more to myself than anything.

But the kid next to me must have thought I was talking to him, because he answered me.

"My dad said it's a controversial new project to install a solar-powered snow-melting system under the school's parking lots that the new principal finally got pushed through," he said. "Apparently, Gomez had been dragging his feet on it all year, worried about the construction causing a distraction and also thinking that all that solar-powered hippy crap never works. Anyway, now they have to hammer out the whole structural base of the east parking lot to try to get it installed in just a few days before winter *really* sets in."

I recognized my detention neighbor. It was Vance Wheeler. His dad was a sixth-grade teacher and had a big mouth at the dinner table, which meant that Vance always had the inside scoop on the school and other teachers.

"Huh, interesting," I said.

"Yeah, sure," Vance said as if he thought I was being sarcastic. "It's like watching a fireworks show with a sugar high."

But I had actually meant it. Perhaps that was why

Gomez was framed? He wasn't approving this project, which could very easily have something to do with the Agency headquarters located a few miles down from where they were breaking up the parking lot pavement. Then again, even if that was why Medlock framed Gomez, it didn't necessarily mean that Pullman was in on it. Maybe Medlock simply knew that Ms. Pullman, who struck me as a lady who knew how to get stuff done and was way more willing to take chances on new things, would push the project through right away.

This was getting complicated. I didn't know what to think or believe anymore. And all I could think about as I sat there and watched the W Construction crew tear up the parking lot, was how much I missed having Agents Nineteen and Blue around to talk to. They had always been there for me, a kind of safety net that I could land in if I needed to.

But now they were gone and I was on my own. Danielle was a great friend, but she was just as inexperienced as I was. There was no net anymore.

I didn't like being the last line of defense. Being a secret agent had been so much easier when there were other agents who knew what they were doing, when it felt like there was a giant machine behind me every step of the way.

I had never seemed so weak. So vulnerable. And it was all because of Medlock. One rogue agent. One man going back on his promise had taken down the whole operation, and basically all that stood between him and world domination was me.

A kid stuck in detention.

CHAPTER 24

A MEETING OF HOODED FIGURES IN THE WOODS PLOTTING CREEPY RITUALISTIC THINGS BETTER LEFT UNSAID

EVEN WORKING WITH REDUCED MANPOWER, THE AGENCY scared me. They could still pull off the impossible. Like, getting a message into my dinner at home that night. How they did that, and made sure that it ended up on *my* plate, I'll never know. I didn't even want to know.

But nonetheless, it was there, in my third bite of stroganoff.

MEET US BEHIND THE GARAGE IN YOUR ALLEY AT 8:19 P.M.

By "us" I had kind of hoped they meant Agent Nineteen and/or Agent Blue. But instead it was Agent Smiley, along with Danielle, who had apparently gotten a similar message in her corn chowder that evening.

"Status report," Agent Smiley said without so much as a wave or greeting of any kind.

We filled her in on everything we'd found so far. What I saw near Agent Nineteen's office. The names we'd crossed off our lists. The names we still had to go—the fact that I'd spotted Junior with a hooded sweatshirt just like the music room intruder's. What I'd found out about the construction site. We told her everything.

And her face never changed the entire time. It remained blank. If it weren't for her occasional nods and blinks, I'd have suspected she was sleepwalking, or dead. When we finished, Agent Smiley didn't offer any sort of compliment. Instead, she just gave us another assignment.

"New objective," she said. "Try and get closer to the construction zone. Find out what is going on there as soon as possible. This is in addition to your ongoing work locating the enemy spy."

"Why can't you investigate the construction zone?" I asked. "You could have a team there right now checking it out."

She stared at me and I wondered briefly if she was trying to decide whether or not to slap me. But if that was the case, she apparently decided not to. Her face remained calm and unemotional when she replied. "We are looking into it independently," she said. "But we'd like you to do so as well. I don't think we need to justify why. That's not how this works. We give an assignment, and then you carry it out. *That's* how this goes."

I sighed and nodded. I wished they trusted me enough to tell me more than they did. But at the same time, that was the reality of being a secret agent. The secrets never ended. Covert was the name of the game. If you didn't like it . . . well, I guess you became Medlock.

"Okay," I said, starting to feel overwhelmed by all of my missions. And never mind school. That was over. I didn't think I'd gotten anything above a D on a test or assignment in weeks. I'd flunk out before I even completed any of my missions at this rate.

"Also," she said offhandedly, "I'm supposed to tell you that Agent Nineteen has regained consciousness and is doing well."

We both perked up at that. "When can we see him?" Danielle asked.

"Soon," Agent Smiley said. "Come to the shed

tomorrow after school for another progress report."

And then she turned and walked away, disappearing into the shadows of the alley.

I looked at Danielle with my eyebrows raised.

"Wow," she said.

"No kidding," I agreed. "Wait, are you saying that about Agent Smiley, or the news on Agent Nineteen, or the additional assignment?"

"Uh, all three," she said. "I think."

"What about Ophelia?"

Danielle shook her head.

"It's not her," she said. "I don't think she even knows that she has an uncle Medlock at all. But even further, I found out she has debate team after school every day, and was there yesterday when Nineteen's office was ransacked, confirmed by three other students and the debate coach."

I nodded, not questioning her further. After how many times she'd saved my skin the past week, I trusted her probably more than anyone else in the world. Even Agents Blue and Nineteen. Danielle and I went back way before the Agency, our friendship cut right through that stuff.

"So that leaves us with Junior," I said.

Danielle shrugged. "Lots of kids have black hoodies, but considering the circumstances, it *is* pretty incriminating. I'll help you keep an eye on him."

"Thanks," I said. "Since I have detention after school, I think I'm going to have to get there early to scope out the parking lot construction. Can you make it?"

"Shoot, I can't," she said. "Dillon would get too suspicious. He's already been asking me a lot more questions than usual lately. If I'm already gone when he gets up early to collect more fungus samples, it's going to be an issue."

"Oh, man, that's right!" I nearly shouted. "I forgot all about that."

"What is it?" she asked.

"I made plans to help Dillon with his weird mushroom collection thing tomorrow morning," I said.

I knew it would upset him to cancel; I'd been basically ignoring him lately with all this Agency madness. But I had to back out—there was no way I could blow off my assignment for some ridiculous mushroom collecting thing that was completely pointless. I had no choice, so I pulled out my phone and sent him a text.

I can't make it tomorrow, sry man . . . don't hate me . . .

I gotta go to school early for xtra help.

"Yeah, he'll definitely be bummed," Danielle said as I typed. "He'd be even more disappointed and suspicious if I take off early now, too. Maybe I will help him instead. Are you sure you can cover the construction thing alone?"

"Yeah, totally. We don't have much choice anyway," I said. "Besides, if you snuck out early, Dillon would probably think you were going to some kind of Meeting of Hooded Figures in the Woods Plotting Creepy Ritualistic Things Better Left Unsaid or something."

Danielle smirked at first and then a laugh burst from her mouth like it had forced its way out. She covered her mouth in surprise, which made me laugh, too. And that's how our night ended, somehow in spite of everything happening, with both of us standing in my dark alley, laughing at nothing like lunatics.

01010101010101010101010101010101010101010101010
01010101010101000010100010101001010101
1010100001001010010101010010101010101
00001   001100101010101010101010
0010   00101010100101010101010
101   CHAPTER 25   10101001010101010101
000   1100101010101010101010

CURSING
YOUR ANCESTORS

IT WAS AN ESPECIALLY COLD MORNING, EVEN FOR NOVEMBER IN North Dakota, which made riding my bike to school instead of taking the bus torturous. I'd actually rather have been getting tortured by Mule Medlock's little psychopathic friend, Packard, than have to spend another minute out in the subzero temperatures. Thankfully there was no snow to add to the misery—it was too cold outside for snow to fall. Yes, that's a real thing that happens in awful places like this.

And don't ever let anyone tell you that people get

used to weather this cold. Trust me, there is no getting used to negative ten-degree weather. It's impossible. It's simply too painful. You don't get used to it, you just get slightly better at surviving it.

There were times just like this one every year, where I cursed my ancestors for settling down in North Dakota instead of a normal state. There were dozens of perfectly normal, nonfreezing states they could have lived in. Why on earth had they chosen this one? But there wasn't much I could do about that now except pedal faster.

By the time I got to the school, I had frozen boogers crusted to my upper lip and it felt like shards of icicles were stabbing my eyes repeatedly. But I couldn't head inside the building just yet. There was still the matter of the parking lot investigation to attend to. Besides, the school doors weren't open for students this early anyway.

I locked up my bike just as the glow of the sun appeared behind the horizon. The sun had not yet risen, but the promise of it doing so soon seemed to warm me a degree or two. My phone vibrated just after I finished securing my bike. It was from Dillon, his first response to me backing out on him that morning.

whatever man i guess Danielle might help me anyway.

I texted a quick reply.

Thnx for understanding. U sure youre not mad?

His response came right away.

Whatever. U do what you have to do I guess.

I sort of got the impression that he was holding back. That he was actually hurt and angry about it all. But I couldn't worry about that at the moment. I had a job to do.

It was still too early for the work crew to have arrived, and it was eerily silent as I approached the construction zone. They had made a lot of progress in just one day. Several large yellow and orange construction machines loomed silently next to a shockingly deep and wide hole in the parking lot.

The hole was probably fifty feet in diameter and at least fifteen feet deep. Pipes and broken concrete were scattered across the frozen ground inside the pit, covered in a sparkling layer of ice crystals—like winter's version of dew. There were several trucks and other equipment with W Construction Co. logos stamped on them surrounding the hole.

I got right up next to the large door on a giant machine that was basically an oversized shovel. I walked around to get a better look inside the pit. And that's when I saw the large plastic bin attached to the other side of the machine.

It was a translucent plastic container that looked to have several rolled-up blueprints inside it.

The container wasn't locked and the lid snapped off easily. I reached inside to pull out a tube when the huge digging machine suddenly sprang to life. The diesel engine roared and gurgled a few feet from my face and I tripped over a loose chunk of cement behind me.

Then, I was falling.

I tumbled backward into the pit, grabbing at the sides, trying to catch myself. The cold and numb hands inside my mittens couldn't really get ahold of anything and I slid all the way to the bottom of the pit. My flailing had slowed me enough to keep from shattering any bones in the fall, but that didn't matter since I quickly discovered that my snow boot had gotten wedged in between two frozen pipes in the dug-up ground below me.

The pipes squeezed my ankle as I attempted to pull free. Then I heard the hiss of hydraulics. The huge shovel started descending right toward me. And I knew that any machine that could tear a hole in this frozen ground would have no problem crushing me like an overripe grape, splattering my insides all over the bottom of the pit like spilled juice.

The shovel moved slowly but steadily. Ten feet away.

Then eight.

Then four.

I yanked at my foot with both hands to no avail.

This was it. There was no escape. My mission and life were about to come to a crushing defeat.

Pun intended.

0101010101010101010110010101010101010101
010101010101000010100101010100101010100
101000010010100101010100101010101010101
000101010101010100110011010101...101010
010101101010001001010101010101...01001
010100010010100101010101010...0101
0010101010101010100110...101010

CHAPTER 26

CAN HUMAN TEETH
CHEW THROUGH HUMAN BONES?

UNLESS I COULD SOMEHOW CHEW THROUGH MY ANKLE IN THE next twenty-five seconds, I was going to die. Once again, the image of my hot insides splattering all over the frozen pit, steaming like stir-fry in the cold air, flashed into my mind.

It would not be a pretty way to go.

It certainly wasn't the hero's death that all secret agents probably hoped for if they were going to die in the line of duty. I had survived two assaults on the hide-outs of dangerous criminals, only to die at the hands of a stupid power shovel. I thought again about the possibility of cutting off my own leg somehow, even as the giant metal scoop descended to just a few feet away. It was so large up close that it blocked everything else from my view, enveloping me in darkness.

But the grisly thought of chopping off my own foot brought with it the easy solution to my problem. A solution so blatantly obvious that I was ashamed it had taken me this long to figure it out. I could have freed myself long before it had come to thoughts of popping like a grape and self-amputation.

I ripped off my mittens with my teeth, exposing my fingers to the harsh air. They dried up and turned pink within a fraction of a second, losing most of whatever feeling the mittens had been preserving. But the adrenaline kept them from shriveling up into useless, shivering fists.

Untying my boot with nearly frozen, clunky fingers that I couldn't feel was not as easy as it might sound. But the direness of my situation helped, as I ripped at the laces. The lowering metal scoop was so oppressively close to me now that I'd have slammed my head against it were I to sit up straight.

Finally, I loosened the laces just enough to allow me

to tear my foot free from the boot. The force of finally breaking away slammed my shoulder into the hard metal of the scoop. I winced but knew there was no time to waste. I spun onto my belly and scrambled up the side of the pit just as the scoop finished lowering and smashed into the ground and pipes where I'd been stuck just a second before.

I sat there and took as many deep breaths as I could manage, the icy air stinging my lungs like poison. Then I shifted my gaze up toward the cabin of the giant machine. It was empty. Whoever had powered up and lowered the scoop was gone.

The hydraulics groaned as they continued to press the scoop into the cold ground. I stood up, my exposed foot already turning into a block of clunky, frozen flesh. After retrieving my mittens, I clambered up to the side of the pit and tried to climb out. There was nothing to grab on to. My painfully cold foot was not helping.

There was a real risk that I could freeze to death inside this pit if I couldn't get myself out. In this kind of weather, a person could get frostbite in a matter of minutes. I wish I was kidding or exaggerating. Do you now understand the insanity of choosing to live in North Dakota?

I assessed my situation, looking all around the pit for

any kind of handhold or ladder or anything I could use to climb out. And once again the solution was so obvious that I had missed it by overthinking the problem.

The giant scoop.

I ran over and climbed up onto the hydraulic arm. It vibrated with energy, since no one had shut it off. Once at the top, I dropped to the ground carefully. My foot was now all the way past pain and just felt completely numb. Instead, the pain was working its way up my leg and into my very core. I climbed into the cockpit and turned the key in the ignition.

Then I hopped down and ran toward the school's front door, desperately hoping that I could catch a teacher arriving for work who would let me inside early before I lost my foot to frostbite.

Although, come to think of it, having a robotic foot like Mr. Blue might be kind of cool. He certainly hadn't seemed that bummed about it. I used this thought mostly as a distraction as I hobbled across the sidewalk.

Just as I rounded the corner, I spotted someone entering the building.

"Wait!" I yelled out.

The figure stopped and looked my way. They waited as I hobbled up.

"Carson?" the figure said in a familiar voice.

"Oh, shoot," I said, recognizing it even though I couldn't see her face under the bundle of scarves that covered it. "Uh, I mean, hi, Ms. Pullman."

LOANER SOCKS

"**W**HAT WERE YOU DOING OUTSIDE WITH ONLY ONE BOOT?" Ms. Pullman asked as she herded me inside the school. "Are you having problems at home, Carson?"

She unfurled the layers of scarves around her face and there was a look of genuine concern on her face. She really seemed worried about me.

"No, it's nothing like that," I said, still limping despite being inside the relatively warm school. "It was just a minor bike mishap."

Ms. Pullman gave me the squinty eye. You know, the

eye of disbelief. Every kid who had ever told a lie to a teacher or parent had probably seen it before. She had a good one. It cut my lie to pieces like a samurai.

"Must have been some mishap," she said.

"Yeah," I said, not really knowing what else to say.

"Why are you at school this early?" she asked. "You know students aren't allowed inside for another twenty minutes. It's dangerous, Carson, to be outside for that long on a day like today."

"My alarm clock must be broken?" I said, disappointed at my own effort.

"Okay," she said, likely pretty cold and tired herself by that time. "Let's just get you to the nurse's office."

Ms. Pullman walked me there. The school nurse, Mr. Looper, still had his coat on when we arrived.

"An injury already?" he said, taking it off and hanging it up in a small closet. "I knew the kids wouldn't fare well in the weather today."

"Carson, you better hope I don't find out that you were up to no good," Ms. Pullman said from the doorway. "I don't think we'd recover from another breach of trust."

Then she left without waiting for an answer. Not that I had one for her anyway.

"Wow, sounds like you might be in trouble," Mr. Looper said.

I shrugged. "I just lost my boot."

"Let's have a look," he said, and patted the padded table. I hopped up and took a seat, extending my foot up toward him. "Oh no, that's going to have to come off," he said, frowning.

"What?" I gasped. Was it really that bad? How was that possible? I'd only been outside without a boot for like five minutes. Ten maximum. Could my foot really have frozen that badly that quickly?

"The sock, I mean," Mr. Looper said. "That sock needs to come off."

He carefully peeled off my crunchy, icy sock as I sighed in relief. My bare foot was red and pink and turning white in places as it adjusted to the heat. Some feeling was starting to return to it, which meant the pain was as well.

Mr. Looper grabbed the top of my foot and I winced.

"Well?" I asked nervously. "Is it frostbitten?"

"No, no, you'll be fine," he said. "You got lucky to catch Ms. Pullman and get inside when you did, though."

I breathed out another sigh of relief. The truth was, he didn't even know how lucky I'd gotten. I'd almost just been squashed like a bug under a huge shovel. I envisioned them carting what was left of me into Mr. Looper's office inside a few buckets. How would he have handled that?

The thought forced out a quick laugh that I tried to cover with my hands, but it was too late.

He gave me a look.

"Sorry, I just now realized how lucky I really am," I said.

"Yeah, whatever you say." He looked at me as if debating whether or not to refer me to the school psychologist. "Do you have different shoes to wear today?"

I nodded, patting my backpack where my regular shoes were stashed. Some kids opted to just wear snow boots around all day during the winter. But I was in the camp of bringing different shoes and changing at the start and end of each day. Who wanted to clomp around indoors in those things?

"Okay, I'll see if I have a dry, warm pair of loaner socks for you," he said, turning to root around inside his supply desk.

I didn't particularly like the sound of "loaner socks" but had to admit that the thought of something warm and dry on my cold, aching foot sounded better than nothing.

"Here we go." He held out a pair of mostly clean-looking black socks.

"Thanks," I said, reaching for them.

"They're clean," he assured me.

I nodded and put them on. Already my foot was feeling better. I put on my sneakers.

"All right, you're good to go, Carson," he said, opening the door for me. "Try to bring those socks back by the end of the week if you can."

"Okay, thanks, Mr. Looper," I said, wrapping my lone boot in a plastic grocery bag and then stowing it inside my backpack.

I left the nurse's office and then started toward my locker through the empty hallways. There was still another five minutes before the school doors would technically be open. Which is what made it so weird to see another kid sneaking around a corner in front of me.

A kid in a black hoodie.

0001010101010101001100101010101010101
1010101010100001010010101010010101010
0101000010010100101010010101010101010
0001010101010100110010101010101010101
0101011010100010010101010101010100100
0101000010010100101010101010010010101010
0001010101010101010011010101010010101010

CHAPTER 28

A JACK DANIEL'S
SHOWER

THE KID IN THE HOODIE STILL HADN'T SPOTTED ME AS FAR AS I could tell.

I crouched and waited, allowing some distance to develop between us. He was also down low, moving cautiously forward, cradling something in the front pouch of his sweatshirt. He got to a junction in the hallway ahead and looked around. I quickly ducked into the doorway alcove of a classroom.

After waiting a few seconds, I tiptoed after him. He wasn't getting away this time. I was going to find out who he was and what he was up to. Was it Junior? It had to be. The figure was certainly too big to be Ophelia, that was for sure.

As I followed him through the deserted school hallways, it didn't take long for me to figure out that he was headed toward Agent Blue's classroom. Even still, I didn't give up my position just yet. I didn't want to jump the gun—I had to catch him in the act, just to be sure.

He stopped at the closed and locked door to Agent Blue's classroom. Most of the teachers were probably already at school, but since Agent Blue had a substitute, his classroom was still dark. Substitutes typically didn't show up any earlier than they needed to.

I wondered briefly how he planned to break in. But it turned out he didn't have to break in at all. He pulled a key ring out of his hoodie pocket and inserted a key in the lock. When he slipped inside the classroom, that's when I made my move. I darted toward the door as it slowly swung closed. I slid feetfirst across the slick, freshly cleaned floor and just was able to jam a foot inside the doorway before it clicked shut.

I stood up and quickly slipped inside the room myself.

The figure spun around. It was Junior. He was standing near Agent Blue's desk, holding a bottle of Jack

Daniel's whiskey. What was he doing? Trying to plant the bottle on Agent Blue and get him fired? With me blocking the doorway, he was now cornered.

Panic spread across his face.

"Gotcha," I said and then immediately felt stupid for not being able to come up with something cooler to say. Maybe something like, "Who's your daddy now, Junior?" But, no, that sounded even lamer and kind of creepy. Maybe "gotcha" wasn't so bad after all.

But it didn't matter either way. Because it turned out there was a lot more to apprehending someone than merely cornering him in a classroom and saying something stupid.

Junior reared back and threw the bottle of booze at my head. I dived out of the way as the bottle crashed into the door and smashed to pieces, spraying shards of glass and whiskey everywhere.

I stood up and recovered, shaking the glass off me, just in time to see Junior charging me, his face contorted into panicked determination. He slammed into me and I went sprawling backward, crashing into the door and then slumping down onto the whiskey- and glass-covered floor.

Junior pulled open the door as I slid across the floor,

still dazed from my head connecting with the hard wood. Then he slipped out into the hallway and was gone, just like that.

But, like I said before, there was no way I was going to let him get away this time.

I sprang to my feet, ignoring the cuts on my knees from the shattered bottle and the throbbing knot already developing on the back of my skull and the strong reek of whiskey that followed me. I'd obviously never tasted whiskey before, but if it tasted even ten times better than it smelled, I'd have no idea why anybody would ever want to drink it.

After collecting my bearings, I burst into the hallway. Several kids nearby stared in shock, not at me but at Junior, who was sprinting down the hall away from where they stood.

The school doors were open and the building was starting to fill up with students, which made running after Junior something of an obstacle course. I spun and wove my way through the startled crowds, keeping my eye on the streak of black hoodie twenty or thirty feet in front of me. I didn't have time to stop and try to explain why I smelled like everyone's favorite drunk uncle.

Junior fled into the gym.

I followed.

We both wove around the orange cones the gym teacher was setting up for first-period basketball drills.

"Hey," was all he managed to say as we ran past him.

Junior was losing ground and he knew it. His pace became more frantic as he headed out the side door and into the empty boys' locker room. He leaped over a row of benches and darted behind a wall of lockers.

I followed. Or, I tried to. I tripped over the edge of the bench, slammed into a nearby locker, and dented the door. But I was able to recover quickly and only lost a few steps as I followed him through the side exit and into the backstage area of the school stage, which was at one end of the gym.

It was almost total darkness since the thick velvet curtain was closed.

I heard a crash ahead of me as Junior tripped over the set of whatever play was currently in rehearsals. I pulled out my phone and switched on the flashlight.

Junior was sprawled out, draped across a row of fake bushes. He tried to get up, but flopped onto the floor instead. I dived on top of him, pinning his arms down, using all of my weight. He was pretty lanky and had no chance to throw me off as he struggled wildly.

"It wasn't my idea," he finally said, "I swear!"

"I know, Junior," I said. "I know. And I'll let you go. Just tell me where he is and what he's planning."

"Who?" he asked as he finally stopped struggling.

"Don't play dumb," I said. "Mule Medlock."

"The milk guy?" he asked, confusion flooding his eyes, erasing the panic.

Mule Medlock had first come to our town under the guise of the owner of a custom milk bar. It had been pretty popular until it closed down. Of course, I knew the real reason it closed down was because I'd managed to foil his plans and drive him into hiding. But that's a whole other story.

"Come on," I said. "Spill it. Medlock. What's he planning? And why did he recruit you?"

"Seriously, Carson," he said. "I'm just doing this for the money. I got paid fifty bucks to put the booze in Mr. Jensen's desk. That's all I know. I just needed the cash."

"And what you did to Agent Nine—I mean, the other Mr. Jensen's music office? What was that all about?"

"Same thing," he said, his eyes wide with genuine fear. "I was paid to go in and mess the place up a bit. That's all."

"Who paid you?" I asked.

"I can't"—he shook his head—"I can't tell you."

I lifted and then slammed his shoulders onto the stage, putting more pressure on them. I felt bad for a moment as he cried out in pain, but then reminded myself that he was working for a known terrorist.

"Tell me," I demanded.

Junior started crying. Tears streamed down his red cheeks as he panted, struggling for breath.

"Don't you know?" he said. "You have to know. You of all people . . ."

I let up on him slightly. *I have to know?* What did that mean? But Junior took advantage of my momentary lapse in restraint and thrust a knee right into my ribs.

It felt like someone had just jammed a broom handle directly in between two of my rib bones and then rattled it around for good measure. I grunted and rolled to the floor, writhing in pain. It hurt even more to do that, so instead I just tried to lie still for a moment. The pain was so sharp it sucked all the breath from my lungs. Which was just fine since it hurt to even breathe.

Junior had gotten to his feet and was running toward the pale green exit sign at the other side of the stage. But I couldn't run after him. I couldn't even move. I thought for a moment that he might have broken one of my ribs.

That I might never be able to move again. But then, slowly, the pain began to subside. Kind of. Enough for me to move again, at least.

I rolled over to my hands and knees; the pain was still immense, but not nearly as bad as it had been just a few seconds before, and it was fading more with each second. I took a deep breath and then stood up.

The faint glow of my cell phone caught my eye a few feet away. I picked it up and shoved it into my pocket before jogging out the same exit Junior had used, down a short flight of stairs, through another door, and out into the school hallway. It was fully packed with kids now. The buses had just arrived, which meant homeroom started in a matter of minutes. Junior had gotten away.

But, given everything he'd said, I was starting to wonder if he was really the guy I was after anyway.

CHAPTER 29

DOES "TAKING CARE" OF GRANDMA MEAN WE HAVE TO KILL HER?

AT LUNCH THAT DAY, I GRABBED DANIELLE AND WE RAN DOWN to the shed by the swallow nest hill. I wished I could have told someone sooner about my encounter with Junior, but I hadn't had a chance. I was already on thin ice with Ms. Pullman after this morning; ditching class would likely earn me a suspension at the very least.

We didn't even bother trying to make up a story for Dillon. He was going to be curious about our no-show at the lunch table, especially after me ditching on him earlier that morning, but we could worry about that later.

We had an enemy spy to deal with.

A few minutes later, Agent Smiley arrived. She didn't invite us down; she merely crossed her arms and waited for our status report with that same grim expression that she always had on her face.

I told both her and Danielle about everything that had happened to me that morning. Investigating the dig site and almost getting killed. Seeing Junior trying to plant booze in Agent Blue's desk. Catching him and getting him to admit that he was paid to do it, but he wouldn't tell me by who. I even included the odd comment he'd made about how I should know, of all people.

Agent Smiley's face never changed. She merely listened, and blinked every once in a while. Then, at the end, she uncrossed her arms and gave a nod, which I'd come to realize was as close to a smile or compliment that Agent Smiley would ever give me.

"It seems our suspicions were right about the parking lot project," she said. "You two keep a low profile for now. We'll take care of Junior. Check back here after school—Director Isadoris has another special assignment for you both."

"What do you mean you'll *take care* of Junior?" I

asked, remembering from several movies that that was often slang for whacking somebody. "You're not going to . . ." I couldn't bring myself to finish.

"We'll handle the situation," Agent Smiley said. "It's no longer any of your concern."

"Yeah, but—" I started, but Danielle stopped me.

"She said she'd take care of it, Carson," she said, pulling at my sleeve.

I glanced at my friend. I knew her well enough to know that look she was giving me.

Drop it.

And so I did. I nodded at Agent Smiley. She said nothing else and simply turned and disappeared into the darkness of the shed, leaving behind just her last exhale swirling in the cold air. Danielle and I trudged over the frozen ground back up toward the school.

"What was that all about?" I asked.

"I'm with you, Carson," Danielle explained. "I didn't like the sound of that either. But I think we need to let them handle this. The whole thing is starting to make me uneasy."

"Starting to?" I said.

She laughed, and then we both fell silent for a few

171

moments. I shivered. It was a little warmer than it was this morning, but it was still stupidly cold outside that day.

"What do you think our special assignment will be?" she asked.

"I have no idea. I just hope it doesn't involve me sneaking around the school and breaking into classrooms again. I have a feeling that if I get caught one more time, I'm never going to be allowed back in school again."

"Don't get your hopes up," Danielle said.

"Right?" I said, smirking.

Except that I definitely wouldn't have been smirking had I known just how accurate her words (and my suspicions) actually were.

CHAPTER 30

THE AGENCY IS ALL

"**W**E NEED YOU TO INFILTRATE THE DIG SITE AGAIN," DIREC-tor Isadoris said down in his office after school that day. "We're running short on leads and we need to find something, anything, relating to the parking lot construction project. Preferably getting those blueprints you mentioned. Also, our intel suggests they keep a project laptop on site. Pullman is not going to get away with whatever she's got planned."

"I really don't think she's involved," I said. "I mean, it just doesn't seem possible."

Director Isadoris shook his head, shook away my comments. Dismissed them as if they couldn't possibly have been right.

"She *is* involved," he said. "I know she is."

"But how?" I asked. "What evidence do you have? You haven't even met her. I have!"

"I don't need evidence," he said, remaining calm in spite of my escalating voice. "Trust me, Agent Zero, I just know."

"Can't you just hack into the construction company's computer system at their office or something?" I suggested. "I mean, the news is always talking about the NSA and CIA spying on the public by hacking their computers. Surely you guys have the same power?"

"We do," Director Isadoris admitted. "And our capabilities should get even better really soon, but that's beside the point. The real problem is that the W Construction company is so small, so relatively new that they don't even seem to have physical offices nearby, or any sort of web presence. All they have are a phone number and PO box listed in the Yellow Pages. Frankly, there is no company network that we can even hack into, so to speak. Which obviously only arouses more suspicion. After all, what sort of company operates in the modern era without some kind of web presence or internet fingerprint? So it'd be better for you guys to simply retrieve those plans manually. And you're the best for the job since you've been there before. Besides, our other agents are unavailable, since the rest of us will be working on the new initiative."

I nodded, knowing there was no use arguing further. He was the boss, after all. And he had been doing this a lot longer than I had. So it was hard for me to sit there and continue to argue that my instincts were better than his. Even if I really did believe I was still right about Pullman, in spite of his rather convincing argument surrounding the W Company.

"When are we supposed to do it?" Danielle asked.

"Tomorrow night," Director Isadoris said.

"And you think they're just going to keep secret plans stashed right at the dig site?" I asked.

Director Isadoris leaned back, his chair groaning under his massive frame. He raised his shoulders and eyebrows in sync in a rare moment of naked uncertainty.

"Maybe, maybe not," he said. "We don't have any choice but to try at this point. Plus, we have a device we can give you that will greatly assist in searching the onsite laptop for hidden or encrypted files." He slid a small plastic case across the counter. "There's a USB device in there for the computer, and also another device that should help you with any locks you might encounter, getting into the files or any of the construction equipment."

I put the case into my pocket and nodded.

"Why tomorrow night?" Danielle asked. "Why not tonight, why not as soon as possible?"

"There are school board meetings tonight," Director Isadoris said. "Which means Ms. Pullman and several school board members will be at the school this evening and may stay to work late. My guess is that the meetings are related to the parking lot construction project. Tomorrow night, the coast should be clear."

I nodded. The coast probably would be clear—not many people hung around schools most nights. Still, I hated the idea of pushing my luck any further with Ms. Pullman if I were to get caught trespassing on school grounds. But if Director Isadoris was right about her, then I supposed it didn't matter either way.

"What about Junior?" I asked.

"What about him?" Director Isadoris said.

"What are you going to do to him?"

"Don't worry about it," he said. "We'll take care of it."

"I'm the one who found him!" I said, trying my best

not to shout. "Don't you think I have the right to know what you're planning to do?"

Director Isadoris stared at me evenly. His eyes looked dead, as if they never had or never could care about what I thought or said or did.

"No," he said.

"For as many times as I've saved this place, for all that I've done for the Agency," I said, "for being one of your last trusted agents left, I get nothing?"

He didn't answer and so I kept going. The way he was handling this was nothing new, so I shouldn't have been getting so upset. But at the same time, he was now saying cryptic things about "taking care" of a witness I had handed them. And something about that, whether Junior was innocent or not, made me feel like I had a right to know what would happen to him. I knew the Agency sometimes had to do ugly things, but I had never been directly or indirectly involved in a murder or interrogation before. And the prospect of that changing was doing things to me. It gave me confidence. It fueled my frustration.

"I'm all you have left, practically," I said, knowing that wasn't entirely true.

Deep down I knew the Agency had a wealth of

resources that I didn't even completely understand. They were just short on manpower at the moment due to the Medlock breach. Likely most of their agents were clean anyway; they were just playing it safe. But in spite of knowing all of that, his next sentence still shocked me.

"Maybe that's true," Director Isadoris said calmly. "But we are also all *you* have left."

I sat there, dumbfounded. What did he mean by that? I realized slowly, however, that he was right. I'd come to live for the Agency, in terms of what mattered in my life, to have that sense of making a difference every day. But even more than that were the greater implications of what he was saying. Our way of life, our very existence might be threatened if Medlock succeeded with his plans, whatever they were. And who would I be to simply turn my back on that when I know I could have helped prevent it? The thought of somehow playing a part in the end of the world, so to speak, was too painful to think about.

This was my life now. I was a secret agent, codename: Zero. He was right: It was basically all I had left.

0010101010101010100110010101010101010101010
010101010100001010010101010100101010100
1010000100101001010101001010101010101
001010101010100110011010101010
1010110101000100101010101000
101000010010100101010010
0101010101010100110010
CHAPTER 31

THE UGLY TRUTH

"P RETTY NEAT, HUH?" AGENT BLUE SAID.

I just stared at him in shock. Maybe I should have cut
my own leg off earlier that day after all.

After my meeting with Director Isadoris, I had asked
if I could visit Agents Blue and Nineteen in the medical
bay again. Turns out, Agent Nineteen had been sent to
another nearby facility for some more specialized care.
But Agent Blue was in the rehab center, working out his
new bionic prosthetic.

He'd just leg pressed over a thousand pounds with

it right in front of my eyes. Twenty reps without even breaking a sweat.

"The hard part is learning to control all of its power," he said, chuckling. "When I walk, I keep making cracks in the floor. But as soon as I get comfortable with it, I can get back to work."

"Wow," Danielle finally managed to say, while I continued to stand there, speechless.

We chatted about our new missions and the recent developments for a few minutes while Agent Blue took a short break from his rehab. I finally asked what I'd really wanted to from the start.

"How much do you trust Director Isadoris?"

Agent Blue furrowed his brow and stared at me for a few seconds. "What happened?"

"Nothing," I said. "I mean, nothing significant. . . . I'm just wondering how much do you trust his judgment. His instincts."

"Carson," Danielle interjected, "maybe it would help if we explained why you're asking about this."

I nodded. I proceeded to explain the Ms. Pullman dilemma to Agent Blue. How everything about her told me she was clean, that she was nothing more than a really good principal brought in to replace a mostly bad one.

But Director Isadoris was convinced she was an enemy agent, in spite of everything I'd told him about her.

Agent Blue nodded while I spoke, almost as if he were agreeing with everything I was telling him. But then, at the end, he smiled at me the way teachers sometimes smile at a student who just tried their absolute hardest at a test but still got a D minus.

"Maybe I can help best by telling you both a story," Agent Blue said, "something I witnessed way back when I was just a rookie field agent. When I say rookie, I mean *rookie*. I think it was just my second week on the job."

He was still seated at the leg press machine. He leaned back and grabbed the side handles as if he needed to brace himself to tell the story. Danielle and I leaned against the bench press next to it. It was rare for Agent Blue to tell a personal story, and I had no intentions of interrupting him now.

"Agent Nineteen was also in his first year on the job," Agent Blue said. "We weren't partners back then. In fact, I barely knew Agent Nineteen at that time. He'd just gotten a new partner, Agent Neptune, who you both now know as Mule Medlock.

"It didn't take long for most of us here to recognize that Director Isadoris had some strange suspicions about

Agent Neptune. Even though Neptune had a flawless background check and exemplary academy record, the director never let him handle any cases with the highest security rating. Agent Nineteen and I knew that there was something going on. However, Agent Neptune never once complained, and did all his work dutifully.

"Still, the director's misgivings surrounding Agent Neptune grew. Before long, Director Isadoris was removing Neptune from almost all fieldwork, and Neptune finally broke. He spoke out openly against the Agency's secrecy, its security policies. He demanded that we declassify the Agency and our operations, claiming that it would only help us do our jobs better. Nobody did that; *nobody* openly challenged Director Isadoris's policies. The director had every reason to terminate Neptune's agent status on the spot."

"Why didn't he?" Danielle asked, breaking our rapt silence.

"Agent Nineteen," Agent Blue said. "Nineteen vouched for Neptune, and managed to convince Director Isadoris to let him stay on as his partner. Agent Nineteen was convinced that Agent Neptune was trustworthy, that he only had the country's best interests at heart, even in those moments. Nineteen basically put his whole career, and even his life, on the line to back up those convictions."

I swallowed. Today wasn't the first time that I'd challenged Director Isadoris in a meeting. I was also getting fed up with all the secrecy. It scared me just how much Agent Neptune and I had in common.

"But don't you think it was maybe Director Isadoris's suspicions that caused Agent Neptune to lose his faith in the Agency?" I asked. "I mean, how could he trust Isadoris, if Isadoris didn't trust him?"

"That might sound plausible," Agent Blue said. "But it's completely wrong."

"How do you know that?" I asked.

"Because Director Isadoris had every right to be suspicious from the beginning," he said. "You probably won't like hearing what I'm about to tell you. But I think it's important you know the whole story."

There was no way I was going to interrupt him now. We both sat in silence and let him talk.

"Agent Neptune was hiding something from the Agency all along," Agent Blue said. "Not just from Director Isadoris but even from his own partner, Agent Nineteen, the one guy who trusted him. Of course, none of us knew what he was hiding then; we didn't know everything until recently, after the events at Mount Rushmore. He was hiding the fact that he had a son. Jake."

It blew my mind that an agent would have to hide having a family. It had never occurred to me before, the impact that this life might have on an agent with a family of their own.

"Agent Nineteen has told us that this explains much of Neptune's behavior in the time before he was presumed killed," Agent Blue continued. "The secrecy was wearing on him. He didn't want to have to lie to Jake for his entire life, the way that Agent Nineteen lied to his children, the way that we all keep secrets from the people we care about. It's the toll this job takes, and Agent Neptune was apparently unwilling to pay it.

"And so that's why he began acting out more and more. That's why he challenged Director Isadoris constantly. That's why the nature of this business, the secrecy of it all, got to him so much. Eventually, it got so bad that Isadoris had to transfer him. He recommended that Agent Neptune be dismissed, but the board transferred him to Chicago instead. Which inadvertently made Medlock even angrier—it separated him from *both* his son and partner, the only two people he cared about. And that's when he officially turned. He started selling secrets to various enemies of the Agency."

"But it's not all Medlock's fault," I found myself saying. "He just wanted to be honest with his son. Is that too much to ask?"

Agent Blue sighed. "You're missing the point. Agent Neptune should have been honest with the Agency from the start, told them about Jake, then this all could have been avoided. The very fact that he was keeping secrets from the Agency was the root of all of these problems. It doesn't matter how Agent Neptune felt about the director's policies or being transferred—there is no excuse for betraying your country."

I nodded, embarrassed.

"So what happened?" Danielle asked.

"Well, as you know, Agent Neptune was killed on assignment in Chicago under mysterious circumstances. Agent Nineteen was there, monitoring his activities, and he witnessed the shooting, which we assume was a double cross by one of his buyers. Agent Nineteen saw them dump the body in Lake Michigan, and so we thought Agent Neptune was dead. . . ."

"So awful," Danielle said, shaking her head. She was right. I couldn't help but shudder; that'd be like me seeing her or Dillon get shot. It was so horrible, I couldn't even bring myself to try to imagine it for a second.

"Anyway," Agent Blue continued, "the main point of the story is that Isadoris was right all along. Right that Neptune wasn't agent material, that he couldn't be trusted, that he couldn't handle the job, that he was hiding something."

I nodded slowly, feeling my sympathies for Medlock fade somewhat but not disappear entirely.

"So," Agent Blue said, standing up, "to answer your initial question: Yes. I trust Isadoris completely. He can be a bit hard to understand at times, sure. Ever since the Neptune incident he's become even more stubborn and secretive. But that's why he's the director. It's his job to keep the secrets so the rest of us don't have to."

I looked down at my shoes. If what he said was right, then that meant that I was completely wrong about Ms. Pullman. And it scared me. If I was wrong about her, then what else might I be wrong about?

If I couldn't even trust myself anymore, then what could I trust?

CHAPTER 32

GINNY AGRICOLE, THE RAT-DEER-PIG

I WENT TO VISIT DILLON LATER THAT NIGHT. PARTIALLY BECAUSE I felt like I needed the relief from how heavy my job as a secret agent was getting and partially out of pure guilt. Guilt over blowing him off several times recently. Even though Danielle told me that Dillon had also been a little distant lately, we both decided as we rode to her house together, that it was probably due to us ignoring him so much.

"So how's the mushroom thing coming?" I asked, as I plopped down onto his bed.

He was sitting at his desk, studying a photo of something with a magnifying glass.

"Oh, that?" he said, without looking up. "I'm over that."

"Really?" Danielle asked. "Just like that?"

I was surprised this was news to her as well—she lived with him, after all.

"Yeah," he said.

"I thought it was the Big One?" I said. "I mean, you were really into it."

"Yeah, well, the results didn't come back as expected," he said. "So I guess that's that. Besides, it could have maybe worked if I'd had more help. You can't crack the Big One alone, you know?"

The sting of his words surprised me.

"You're right," I said. "I'm really sorry. Really, I am. I'm just . . . I mean it's hard. This new principal is putting a lot of pressure on me to turn over a new leaf and part of that means getting my grades back up. So I've just been really busy focusing on that. I'm sorry, man, I promise by this summer I'll be around a lot more."

Dillon finally looked up from his desk. He spun around in his chair to face me. And right away I could tell that he felt bad for making me feel so guilty. Which of course was only making me feel even *guiltier* since I'd just lied to him . . . again—and in a really heartfelt way, no less.

"It's all good," he said, cracking a smile. "I'm onto something new anyway. Something that I think is actually better. Not bigger, but definitely better. In a hilarious way."

I grinned back. Now this is what I needed: just some good old-fashioned Dillon Conspiracy stuff.

"What do you got?" I asked, truly excited to hear about a theory of his for the first time in at least a few months.

"I think our neighbor has genetically manufactured a strange new animal," he said.

"Which one?" Danielle asked with legitimate interest. I could tell she needed this as much as I did.

"Mrs. Walker, across the street," Dillon said. "Her *dog*, Ginny Agricole, isn't really a dog at all."

"What is she then?" I asked.

"It's a rat, deer, and pig spliced together in a way that roughly resembles a dog," he said.

"What proof of that do you have?" I asked, grinning so wide now I couldn't wipe it away if I tried.

"Well, for starters, just look at it!" he said, thrusting the picture he'd been examining my way.

Danielle and I looked at it together; and for the first time ever, we both thought that one of his crazy theories might just be correct right away upon hearing about it. The picture of Ginny Agricole did sort of look like a dog. But it was definitely the weirdest dog I'd ever seen. It was light red or tan in color like a deer; had a deer's long, spindly legs but the face, tail, and ears of a huge rat; and, to top it all off, the naked, rotund, pink belly of a pig.

After just a few seconds, we both burst out laughing at the little mutant dog. Then Dillon joined us. And that's how the best night I'd probably had since joining the Agency ended: me and my two best friends sitting on Dillon's bed, laughing at all his photos of the neighbor's strange little dog.

0010101010101010100110010101010101010101010
101010101010000101001010101001010101010
0101000010010100101010100101010101010101
0001010101010100110010101010
1010110101000100101010101001
0101000010010100101010101010
0101010101010101001110

CHAPTER 33

THE ORGANIZATION
OF SAD CLOWNS
WITH AWESOME BEARDS

Junior was not at school the next day.

Which, to most kids, wasn't a big deal. Hardly anybody noticed. That is, until a few rumors started spreading. It started with his best friend, Matt, who had inside information, being his best friend and all.

"Carson," Danielle whispered to me at the lunch table, "apparently his parents don't even know where he's at. That's what Matt says."

I tried to block it all out. I didn't even want to know. To consider the possibility that the Agency had made a kid disappear because of what I'd told them. I'd much rather have just sat there and listened to Dillon's crazy theories on Junior's disappearance.

"Of course his parents don't know where he is," he said, speaking over our table of friends. "Junior was actually a member of a secret organization of sad clowns with awesome beards called the Secret Organization of Sad Clowns with Awesome Beards. Or SO-SCAB, as it's known among its members. Which is sort of gross, but I guess that's the kind of joke a clown makes when he's sad. Anyway, SO-SCAB initiated Junior last night and then he grew a beard overnight. Which probably freaked him out somewhat . . ."

Everyone else laughed as Dillon continued his story. I wanted to find it funny. I wanted to believe it was true. I forced a laugh just to look normal. But deep down, I wasn't finding any of this funny. Because I had my own suspicion about what had happened, and I knew mine was probably right.

My theory was that the Agency had kidnapped Junior and was holding him somewhere. Probably interrogating him. The thought that the Agency would interrogate a twelve-year-old kid made me want to puke. What if

Junior wasn't working for Medlock? And even if he was, what if he was just Medlock's pawn, working for the money with no actual idea what he was doing? Would the Agency even think about that before they put the screws to him?

"Did you hear me, Carson?" Danielle hissed in my ear.

I turned to face her. My panic was reflected in her expression. She was scared, heartbroken, worried. Sickened.

"What have they done to him?" she asked.

"Maybe," I whispered, ignoring my own gut feeling, "maybe it wasn't the Agency at all. Maybe Medlock's guys grabbed him? To keep him from talking?"

I'd meant for the alternative to be comforting, but as soon as the words left my mouth, I realized that would be even worse.

Danielle looked close to tears now. This wasn't a game—each side was just as likely as the other to capture and harm a kid in order to accomplish its goals. And I suddenly wasn't sure I wanted to be involved in any of this anymore.

But I knew that it was too late now. I was in this thing whether I wanted to be or not. And I also knew that the only way I was going to get any answers or help to end this mess once and for all was to keep completing my missions, to keep working to help the Agency apprehend Medlock.

And so that's what I was going to do.

0100101010101010101001100101010101010101010
1010101010101000010100010101010010101010
0101000010010100101010010101010101010
0001010101010101001100 10101
0101011010100010010 100
0101000010010100101 010
0001010101010101001 101

CHAPTER 34

DEEP STAR 7

THE CONSTRUCTION SITE LATER THAT NIGHT LOOKED A LOT LIKE it had the other morning except for three things:

The hole was deeper and wider as they had demolished a lot more of the parking lot.

There were a few new construction equipment machines, a small utility shed near the pit, and what looked to be a power drill of some sort like they use to find oil underground.

Danielle was with me this time, which made the

whole scene of destruction in the darkness look a lot less ominous.

We worked our way around the huge pit of broken-up concrete toward a small mobile shed that the construction crew had apparently installed the past few days to house some of the supplies. We pressed our faces to the window on the door and then shined our flashlights inside.

Jackpot.

The tube of blueprints sat leaning against a small desk. Additionally, a laptop computer sat on the desk and several folders stuffed with papers lined a small shelf behind it. There was a treasure trove of targets inside that might end up proving useful.

I was just about to get started on the shed lock, when Danielle suddenly pulled me aside.

"Someone's coming!" she hissed, her eyes wide with panic.

We quickly ducked behind a nearby bulldozer.

The beam from a flashlight showed up on the ground right where we'd been standing just a few moments before. It shrank and condensed as the person holding it neared. The question was, Who else would possibly need to be at a school parking lot construction site at 1:00 a.m.?

Before we even saw the guy, we heard whistling. It wasn't menacing or taunting in any way. It was cheerful. Almost pleasant. And the dude was a pretty good whistler.

He switched off the flashlight when he got to the shed's front door. It was a large guy wearing jeans, a Carhartt jacket, and work boots. He looked exactly like you'd expect a guy visiting a construction site to look—except that that's exactly how an enemy spy cell would want it to look, so we both knew it meant nothing.

Danielle and I watched quietly as the guy entered the shed and flipped on a flashlight. He came out several minutes later holding the laptop, the roll of blueprints, and several file folders. They'd beaten us to the punch! Had Medlock known about our mission somehow? I supposed it was possible, except, if that were true, then we'd both probably be dead or captured by now. If they had known we'd be there, they likely wouldn't just let us go like this. They'd have waited and then nabbed us red-handed in the act of stealing.

"What do we do now?" Danielle whispered.

"I don't know," I admitted. "But he's walking toward the school now . . . which is weird, right?"

Danielle nodded. We stayed behind the bulldozer

for now but kept an eye on the man as he carried what was supposed to be our score toward the school's front entrance. He had a set of keys and unlocked the front door with them.

"What the heck?" Danielle said.

"We better see what he's up to," I said.

We dashed from the bulldozer to the bushes near the front entrance.

"Should we go in after him?" Danielle asked.

I really wasn't sure. If the guy was an enemy agent, then it'd probably lead to a shoot-out. And then death since we had nothing to shoot back at him with. If he was just a normal construction worker, then he'd call the cops, which would end in us getting arrested. Neither scenario seemed to play out too well for us.

But then a light above us switched on. He was in the administration office area. We shifted over to the school wall below the administration office windows.

"I'm going to take a quick peek," I said.

Danielle shook her head.

"I have to," I said. "We need to know what's going on."

I didn't wait for her approval. I simply turned around and poked my head quickly above the windowsill into the office area. The guy was just exiting Ms. Pullman's office. Empty-handed. I ducked back down.

"He dropped it all off inside Pullman's office," I whispered.

"Really?" Danielle said. "That's weird."

I nodded. We waited there quietly until the man exited the school again. He walked over to a red W Construction pickup parked across the street, and drove away.

"Now what?" Danielle asked.

"I suppose we should finish the mission," I said.

"You're not suggesting . . ."

"Yeah," I confirmed. "We have to. We're here to get that data, and I don't think it changes anything that it's now in Pullman's office. I'm pretty sure Isadoris would still want us to go after it."

Danielle looked unconvinced.

"Look, you can stay out here, just keep watch for me," I said. "I'll be in and out. We're already here; we know our objective is in there. Besides, this might be my only chance to prove Isadoris wrong about Ms. Pullman."

"Okay, you're right," Danielle said. "Let's do it."

Getting into the principal's office was a lot easier than usual. I didn't even need to pick any locks. One of the devices in the plastic case Isadoris had given me was this insanely powerful magnet shaped like a small gray bar of soap with a curved handle on one side. And the new window Ms. Pullman had installed in her office had a metal lock mechanism just inside the frame. All we had to do was press the magnet against the window frame, hit the activation switch, and then pull the magnet along the outside of the windowsill until we heard the lock slide open. It was about as easy an infiltration as I'd ever done.

I climbed inside the office and commenced with the search. The laptop and folders were all sitting on top of her desk. As if he'd merely been dropping them off to her. I decided to just take it all instead of trying to read and document it all right then and there. I gathered up the files, blueprints, and computer and then handed them outside to Danielle.

"Okay, let's go!" Danielle said.

I was about to climb out, but then whirled around and looked back at Ms. Pullman's computer. I wrapped my fingers around the USB device Director Isadoris had given me. Agent Smiley had given me a more detailed rundown of how it worked before we left and had said it would make searching a computer for any encrypted secret files easy and fast. I knew what I had to do.

"I need a few more minutes," I said to Danielle.

"What!" she hissed. "Are you nuts?"

"I have to do it—just wait here," I said, turning back to Ms. Pullman's desk and computer.

If there was any way to clear her name or find out for sure who was right about her, me or Director Isadoris, then I knew I had to run a spy scan on her computer itself. Even if the stuff we just took was incriminating, it couldn't be directly linked back to her. After all, we just saw some guy deliver it in the middle of the night. He could have been planting it—we don't even know if she's ever seen any of that stuff before. But a scan of *her* computer would be irrefutable.

The first step was to switch on Ms. Pullman's computer. It booted up and then a school verification page appeared, asking for a username and password. I plugged the little device Director Isadoris had given me into the USB port on the computer.

A small black box filled with green text popped up on the window. Numbers, words, and symbols flashed across the screen in a flurry. Not that I would have had any idea what the text meant had it been moving slowly enough to read.

Several seconds later, the box disappeared, and the username and password fields autofilled:

Username: jlpullman

Password: •••••••••

I clicked the log-in button.

Her desktop filled the screen. It had been that easy. I marveled at how much ruckus the Agency could cause with their high-tech devices and seemingly endless resources if they ever decided to stop being the good guys. Then I had to suppress a bitter laugh as I realized that's precisely what had made Medlock into such a dangerous and effective enemy.

Another pop-up window appeared, asking to perform a system file scan. The program would automatically search through the entire hard drive for anything related to Medlock or the Agency.

While the search ran, I turned my attention to her desk. I picked the locks on her desk drawer and riffled through all of her folders and papers, looking for anything unusual. Ms. Pullman was insanely organized. Everything was stacked and sorted so neatly, I was convinced she was going to notice if even a single corner of a page was creased. And so I was extra careful while handling everything.

There were simple memos, printed emails, notes from teachers—all the various junk you'd expect to find in a school administrator's office. There was a whole file cabinet full of permanent records, each folder labeled with a student's name.

I lifted the files out and looked underneath them for hidden compartments, and then carefully put them all back into place. I did this for several drawers full of folders. Near the end, I saw the one labeled: *Fender, Carson.*

I glanced at the computer screen across the room. The status bar was only a third full. I had time for a quick peek, right?

I opened the file. Right on top was a page of notes, handwritten by Pullman, dated that day. The notes were in all capital letters that were neat, sharp, and consistent, almost as if a machine had written them.

CARSON CONTINUES HIS OLD HABITS. BUT I DO SENSE A STRUGGLE. IT'S ALMOST AS IF HE DOESN'T WANT TO CAUSE TROUBLE BUT CAN'T HELP HIMSELF SOMEHOW. AS IF AN EXTERNAL FORCE IS MAKING HIM ACT OUT IN SOME STRANGE WAY. HE IS MOST CERTAINLY VERY SPECIAL, THE TYPE OF KID WHO COULD GO ON TO ACCOMPLISH SOMETHING GREAT. HE HAS THE SELF-AWARENESS AND SHARP EYE FOR DETAIL OF SOMEONE TWICE HIS AGE. NOT ONLY THAT, BUT HE HAS A STRONG SENSE OF MORAL JUSTICE AND AN IMPECCABLE CODE OF ETHICS AS

WELL. IT SEEMS COUNTERINTUITIVE, GIVEN HIS BEHAVIOR, BUT I KNOW WHAT I'VE SEEN. HE REMINDS ME A BIT OF MYSELF. HE KNOWS WHAT RULES DO AND DON'T MATTER. HE IS DRAWN TO ALWAYS DO THE RIGHT THING, REGARDLESS OF CONSEQUENCES. I DO NOT WANT TO GIVE UP ON HIM; HE IS A COMPASSIONATE, THOUGHTFUL INDIVIDUAL. I FEAR THAT EXPELLING HIM COULD NEGATIVELY ALTER HIS TRAJECTORY, BUT IT'S UNFORTUNATELY SOMETHING I WILL NEED TO DO IF HIS BEHAVIOR DOESN'T CHANGE.

I was speechless. I picked up another note.

I ALSO GET THE SENSE THAT HE HAS A SECRET. THAT HE IS HIDING SOMETHING, FROM EVEN HIS FRIENDS AND FAMILY. HE SEEMS CONSTANTLY DISTRACTED BY SOMETHING THAT HE PERCEIVES TO BE FAR MORE IMPORTANT THAN ANYTHING SCHOOL RELATED. PERHAPS HE IS STRUGGLING WITH AN ISSUE AT HOME OR WITH AN UNIDENTIFIED EVENT FROM HIS PAST? WHATEVER IT IS, I HOPE I CAN GET TO THE BOTTOM OF IT BEFORE LONG. I WILL CONTINUE TO MONITOR HIS ACTIVITIES AND GIVE HIM AS MUCH ATTENTION AS I CAN WITHOUT SEEMING TOO OVERBEARING. CARSON IS LIKE NO OTHER STUDENT I'VE EVER ENCOUNTERED AND IT WOULD BREAK MY HEART, PERSONALLY AND PROFESSIONALLY, TO LOSE HIM AS A STUDENT.

It was here that I had to stop reading. Partially because I was feeling too guilty and embarrassed to continue, and partially because the computer behind me had just beeped.

I never should have looked in the file.

Something about reading her personal notes about me had felt like the worst thing I'd ever done. Worse than lying or cheating or any of the pranks I'd pulled. It had been an invasion of Ms. Pullman's privacy. And, beyond that, she really seemed to care. She was invested in me as a person. I was used to having a principal whose sole professional purpose was to see me expelled.

I knew then that I didn't even need to turn around and see what the results of the computer scan would be. There was no possible way she was connected to Medlock. It wouldn't make sense. I knew that everyone believed Director Isadoris to be some kind of psychic superspy, but he's still human. He can't *always* be right. And he wasn't right now.

After quickly putting my file back into place, I spun around and moved back to the computer. A small pop-up box sat in the center of the screen:

Scan completed. Results:

3 suspect files located

All files successfully downloaded and decoded
Click file name to view suspect files
Click Save to exit

I looked at the list of files. Two of them had mostly indecipherable names, like 43GHYE22.exe. One of them, however, was labeled Project Deep Star 7. I clicked the file name to open it.

What appeared on the screen in front of me sucked all the air from the room. It gutted me like a fish on a filleting table, complete with greedy, squawking seagulls to mop up the extra bits.

Much of what I was seeing was too complicated for me to fully comprehend. There was a lot I didn't understand or that seemed completely foreign. But the purpose of Project Deep Star 7 was still quite obvious. The endgame was as clear as a glass of filtered water.

The project was to drill down into the ground, right down to Agency headquarters, which was labeled on the plans, and destroy it.

And the lead Project Manager was also very clearly labeled within the documents.

Jayne Pullman.

CHAPTER 35

SENTIENT TIRES
THAT EXPLODE HEADS

"**W**HAT DID YOU FIND?" DANIELLE ASKED AS I STUMBLED OUT of the office window.

I was so disturbed that I was literally shaking. Which is why I lost my footing and went sprawling to the ground. Danielle gave me a worried look before turning to close and relock the window from the outside. Then she helped me to my feet.

"Seriously, Carson, what's wrong?"

"It's her," I managed to spit out. "Isadoris was right."

"What?" Danielle asked, but she'd heard what I'd said. I

was silent, still very much in shock. And I was embarrassed. To have been fooled so easily into trusting someone. It was like what happened with Jake all over again.

"Come on," I finally managed to say, slinging my backpack over my shoulder. "Let's get down to the shed."

Danielle didn't ask any more questions. She just kept walking. I followed on legs that were still sort of wobbly and gooey from the adrenaline of the discovery.

We got to the shed and stood outside, knowing we likely wouldn't have to wait long. The Agency was expecting us, after all. What surprised me, though, was who eventually opened the door.

"Agent Nineteen!" I practically shouted.

He put his finger to his lips and then beckoned for us to step inside the small maintenance shed that doubled as the secret entrance into the Agency headquarters.

"Nice to see you both," he said with a thin smile once we were inside the privacy of the shed. "Did you find anything?"

"You could say that," I said.

"Nice work. You can fill me in once we're inside." He stepped onto the waiting elevator platform. "I've never seen Director Isadoris so anxious. He's basically chewed through a dozen boxes of pens."

A pop song from a recent animated Disney movie suddenly filled the space and interrupted our conversation. The shed had surprisingly good acoustics.

"Sorry!" Danielle said, pulling out her phone. "I better take this?"

She said it more like a question than a statement as she looked at Agent Nineteen. He nodded and drew his hand back away from the elevator switch.

It was Dillon. From the sound of it, their mom was not happy that she had snuck out that night. It also sounded like Dillon was in full-on conspiracy mode.

"No," Danielle said into the phone with a scoff, "I did not sneak out to do that. And I don't know where you even came up with the idea of an army of sentient tires that can explode people's heads telepathically. Do you know how ridiculous that sounds?"

Agent Nineteen and I exchanged a look and he couldn't suppress a grin.

"I didn't tell you where I was going because I knew you'd act like this!" she said. "Plus, I really didn't think you'd want to come with me on a study date with Eloise." There was a pause and Danielle's eyes widened. "Oh, you did?"

She sighed and shook her head.

"He must have already called Eloise," I whispered to Agent Nineteen. "Classic Dillon move."

Finally she hung up the phone and confirmed my suspicions.

"Well, he knows I'm lying," she said. "So I gotta get home and try to talk my way out of this before it gets out of hand."

"Carson can fill you in tomorrow," Agent Nineteen said as he walked over to open the secure shed door for her.

But there was something in his tone that seemed off to me. Like there was more he wanted to say but couldn't. Or maybe Dillon was starting to rub off on me in the wrong ways.

Danielle shook her head and waved as she stepped outside. "Sorry, Carson."

"No," I said, "I'm sorry that you have to take on most of the work of keeping Dillon in the dark about all this."

She shrugged. "I'm his twin. It comes with the territory."

We finished our good-byes and then a short time later, Agent Nineteen and I were zooming down into the earth toward Agency HQ. Just like old times.

0010101010101010100110010101010101010101010
0101010101000010100101010100101010100
1010000100101001010100101010101010101
0010101010101010011001 101010
1010110101000100101 01001
1010000100101001010 0101
0010101010101010011 1010

CHAPTER 36

THINGS BETTER
LEFT UNSAID

LUCKILY FOR ME, DIRECTOR ISADORIS WAS A GRACIOUS WINNER. He didn't gloat or say I told you so or even reprimand me for doubting him when he'd been right all along. Instead, he merely nodded occasionally while I told him what was on the USB drive in the backpack I'd just handed over. I'd left out the part about what I'd found in Ms. Pullman's files about me, but that didn't mean I'd been able to stop thinking about it.

"Nice work, Agent Zero," he said at the end and then handed my backpack containing the USB drive and the construction laptop, and the tube of blueprints to an agent standing behind him.

The agent went back over to the small table behind Director Isadoris, where he and Agent Smiley were clacking away steadily at their laptops. Agent Nineteen sat next to me across from Director Isadoris.

"I'm still not sure whether to reprimand or reward you for going outside mission parameters to get this information," Director Isadoris said. "Infiltrating Ms. Pullman's office could have been dangerous. A necessary risk perhaps, but that wasn't for you to determine."

"I can still hardly believe it's true," I said, not really caring about a punishment or reward either way. I was in shock.

"Well, if spotting the bad guys were easy," Director Isadoris said, "there'd be little need for an Agency like ours."

I knew he was trying to make me feel better, but it didn't work. Because I wasn't upset about being wrong. I was upset about Ms. Pullman.

"So, the plan is to blow this place up," I said quietly. "Shouldn't we, like, be evacuating now or something?"

"We can't do that," Director Isadoris said. "I'm not running away. We are going to face this head on and stop

Medlock once and for all. If we evacuate now, it might tip him off."

"We can still face him head on without sitting around here waiting to get blown up," I said.

"Agent Zero, I'm telling you we can't evacuate," Director Isadoris said.

"Why not? Wait, let me guess, it's *classified*?"

Director Isadoris actually smiled at me. It was entirely humorless, but it was still a smile.

"You're right, it is classified," he said. "But I'll tell you anyway. It's because this base houses the main standby backup system for the nation's entire defense network. We can't evacuate without presidential approval. So for the time being, we stay put. Besides, their little hole up there is still a long way from being deep enough. I don't even need to see those plans to know that. Trust me, when the time comes that it's necessary, we will evacuate. But only then."

I nodded, not finding a reason to argue the point any further. Especially since I needed something from them. I didn't want to waste my energy arguing over protocol semantics.

"So, I did *this* for you," I said. "Now you need to do *something* for me."

Agent Nineteen shifted in his seat beside me.

"Agent Zero, I hardly think—" Director Isadoris began, but I didn't let him finish.

"Listen to what I have to say before you automatically say no," I said. "You owe me at least that much."

Director Isadoris tilted his head and then leaned back in his chair and said nothing. I took that as my cue.

"I need to know what you did with Junior," I said. "I do pretty much everything you ask me, mostly without question and with very little information. And now one of my missions has resulted in his disappearance. I want to know why."

I waited for an answer. Neither Director Isadoris nor Agent Nineteen spoke.

"What?" I continued. "Are you afraid to tell me? Do you even know if he's working with Medlock? Or did you kidnap some innocent kid?"

"Carson, that's enough," Agent Nineteen said.

"I'm afraid these are details we're just not free to discuss with you," Director Isadoris said. "But I assure you that we're treating Junior as the situation demands."

"Stop giving those vague answers," I said. "I *need* to know."

Something changed in Director Isadoris just then.

That blank stare left his face and it seemed like he was really looking at me as a person instead of merely another agent for the first time that night.

"Carson," he said, "I am being completely honest with you when I say this: It's truly better that you don't know the details surrounding the investigation. It's for your own protection. You will be involved soon, I assure you; in fact, we *need* your help with the next phase of this mission. But as to how we got there . . . it's better left unsaid."

Agent Nineteen nodded beside me.

That's when I lost it.

I knew it was unprofessional. I knew I would be in danger of getting dismissed. I knew it was foolish to lose my cool in front of my boss, especially when your boss is a seven-foot-tall grizzly bear of a man. But I simply couldn't help it. The months of frustration that had built up inside me finally erupted out of my mouth in a scream. I screamed so loud that my throat stung like I had just poured acid down my esophagus.

I must have stood up, because I remember Agent Nineteen pulled me back into my chair while I tried to catch my breath so I could yell some more. But I didn't have it in me. So when I spoke again next, it came out in more of a hoarse whisper.

"You tell me what's going on or I'm walking," I said. "I mean it, I'm out. You can't just ask people to do things for you, and then make kids disappear and expect everyone to be cool with that. Because I'm *not* cool with it. And I won't let you do this. Even if that means going to the local police or the FBI or the NSB. They'll listen to me. Someone will, eventually. You know it and so do I. Now tell me what is going on."

Director Isadoris was quiet for a long time. He just sat there, staring at me, unblinking, unflinching. His eyes burned and they almost seemed superhuman in that moment. They glowed with intensity. He was upset, and why shouldn't he be? He was working to save the world.

But so was I. And in order to do that, I needed to know what had happened to Junior.

Finally, he nodded.

"Okay, fine, we'll tell you everything," he said softly. "But just remember—this was your choice."

0010101010101010100110010101010101010101010
0101010101010000101001010100010101010100
1010000100101001010100010101010101010101
0010101010101010011001 101010
1010110101000100101 01001
1010000100101001010 0101
0010101010101010011 1010

CHAPTER 37

WHAT COULD BE WORSE
THAN TORTURE AND DEATH?
JUNIOR WILL TELL YOU

DIRECTOR ISADORIS AND AGENT NINETEEN SILENTLY LED ME TO a nearby room. At first, I was worried they were taking me to some kind of morgue. Or maybe a torture chamber. But it ended up just being a small, concrete room with a single plastic table in the center.

It looked like a police interrogation room from the movies, except this one didn't have a mirror or any one-way glass. Instead, it was just plain concrete from floor to ceiling.

"Have a seat." Director Isadoris motioned to one of

the four chairs at the table.

I sat down. He and Agent Nineteen sat down across from me. Agent Nineteen set a thin laptop computer on the table between us and then opened it. He spun it toward me so I could see the screen.

"Are you sure you want to see this?" he asked me.

I remembered being present in the room while Mule's psycho little henchman Packard tortured my friend Olek just a few months ago. If I could witness that, I was sure I could handle this.

"Show me," I said.

Agent Nineteen glanced at Director Isadoris. Director Isadoris merely gave a single nod back. Agent Nineteen pressed a button and then a video filled the computer screen.

It was Junior. He was sitting at a table in a room not unlike this one. In fact, it might even have been the same room. And he wasn't being tortured and hadn't been drugged or anything like that. In fact, he had a soda and chips in front of him and was calmly answering questions like everything in the world was okay.

And at first I didn't get it. Why had they been so scared to show me this? It didn't make sense. This was, like, best-case scenario. Junior was unharmed and cooperative. And apparently being fed just fine.

"Junior, look at me," an offscreen voice in the video said.

Junior redirected his gaze from his bag of chips toward the voice.

"We're going to ask you some control questions first," the interrogator said.

"Control?" Junior said.

"Yeah, just a few basic questions to show you're in the right state of mind and in good health."

"Okay, sure," Junior said.

They first asked him where he lived and what his name was and his parents' names and ages and a whole bunch of questions that they already knew the answers to, no doubt. Junior responded to each one calmly and easily. He seemed a bit nervous but otherwise okay.

Then came the real questioning. The questioning surrounding his involvement with Medlock and the events of the past few days. And they basically didn't even need to ask many questions. Junior seemed more than happy to give up everything he knew.

And that's when he dropped the bombshell that basically blew up my little personal universe:

"I've only worked with one person, really," Junior said,

"I even have another meeting with him tomorrow for a new job. It was this kid at my school named Dillon. He's got a twin sister named Danielle, too. But it was Dillon who paid me to do all those things."

0010101010101010100110010101010101010101010
010101010100001010010101010010101010100
1010000100101001010101001010101010101
0010101010101010011001   10101
1010110101000100101   1001
1010000100101001011   0101
0010101010101010011   1010

CHAPTER 38

WHO IS BETRAYING WHO ANYMORE?

AFTER THE VIDEO, I JUST SAT THERE AND STARED AT THE blank screen for a long time in silence. To their credit, Agent Nineteen and Director Isadoris gave me the time to do so. They sat across from me and waited patiently.

"It can't be true," I finally said. "It's not, is it?"

They looked at each other and then back at me. Clearly, this wasn't some practical joke or master prank.

"We're investigating the matter," Agent Nineteen said.

"Maybe it's some kind of innocent prank Dillon is

pulling," I suggested, knowing how unlikely that was even as I said it.

"Of course, nothing is outside the realm of possibility," Director Isadoris said. "But you have to admit it would be a reach to assume anything but direct involvement by Medlock. For Gomez and both Mr. Jensens to be targets, as well as the new evidence surrounding Ms. Pullman, it would be a pretty remarkable and unlikely coincidence for it all to be an innocent prank."

It couldn't be true. There was no way. I knew I just needed to talk to Dillon first; I could straighten this all out. Figure out what he was thinking, if he even knew who Medlock was. If I could only talk to him, tell him the truth like I should have from the very start, then it would undo the damage.

"So . . . what's next?" I asked.

"Well," Director Isadoris said, "you heard the last part, about how Junior had a scheduled meeting with the contact tomorrow afternoon, right?"

"Yeah," I said, afraid of what was coming next.

"Carson," Agent Nineteen interjected. "You know Dillon. He trusts you. He won't run if he sees you there."

"You mean . . ." I said, not able to finish. But Director Isadoris had no problems finishing for me.

"Yes," he said. "We want you to go to that meeting. Help us bring Dillon in safely. If we can get him into our custody, he may be able to lead us to Medlock. It's obviously imperative that we find out where he is before he executes his plan."

"But can't you just have an agent at the meeting place in hiding?" I said. "And grab Dillon before he even realizes what is going on? Or even just grab him tonight or tomorrow morning before school, like you somehow did with Junior?"

"It's not that simple," Agent Nineteen said. "We're hoping that Dillon is coming to this meeting with intel we can use. Or he may even show up with Medlock himself. Either way, I think you get the point: It may be to our advantage to have him keep the meeting and not just apprehend him beforehand. And we're asking you because we'd never be able to get away with an adult agent taking him into custody without compromising the whole thing—the meeting is in a public place, the Arrowhead mall, in the middle of the day. If you were present, however, that changes things. If you could somehow get him to an isolated location, or perhaps administer the tranquilizer yourself—"

"Tranquilizer?" I shouted. I just didn't think I could

do it. Knock out my own best friend? There was no way.

"Before you say no," Director Isadoris said, "think about the consequences. This could be our only chance to get to Medlock. You know what happens if we don't— he might be able to execute his plan to blow up the Agency, or at the very least formulate another devious plot while we're busy preventing that first one. This has to *end*, Carson, and you can help make that happen."

"How can you be sure Dillon will even show up anymore?" I asked, looking for a way out of this. "He has to know Junior's been compromised by now."

"We think he'll still show," Agent Nineteen said. "We've been having Junior stay in contact with him via text, telling Dillon that the rumors around school about him are hilarious since he was merely away at a funeral for a distant family member. We're pretty sure Dillon bought it."

That didn't sound like Dillon; he never bought into anything at face value. But then again, maybe the whole conspiracy theorist thing was a ruse all along. Maybe it was an act. If what Junior said was true, if Dillon really was working for Medlock, then maybe I didn't actually know my best friend that well at all.

"Can I talk to him first?" I asked. "I'll see him

tomorrow before the meeting. Can I at least have that? Maybe I can get him to come in willingly."

"I'm afraid we can't let you do that, Carson," Director Isadoris said. "If you tip off Dillon in any way that we are on to him, it could blow whatever little chance we have of getting to Medlock. We don't know how deep into this Dillon is. He could be Medlock's coconspirator, for all we know. You're not to speak to him until his scheduled meeting with Junior, understand?"

"But I have to," I said. "I mean, not about all this, but he's my best friend. If I ignore him at school all day tomorrow, he'll definitely know something is up."

"We suspect that won't be a problem for you," Agent Nineteen said.

"What do you mean by that?" I asked.

"You'll find out tomorrow," Director Isadoris said.

What did they know that I didn't? It was always something with these guys. I could see why Medlock got fed up with this job. Is that why Dillon was helping him? But what about all the innocent people Medlock had hurt? Had Dillon helped him then, too? Unless he simply didn't know . . .

But there was nothing I could do about it now. So I just nodded.

"Good," Director Isadoris said. "Remember: No matter what, we need you to keep your cool and reveal nothing if you happen to see Dillon or Danielle before the meeting tomorrow, right?"

"Right," I said.

0001010101010101010100110010101010101010101010101
1010101010100000101001010101001010101010
0101000010010100101010010101010101010
0001010101010101001100110101010101
010101101010001001010010101
01010000100101001011010
0001010101010101010011010

CHAPTER 39

FINALLY, THE END

THE BUS RIDE TO SCHOOL THE NEXT MORNING TOOK FOREVER.
I was exhausted, having lain awake all night thinking
about Dillon. Could he really be working with Medlock?
If so, why? And what would I find when I got to school?
Would I be able to keep a straight face with Dillon and
Danielle? Was the Agency going to assault the school
and take out Ms. Pullman? Does the school even exist, or
had it really just been a hologram the whole time? Maybe
I was even more tired than I thought.

I'd debated calling Danielle that night after getting

home, but had decided against it. It would have been disobeying a direct order, after all.

Great secret agents didn't disobey direct orders. Though I wasn't sure I even qualified as a competent secret agent anymore.

When the bus finally pulled into the parking lot, the school looked just as it always did in the morning. Kids hurried inside the doors trying to escape the harsh cold. I did the same thing. I went to my locker like usual, and then found my way to homeroom like usual. And the day continued, like usual. No Agency raids, no disappearing kids or teachers.

I even spotted Dillon once in the hallway. It was only from a distance—he hadn't seen me. Which was good because then I didn't need to avoid him or pretend to have not seen him. It really wasn't all that unusual for us to not see or talk to each other until lunch, especially lately with how distracted we'd both been.

That's when it occurred to me that his recent Master Theory had probably been code for his plan with Medlock. I tried to swallow, but my mouth had gone completely dry, so I just coughed instead.

It was right in the middle of second period when the shoe finally dropped. It started with the intercom in our classroom crackling on.

"Mr. Wright?" the secretary's voice said.

"Yes?" Mr. Wright answered.

"Can you please send Carson Fender down to the office?"

"Sure thing." Mr. Wright and every kid in the class turned to look at me.

"Make sure he brings all of his things. He won't be returning today," the secretary added.

"You heard the lady, Mr. Fender," he said without getting up from his desk.

I ignored the stares of my classmates as I trudged out of the classroom. This wasn't an unusual occurrence. I got called down to the office a lot. But it felt different this time. Darker. As if this were all happening in a movie and some sort of eerie filter was on the lens.

Somehow, I think I knew I was doomed before I even got down to the administration office.

"Head on in," Mrs. Bradshaw said, motioning toward Ms. Pullman's office.

Her usual smile and bright eyes were absent. Instead she looked at me coldly, as if I were a dead fish and not a student. That was the second sign that something was seriously wrong.

Upon entering Ms. Pullman's office, my true fate became immediately apparent.

Both my mom and dad were already there, seated across from Ms. Pullman. It was rare to get my dad away from work. It would have probably taken either a death in the family or else . . .

My dad glared at me.

My mom was crying.

And right then I knew I was finally going to be expelled.

0010101010101010100110010101010101010101010
010101010100001010010101010100101010100
1010000100101001010100101010101010101
001010101010100110011   101010
1010110101000100101   01001
1010000100101001010   0101
                                             101

CHAPTER 40

ME, ALONE

IT WAS LIKE DÉJÀ VU FROM THE NIGHT BEFORE, SITTING THERE in Ms. Pullman's office watching a video on her computer monitor. Except now, instead of Agent Nineteen and Director Isadoris looking on, it was my parents. And instead of it being a video of a kid giving up his spy contact, it was a security video of me breaking into Ms. Pullman's office.

She had video evidence. There would be no lying my way out of this.

So I had to deal with the uncomfortable business of

watching my parents watch me commit the ultimate offense. A criminal offense. While at the same time, I had to sit there and pretend that Ms. Pullman wasn't what she really was: one of the most brilliant evil masterminds I'd ever known. Even now that she knew that I must know her secret, she kept up the act like a true pro.

"What exactly were you doing?" she asked me. "And why would you take the parking lot project blueprints?"

She actually looked upset, like she wanted to cry. Like all those things she'd written about me in her file were true and not just a part of her cover.

"Does it matter?" I asked. "Will it change how this ends?"

My answer just made my mom sob harder. My dad's hand gripped the seat back behind me so hard, I thought the wood might splinter in his hand.

"Well," Ms. Pullman said softly, "it might affect whether I decide to pursue criminal charges or just leave this at a simple expulsion."

"I was . . ." I stopped, not sure what to say.

Technically I had only taken the blueprints. I hadn't pulled a prank or vandalized anything. So what good reason was there for me to break into her office, mess around on her computer, and then take some random construction materials? It ultimately didn't matter what I said, since she likely knew the real reason. But at the same time, I could make a good show in front of my parents.

"I was trying to break into the computer to change my grades," I finally finished. It was a believable lie. My grades had basically fallen off a cliff since I'd become a secret agent. "And I only took the blueprints to hide my tracks. A diversion of sorts."

"Carson, what do I always tell you about shortcuts and hard work?" my dad said, his teeth clenched.

"Yeah, yeah, I know," I said, forgetting exactly how his lame saying went.

"Regardless," Ms. Pullman said, somehow taking command of the room again in spite of the fact that she was speaking the softest of everyone, "you had to have known breaking into my computer wouldn't actually work, right, Carson? We both know how smart you really are."

My mom looked up briefly at the compliment, but then looked down and dabbed at her eyes again.

"Moving on," Ms. Pullman said. "We saw someone else on the security footage from outside my office. I'd like you to tell me who it was."

It was true that Danielle could be seen on one of the

outside security cameras. But it had been dark. The outside camera shots must have been inconclusive, which is why I was the only one here.

"No one," I said.

"Carson!" my dad said. "If you were doing this with someone else, you are going to tell us who, right now."

I sat there and said nothing. I didn't care if they threatened to arrest me right there on the spot. There was nothing they could say or do that would make me give up Danielle. It felt like her trust in me was the last honest thing left in my life. I needed to hold on to it for all I was worth or I'd likely never be able to trust another person ever again.

"It's probably his little friend," my dad said to Ms. Pullman. "You know, that little weird one. Danny?"

Most parents probably knew their kids' best friends. But my dad was hardly ever around. He was always working and so he actually knew very little about my friends. Even less now that I had become a secret agent.

"*Dillon*," I said. "His name is Dillon and he isn't really my friend anymore."

"What if I told you the difference between the school pressing criminal charges or not would be you telling us who your associate is?" Ms. Pullman said. "Would you tell me then?"

"So you're blackmailing me now?" I said.

My mom gasped, and my dad sat there, opening and closing his mouth as his face got more and more red. I knew I was being aggressive. But I was just so tired of being lied to by everyone that I didn't care anymore. Ms. Pullman could go lick an old boot, as Olek might have said were he there. That was a friend I knew I could always trust. Olek was about as straight up honest as anyone I'd ever met. I'd have done anything to have been able to see him right about then.

"Watch your mouth," my dad finally said. "You're already in very big trouble as it is."

"Gee, you think?" I said, not being able to help myself. "Brilliant deduction, Sherlock."

"Carson!" my mom sobbed.

"I'm sorry," I said, meaning it. "Dad, Mom, I am really sorry. I'm just . . . I didn't mean for this to happen. I made a mistake. But no matter what you threaten me with, no matter what you say, I'm not ratting out my friend. They helped me because I asked them to. It wasn't their idea. It was all mine. It'd be wrong to get them in trouble."

Ms. Pullman looked at me, and there was something strange behind her expression. Like always, I had no idea what she was thinking.

"Very well, then," she finally said. "I'll be getting in touch with the local authorities. I'm sorry it had to end this way. I truly am."

I couldn't even look at her as she said this. Because we both knew that wasn't true. It was just another filthy lie. I'd heard so many of them now that I practically couldn't tell the difference anymore.

0010101010101010011001010101010101010
010101010100000101001010100010101010
010100001001010010101001010101010101
0010101010101010011001   101010
010101101010001001010   100
010100001001010010101   010
001010101010101001101   010

CHAPTER 41

NEBRASKA IS NOT
THE WORST PART OF NEBRASKA

$\int$

IT WAS ON THE CAR RIDE HOME THAT THE REAL UGLY TRUTH HIT me: The Agency had known I was getting expelled. That had been what Director Isadoris and Agent Nineteen had hinted at the night before. But I suppose it would have been too much for me to expect them to stop it somehow.

But I do wish they could have at least warned me. I could have handled the news. Probably. Either way, I was annoyed that they would even ask me to complete another mission breaking into school property being that close to expulsion. And they had to have known about the school's new security cameras.

"Are you listening to me?" my dad said from the front seat.

My mom was following us in her own car. My dad had insisted on me riding with him. He wanted to spend the car ride home yelling at me so he could get back to the office as soon as he dropped me off.

"Sorry," I mumbled from the backseat.

"That's all you have to say?" he said. "I just told you that you're being sent away to military school in the morning and all you can offer is a limp *sorry*?"

"Wait, what?" I said.

"Yeah, that's right, Carson," he said. "First thing tomorrow morning you're off to Nebraska. You'll be attending the Omaha Military Reformation Academy for Boys. So you'd better spend the rest of your day packing."

This news hit me like a punch to my gut. I was done. Finished as an agent. Finished as a student. Finished as a member of my family. I'd be out of the picture in less than twenty-four hours.

But it still left me with enough time to complete my one final mission: helping the Agency capture my best friend. Or *former* best friend.

"We're hoping the judge will be lenient if he knows

you're attending a military reform school," my dad said.

I sighed.

"Yeah," my dad agreed, "you really botched this one."

I was tired of listening to him lecture me. So I said nothing else, hoping he'd shut up. But he didn't. He just kept going. Not that I would keep listening.

Instead, I pulled out my phone.

"What's that?" my dad yelled from the front as we pulled into the driveway. He looked back and saw me looking at my phone. "No you don't."

He reached back and snatched it from my hands. Then he got out of the car and smashed my phone on the driveway. He stomped on it several times until it was in at least fifty-three pieces. He pointed a finger at me through the windshield.

"No more phone, no more internet, no more computer," he said. "Go to your room and pack and then stay there until dinner. Got it?"

I nodded and got out of the car. Though, the truth was, I had no intention of obeying his orders. I'd have to sneak out of my house a little later on if I was going to make it to the meeting with Dillon.

CHAPTER 42

THE OLD REVERSE SANTA CLAUS TRICK

AT 2:37 P.M., I SET MY PLAN IN MOTION.

It started by placing a phone call to our house phone. Which was a lot harder than it might sound, because my dad had smashed my cell phone to pieces, then he had taken my computer, TV, PlayStation, and landline phone out of my room before he'd left.

But, thankfully, he had forgotten about the handheld gaming system I had stashed in my bedroom closet. It was hard to blame him, though; he was never really around to see me playing it.

Besides, even if he had remembered I had one, he likely had no idea what it was capable of. I'd pulled it from the closet after getting to my room, connected to our house Wi-Fi, and downloaded the Skype app. I was then able to call my parents landline phone later that afternoon. Thus began phase one of my escape plan.

My escape had to be arranged so precisely because my psychotic dad had actually superglued my bedroom window closed before he left to go back to work. And my mom was sitting out in the basement den watching TV with a full view of my bedroom door and plenty close enough to the stairs to block them before I could run past her.

We had a cordless phone, but I knew my mom wouldn't have it downstairs with her since nobody ever called the landline anymore. Honestly, I'm not even sure why my parents still had one.

My hunch paid off. I heard my mom get up and run upstairs to answer the phone a short time after I'd dialed the number. This was it; I needed to make my move, I'd only have a few seconds.

I set down my gaming system with the call still connected and then ran out into the basement den.

"Hello?" I heard my mom say upstairs. "Helloo-ooo?"

She had already answered the phone. Man, she'd gotten there quickly. Did the prospect of getting a call on the landline really excite her that much that she felt the need to run to answer it? Either way, it meant I had mere seconds before she'd be back down here and the whole thing would be a bust.

"Hello? Anyone? Is anyone there? Is that you, Mom? Is your mute button on again?"

I ran over to the fireplace and pulled open the glass doors slowly so they wouldn't creak.

"Who's calling?" she said loudly. "This is your last chance before I hang up."

I climbed inside the fireplace. It was a lot tighter squeeze than I expected. But I fit, sort of, and that's what mattered. I pushed at the outer folds of the glass doors until they would appear closed at a glance. Then I pressed my palms against the inside of the chimney. It felt grainy with soot. I could barely breathe and already I could feel sweat trickling down the back of my neck in spite of the drafts of cold winter air gusting down on me.

I tried not to cough as I wedged my feet against the inside of the chimney and inched my way up. Loose soot and dirt fell around me, into my face and hair. Slowly but surely I worked my way up the narrow chimney.

The irony, of course, was that had it been any wider it would have been a lot harder to climb. But it was so narrow that I would have had to *try* to actually fall back down it. So I could stop and rest as much as I needed, wedged in the narrow space, without having to worry about losing any progress. And I needed to rest a lot, because climbing up a chimney is as hard as it sounds times a hundred.

But it was necessary.

I had one last Agency mission to complete, after all.

About halfway up, the coughing started. I just couldn't hold it in any longer. My lungs burned from all of the ash in my mouth. My knees and hands ached from the constant pressure of pushing up my body weight inside the old brick chimney. But still I pushed on.

The last part, pulling myself completely free from the small chimney opening, turned out to be the hardest part. My muscles were completely spent from the climb. I rolled off the chimney into the snow on the slanted roof. It was deep enough to keep me from sliding down the slope and onto the pavement below me. My arms and legs and face were covered in black ash. I looked like I'd been tarred and feathered except that the guys doing it had forgotten the feathers. But, oddly enough, the soot jacket seemed to be helping with the cold somewhat.

After crawling my way toward the edge of the roof, I peered over the side. Our house was just two stories, but from the top it felt like it was ten. I worked my way over to the gutter drainpipe that ran down the side between the house and the garage. I had no idea if it could hold my weight, but the only alternative was to simply jump. And that certainly didn't seem like something I could do without breaking several dozen bones. While still on my hands and knees, I grabbed the lip of the gutter and slowly swung one leg over the side of the house. I froze, not really sure if I actually wanted to put the other leg over the edge.

Don't look down.

Don't look down.

Whatever you do, Carson, don't look down.

I looked down.

The white snow spun below me. I felt like I was going to pass out. I managed to snap out of it before I did, but the damage was already done. My hand slipped on the slick, ice-coated roof and then I went sliding off the edge.

0010101010101010100110010101010101010101010
010101010100001010100101010100101010100
1010000100101001010101001010101010101
0010101010101001100101010
1010110101000100101001001
1010000100101001011010101
0010101010101010011

CHAPTER 43

PROFESSIONAL FALLER

THE GOOD NEWS WAS THAT THIS WAS HARDLY THE FIRST TIME I'd found myself falling toward my death. In fact, by my count, this was at least the fourth or fifth time I was in the middle of falling several stories since becoming a secret agent. And so, my limbs instinctively moved on their own and my hands grabbed the lip of the gutter.

I dangled there for several seconds. The cold was eating away at my grip, but it didn't matter since the gutter wouldn't be attached to the house for much longer, anyway.

A loud creak was the first warning that the gutter

could not actually hold the weight of a thirteen-year-old kid. The second wasn't so much of a warning as it was me simply falling backward again, this time towing the torn metal gutter with me.

I landed on my back with a solid thump. I struggled to breathe, the wind completely knocked out of me. Surely, though, that was the least of my problems. I'd just fallen nearly two stories onto my back; I had to have cracked a vertebrae or two. Maybe shattered my pelvis.

But as my breath slowly returned, I realized that despite a sharp aching in my tailbone, I was mostly okay. I could move my arms and legs and didn't feel any blood flowing from my skull.

I rolled out of the mound of snow, shivering, in pain, but still somehow alive and functioning. Surviving the fall, however, still didn't change the fact that I still had a lot to worry about:

- I'd just been expelled from school completing a mission for the Agency.
- Tomorrow morning I was headed off to some military academy in Nebraska where the hardened student populace probably ate puny punks like me for bedtime snacks.
- Mule Medlock was still on the loose and was

planning to blow up Agency headquarters.

- My best friend in the whole world was allegedly helping Mule Medlock pull off his evil plans for some inexplicable reason.
- I was currently on my way to go stab my friend in the back and help the Agency capture him. The fact that it was all in an effort to save the world didn't really make it feel much better.

I was starting to think I might have been better off landing on my head when I'd fallen, all things considered. But of course that was ridiculous. Because if that had happened, then I'd never get an answer to the most troubling question of all:

Why did Dillon join Medlock?

As I shook off the cold, I started jogging toward the rendezvous spot. One way or another, I was going to get an answer to the question. I just hoped it would be before the Agency made their move, or I might never see Dillon again.

0000101010101010101010011001010101010101010
010101010101010000101001010101001010101
1010100001001010010101010010101010101
0000100011001010101010101010
001000101010100101010101010
101010100101010101010
000110010101010101010

CHAPTER 44

THE DIRT MALL

THE SECRET LOCATION WASN'T REALLY THAT SECRET, WHICH WAS
probably the point.

Junior and Dillon had planned to meet in the middle
of a nearby shopping mall. Although, calling the Arrowhead Shopping Center a "mall" was a stretch, even by
Minnow, ND, standards.

Minnow had a real retail mall, complete with a Gap
and a sporting goods store and Barnes & Noble and all
that stuff. This was North Dakota, so the mall wasn't
nearly as big as the huge multistory malls you see in

movies and TV shows, but it was big enough to be called a mall nonetheless.

The Arrowhead Shopping Center, on the other hand, used to be the "big mall" in Minnow until the late 1980s. Since then it had basically been turned into a big building housing a few creepy, weird businesses and a lot of empty space. Most kids called it the Dirt Mall.

The grocery store at the far end kept the place well trafficked enough to still be considered a public place. And I noticed all of these people staring at me as I passed them. I glanced at my reflection in the window of a store. I looked like I'd survived a fire, then a World War II battle, a swim through tar pits, then trekked alone through the Rockies, and finally battled a dragon inside a volcano. My entire body was still covered in black soot. But the combination of sweat and snow had caused it to run somewhat, giving it a streaky look, like I'd coated my body in eyeliner and then cried through all my pores.

Dillon stared at me with his mouth agape as I approached him near the benches and plants at the center of the mall.

"What are you doing here?" he asked. "And what in the world happened to you?"

Normally I'd have laughed or at least smiled at his

shocked expression. But given the circumstances, I could barely even look at him.

We just stood there, ten feet apart, and stared at each other. And in that moment, that long pause, I knew it had to be true. He was working for Medlock, and I was working for the Agency. We both knew it. He knew who I really was and I knew who he really was. Nothing else needed to be said. But I said it anyway.

"How could you?"

"*Me*?" Dillon said, shocked, the real pain of discovering your best friend lied to you pouring out of his eyes like lasers. "What about you?"

He took a step back. And that's when I noticed a couple walking toward us from the grocery store carrying several large grocery bags. Except that it wasn't just a random couple. It was Agent Smiley, flanked by another agent. This was it; the Agency was making their move.

That's when I knew I couldn't do it. I couldn't just stand there and watch them arrest my best friend. It didn't matter who he was working for. I had been lying to him all year; if I'd told him who I was and what I was doing, none of this might have ever happened. It was my fault. And I wasn't going to let him take the fall for it.

I pulled the small tranquilizer gun the Agency had

given me from my jeans pocket. Dillon's eyes grew wide as he saw it. I ran toward him and he stood there, staring at me with a mixture of shock and heartbreak on his face. He still hadn't spotted the two agents coming up from behind him with their own tranquilizer guns.

Instead he was focused on me, clearly still thinking that I was there to capture him. Which, to his credit, I had been.

But not anymore.

Instead I dived at him, right as Agent Smiley fired. I slammed into Dillon as the dart sailed wide. It embedded itself in the bench behind us and we crashed to the floor behind a large, fake plant.

"Dillon, run!" I said, rolling to a crouch.

I pointed my own weapon at the approaching agents, closed one eye, and fired two shots. The first dart hit the male agent right in the chest. He dropped like dead weight before he'd taken two more steps. The second dart hit a bag of groceries Agent Smiley held up as a shield. Several bystanders nearby screamed and headed for the nearest exit.

Dillon was on the ground next to me, staring up with a look of confusion.

"What are you doing?" he asked.

"Saving you," I said. "You're still my best friend, no matter what. Come on."

I grabbed his shirt and pulled him around to the other side of the fake plant, shielding us from Agent Smiley.

"I'm going to fire some shots," I said. "When she dives for cover, you make a break for that exit. I'll be right behind you."

Dillon nodded, his eyes wide, finally seeming to snap out of his confused daze.

Then his nod turned into a shaking head.

"No," he said. "We need to go this way."

He pointed at the other exit across the hall.

"Fine, let's go," I said.

I rolled out from behind the plant and then fired another dart toward Agent Smiley. Her reflexes were inhuman; she easily dived out of the way, then raised her own weapon toward me.

It surprised me how fast my brain was operating in that moment. It was more than just simple reflexes. Somehow in that split second before she fired, my brain registered that she was too skilled for me to simply try to dive one way or another. She'd recognize my movements and lead me easily. So instead, my brain signaled to my legs to hip fake to the right ever so slightly, then quickly spring back the other way, toward the exit Dillon had already made it halfway to reaching.

And, shockingly, the double move worked.

That one extra motion caused Agent Smiley just enough of a hitch in her shot to fire wide left. Which gave me just enough time to raise my weapon again and let off a barrage of darts. She hit the ground hard behind the bench between us and didn't get up.

I turned and sprinted after Dillon, who was outside the mall now, but waiting for me with the door open. I grinned at him. He grinned back, but then it quickly faded. His eyes grew wide.

I spun around, shocked to see Agent Smiley half standing, half leaning against the bench. A dart stuck out from her arm. She should be unconscious. Maybe she was a robot after all.

But her eyes betrayed her; she was losing her battle with the potent tranquilizer that had dropped her partner in under two seconds.

She used whatever energy she had left to raise her gun and let loose one final shot. The shock of seeing her fight off the dart's toxin for so long slowed my reaction time just enough. Before I could even so much as attempt to dodge, I felt a soft thump on the right side of my chest.

The shock and mild pain caused me to stumble, and I fell at Dillon's feet half inside the mall and half out in the cold late-afternoon air. I stared up at Dillon's shocked and panicked face in disbelief.

"Carson, get up!" he yelled.

But his voice was already fading. It sounded like I was under water and he was screaming at me from somewhere above the surface. I could barely hear his words. My eyelids felt as if they were being pushed closed by a pair of invisible fingers.

The last thing I felt was Dillon dragging me the rest of the way outside.

And then, it was all gone.

CHAPTER 45

HOP TO IT, BRUCE DERNS

"**S**HOULD WE TAKE HIM TO THE HOSPITAL?" A VOICE ASKED somewhere in my dreams.

It was a girl's voice. Familiar, but I couldn't quite place it.

"You know we can't do that," a boy responded.

"But I'm worried about him," the girl said. "Besides, I don't like it here. It's making me uneasy. Why did you bring us here?"

"Because I knew it was safe," the boy said.

I groaned.

"See?" the boy said. "He's waking up, he's fine."

"Carson?" the girl asked. "Carson, come on, wake up!"

A hand shook my shoulder and I groaned again.

"Stop it," I mumbled. "My head hurts."

"What did he say?" the girl asked.

"I don't know," the boy responded. "Something about bop-it Ned hurls?"

"No," the girl said. "That makes no sense. I think he said, 'Hop to it, Bruce Derns.'"

"Why would he say that?" the boy said.

"I said, my head hurts," I repeated slowly, struggling to enunciate every word.

"Yeah, it probably does," the boy said. "You smacked it on the cement pretty good when you went down. You're lucky Danielle showed up. I never could have gotten you here alone."

Finally, my eyes fluttered open. It was just a dim haze at first, but then the faces above me came into focus. It was Danielle and Dillon, staring down at me. I was lying on something relatively soft. I tried to sit up, but a wave of fresh stabbing in my forehead forced me back down.

"Just take it easy, Carson," Danielle said.

"Whaddaryoudoinghere?" I mumbled.

"Saving you two idiots, apparently."

I tried to look around. We were somewhere dark. And quiet. I couldn't hear anything but our own voices. No traffic, no birds, no nothing. My vision was still too blurry to make out much of anything that wasn't right in front of me.

"Where are we?" I asked.

"Bonanza," Dillon said.

"Bonanza?" I repeated.

"Yeah, Bonanza. That's one of those words, isn't it? That's kind of fun to say? Bonanza. Bo-*nan*-za. Bo-nan-*za*."

"This is hardly the time," Danielle said.

Bonanza was an old restaurant in Minnow that had been closed down for a few months. The old building had been sitting on Broadway, dark and vacant, ever since. It had been a family favorite—it was the type of place that was a steak house and buffet all in one. The sort of place my dad loved. If my dad had a sense of humor, he might have held a fake funeral on the day it closed down.

But now that it was gone, the place was all but forgotten.

I attempted to sit up again, more slowly this time. And the rush of pain that flooded my headed was duller, more bearable. I sat up and found myself in an empty red booth with no table.

It was dark outside, and there were no lights on in the abandoned restaurant, but there were enough windows to allow me to see that the place had been half demoed. Most of the tables and chairs were gone. The giant buffet in the center of the room was just a barren framework of old wood. Most of the booths had been torn out, except for three or four.

Dillon and Danielle stood next to the booth and watched me uneasily.

"Are you okay?" Danielle asked.

"I think so," I said. "What happened? How did you get here? Did Dillon call you?"

"It was the Agency . . ." She stopped, looking uncomfortable. Danielle rarely had a hard time speaking her mind. "They sort of tasked me with following you."

"What?"

"Yeah," she said. "They told me they were worried about you having a secret motive. I didn't ask why . . . but I should have. I'm . . . I'm sorry, Carson."

And just like that, I felt like passing out again. The Agency actually suspected *me* of having turned? It just didn't seem possible. But Director Isadoris had hired my own best friend to spy on me while I was spying on my other best friend who was the first best friend's brother.

It was like a classic Spy Triangle. A spyangle.

And the worst part was, they'd been right. They were right to be concerned about my loyalties. What I'd done finally hit me. I was finished. I'd actually helped an enemy agent escape and had shot two of my fellow agents with tranquilizer darts. There'd be no coming back from that.

I was Agent Zero no more.

CHAPTER 46

THE TRUTH BEHIND
ALL CONSPIRACY THEORIES

"**S**EE?" DILLON SAID. "THIS IS EXACTLY WHY MULE MEDLOCK wants to expose these guys. They're hiring their own agents to spy on each other! What the Agency is doing is wrong."

"That's exactly what a lying backstabber would say," I said.

"Takes one to know one."

A classic comeback, never more cutting than it felt right then. And accurate, I had to admit. I had lied to him for a long time. Maybe it was time for that to end.

"You're right," I said. "And I'm sorry. I thought I was protecting you. I should have told you I was an agent. . . . I should have told you everything. But it's still no excuse for what you've done. Working for a terrorist, someone who's trying to bring down the government . . . Dillon, what could you possibly be thinking?"

Dillon paused, furrowed his brow, and then sat down next to me on the booth bench.

"Wait, what are we talking about?" he said, genuinely confused.

"You are working for Mule Medlock, right?" I said.

"Well, yeah, but he's not the evil one here," Dillon said. "The Agency is. They have a secret base under our hometown; they keep us under surveillance twenty-four hours a day; they can do whatever they want, whenever they want, and don't answer to anyone!"

"Not now with your theories . . ." I started, but then stopped. This wasn't some crazy theory. This is what Medlock must have told him. And I suppose it was true.

But that still didn't change the fact that Medlock was the bad guy here.

"Don't you know what Medlock has done?" I said.

"He was going to kill Olek's parents."

"Olek's parents?" Dillon said. "What are you talking about?"

"All that business at the fairgrounds earlier this year? That was Medlock. He kidnapped Olek and was using him as a ransom to have his parents killed so they couldn't testify against several known, dangerous terrorists. Or did Medlock forget to tell you about that?"

"It's true, Dillon," Danielle said quietly.

Dillon seemed truly shocked. And so I said nothing, giving him time to digest the truth for once.

"He told me you guys would do this," he finally said.

"Do what?" Danielle asked.

"Make up a bunch of lies to try to justify your actions," Dillon said. "Once a liar, always a liar."

"Dillon!" I nearly shouted, and my voice echoed through the empty restaurant. "I'm not lying to you now. I swear it. I'm your best friend, you have to trust me. Medlock is bad news."

"*Trust* you?" Dillon said. "Why would I? Besides, you're not my best friend anymore. Best friends don't tell dozens of lies to each other without even batting an eye. Best friends don't keep secrets from their best friends, like the existence of a freakin' covert fascist group operating in our own hometown. When Medlock finally told me yesterday that *you* were the kid the Agency hired to do all its dirty work, I just . . . I could hardly believe it. I didn't want to. But then he showed me the tape of you breaking into Ms. Pullman's office to get into her personal files and frame her for treason."

"Me?" I yelled. "No, she's the one who is going to blow up the headquarters. We found these plans in her office—"

"Carson, listen to what you're saying. Ms. Pullman has some evil plan to blow up the secret government base underneath our school? You sound like . . . well, you sound like me."

I closed my mouth. He clearly wasn't going to believe a word I said anymore. And it was hard to blame him. I had told him more lies than truths the past few months, after all. There was no denying that.

"You know that I know most of my theories are bogus, right?" Dillon continued. "I'm in on the joke most of the time. The reality is that chaos frightens me. The idea that there is no one person or group in charge, that the world is completely random, terrifies me more than you can imagine. So it comforts me to always believe there is a purpose behind everything that happens in the world.

That everything is connected. That's why I make up my theories—even though I know most of them are not true, they make me feel better. And everyone always thinks I'm crazy. But Medlock didn't. He was once afraid of the same thing I was. That's what led him to join the Agency in the first place. But soon after that, he learned something: The scariest thing isn't no one being in charge. It's the wrong person being in charge."

I didn't say anything for several moments. I let what he said really sink in. And I suddenly felt even guiltier. Guilty for never taking Dillon seriously. For treating him like a cartoon character in many ways instead of a real, true best friend.

"I get that," I said. "I really do. And I'm so sorry I never tried to understand all of that before. But what Medlock is planning will put millions of people in danger. He may think what he's doing is right, but putting all those people at risk is not the answer."

"Is that what the Agency told you?" Dillon asked with a grin, like he was in on some ultimate truth that I didn't know yet. "They've been lying to you from day one and you've bought every word of it. You guys really don't know, do you?"

"Know what?" Danielle said.

"You guys don't know what really happened between Medlock and the Agency," Dillon said, looking at Danielle and then back at me in genuine surprise.

I opened my mouth to say something, but realized I had nothing to say. If Dillon was telling me that there was something the Agency wasn't telling me, I couldn't deny that he was probably right. As crazy as it sounds, I think I was going to have to start listening to Dillon.

"You need to know what happened," Dillon said. "But I can't tell you myself. It's better if you just hear it directly from Medlock."

.

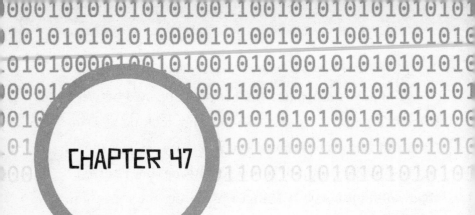

CHAPTER 47

A THANK-YOU IS IN ORDER

"**W**HAT?" I ASKED. "MEDLOCK IS HERE?"

My head swiveled around, expecting to find a gun pointed at my back. But there was nothing there but the dark cashier's table at the entrance where lines of people used to stand, waiting to get in the door. I looked back at Dillon.

"This way," he said, standing up.

Danielle looked calm, but I could see in her eyes that she was as scared as I was. She shrugged and moved to follow him.

Dillon led us into the abandoned kitchen, which still smelled like grease and meat and fried stuff, despite being nothing more than a hollowed-out shell with none of the appliances or kitchen equipment left inside. The smell would probably never go away.

Standing near the back, on a lighter portion of tile where a huge fridge must have once rested, was Medlock. It was hard to make him out completely in the darkened kitchen—he was barely more than a silhouette—but I could see his eyes and they practically lit up like an evil flashlight. I flinched instinctively.

"Hello again, Carson," he said to me. Then he turned toward Danielle. "And you must be Dillon's twin sister?"

Danielle nodded slowly. This was her first time meeting Medlock since knowing he was an evil enemy spy, but we'd all met him a few months ago when he'd been posing as the kindly owner of a pretty fantastic custom milk bar and ice cream shop.

"How could you do this?" I asked Dillon. "You set us up."

"Oh, please," Medlock said. "Give him a break, will you? If I wanted to capture or kill you, I could have easily done so anytime I wanted. It would have been as simple as having one of my men make you disappear after school one day, right?"

I didn't respond, but admitted to myself that he made a good point. What had been stopping him from doing that all this time? Or from capturing me for interrogation? It's not as if I was under protection when I was riding home. I had been continuously thwarting his plans for months now, why let me continue to do so, unless . . .

"You used me again, didn't you?" I said.

I was referring to way back when I'd first gotten mixed up with this whole spy thing. Medlock had purposefully gotten me involved and then used me to help him get to Olek, the kid I was supposed to protect. And his genius plan had almost succeeded. Then just a few weeks later, he used me to help him get his hands on a weaponized virus. And once again, he'd been just a hair away from making it happen.

Medlock smiled at me.

"This time," he said, "I've actually succeeded. My plan is already in motion; it's too late to stop me now. And, yes, to answer your question, you were once again vital to its success. So, I suppose that means a thank-you is in order. Thank you, Carson. I really mean that."

"How?" I said weakly, shaking my head.

"We'll get to that later," Medlock said. "After all,

everything up until now has just been phase one, the setup for what I—no, *we*—really need to accomplish, which is to stop the Agency before they destroy this planet in the name of justice."

"What are you talking about?" Danielle asked. "The Agency is working to stop *you* from destroying the world."

"You know, Dillon told me you were smart, Danielle," Medlock said. "But if the Agency has you this blinded, I'm not sure if I believe that."

Danielle stared at him with her mouth open. She looked at me, but I had nothing to say. There was no way Medlock was actually the good guy, right? Not after the things I'd seen him do—such as torturing my good friend Olek. Good guys didn't authorize the torture of twelve-year-old kids, no matter what the reason, right? Then again, the Agency had kidnapped Junior, and was holding Jake against his will in some secret location. . . .

"You're starting to see now, aren't you?" Medlock said, reading our expressions like flash cards. "Has Dillon told you the truth about me yet? About what really happened between me and the Agency all those years ago?"

I shook my head.

"I told them you would tell them," Dillon said.

Medlock's smile faded. He looked down at the floor as if he were fighting off tears. Then he looked back up at me and pulled aside his bangs, revealing the scar on his forehead. The scar from the bullet that had supposedly killed him years ago.

"It's time you know who really did this to me," Medlock said.

"It was the terrorists you were selling secrets to," I said. "Agent Blue already told me that story. He said Agent Nineteen felt responsible since he was there but wasn't able to stop them."

Medlock scoffed suddenly, making me flinch.

"That's what he said?" Medlock said. "Well, he told the truth about one thing: Agent Nineteen *should* feel responsible. Since he was the one who pulled the trigger."

CHAPTER 48

BALONEY STEEPED
KOOL-AID

ALL I COULD DO WAS STAND THERE AND SHAKE MY HEAD. I knew Agent Nineteen too well for that. He would never shoot his own partner and friend in the head. Or *anywhere*, for that matter.

"It's not true," I said. "You're a liar. I'll never believe that."

Medlock stood there and smiled at me smugly. It was the sort of smile that people used when they knew something no one else did. The smile of someone who'd just won a bet.

And it was like a dagger to my gut.

"What exactly did they tell you, then?" Medlock asked. "It'll be sort of fun to hear what kind of baloney they steeped into your Kool-Aid."

"They told me you were upset because you didn't think Director Isadoris trusted you," I said. "That you were more and more critical of the Agency's policy of secrecy, especially when it came to lying to your family and to Jake. That's when you cracked, betrayed the Agency, and started selling confidential information to the highest bidder. They sent Agent Nineteen to Chicago to monitor you. But one of your deals went bad and one of your buyers shot you in the head."

Medlock nodded slowly.

"Not bad," he said quietly. "That's a pretty good story. Very believable. But here's what actually happened.

"I *was* unhappy with the Agency and Director Isadoris—that much was very true. Most of it had to do with my son, Jake. I knew I couldn't tell my family about who I was, about what I did. I knew that when I joined the Agency, long before Jake was born. But when I told the Agency about Jake, Director Isadoris didn't trust me to remain quiet, and forbade me to be a part of Jake's life. To ever speak to or even see him again. They said it was too risky, that it might compromise my cover, but I knew that they simply didn't trust me. They don't trust anyone. They cut me off from my own son, all in the name of national security."

A long silence followed. And I realized he was waiting for us to answer. He wanted us to acknowledge that what the Agency had done was awful. And, I hated to admit, he was right. It was horrible. To separate a dad and son to protect a cover identity seemed a little extreme, but such was the nature of being a spy. I was starting to realize that more and more with each passing mission.

"It's awful," Danielle agreed.

I shot her a look.

"Well, it is," she said.

"Right?" Dillon added. "These are the people you two are working for. And this isn't even the worse part."

"He's right, it's not," Medlock said. "The real kicker is this: I never once had dealings with an enemy agent. I never sold *one* secret. When I was transferred to Chicago, yeah, I was devastated. No one trusted me, no one stuck up for me. But I would *never* turn around and start selling Agency secrets to enemies of the state, just for some sort of petty revenge. Not ever. You want to know what I *really* did after my transfer to Chicago?"

I nodded. My knees felt weak. And Danielle's expression matched how I felt. Sick.

"I quit," Medlock said. "That's all I did. I simply walked away. I disappeared from my post, left my job behind. I just wanted out so I could get back to Minnow and get my family and then hopefully we could make a clean break. Get away to Canada or something so we could be together. Was that too much to ask? Turns out, it was. Once you're in, you're in for good. The Agency doesn't let you walk away. When you retire early, *they retire you early*, understand?"

I shook my head. I mean, I understood what he was saying, I just didn't want to believe it.

"But they let *me* walk away after my first mission saving Olek from you," I said.

"Carson, you know about the Agency, yes, but how much do you *really* know? They've never let you in on any real secrets, have they? Ever really trusted you? And if you were to share anything you'd learned, no one would believe you. Such is the case with all of their kid agents."

"Wait, wait, wait," I said. "They have other agents our age working for them?"

Medlock gave me that smug smile again.

"Ah, they gave you the old, 'we never usually do this'

line, right?" Medlock said. "Yeah, they use that one a lot. And technically, it's sort of true. Not many kids are made field agents or brought in as quickly as you were—there were extenuating circumstances in your case. But the Agency starts recruiting potential agents at a very young age. You know I was originally recruited when I was fourteen? I wasn't all that different from you. After all, kids and teenagers are way easier to manipulate than most adults. They're too young to understand what's happening, too inexperienced to be suspicious of such an organization. It was only later, after I'd become a full-fledged agent, that I found all of this out. Which means I knew that once they realized I was trying to quit, they'd send out an agent to *retire* me."

"But why send Agent Nineteen?" Danielle asked. "Why would they make your own partner do it?"

"Because they knew he was the only person I'd trust enough to let get that close. I could have stayed hidden, gotten Jake, and made a clean break somewhere. But I trusted Agent Nineteen. So I agreed to a secret meeting with him—that was my biggest mistake, I suppose."

"And so . . ." I said, but couldn't bring myself to finish his story for him.

"That's right," Medlock said, his voice tightening

from the emotion of reliving what was surely the worst moment in his life. "I met up with Agent Nineteen on the Navy Pier in Chicago, thinking he was going to help me get my son and get away. Thinking he was more of a true friend to me than he was a loyal pawn of the Agency. I was obviously wrong. You can't imagine the pain of looking your supposed best friend in the eyes right at the moment that you realize he's lied to you. Right before he pulls the trigger."

I looked at Dillon. He looked back and then we both looked away. In that moment, I actually pitied Medlock. Dillon and I had lied to each other, yes. But I knew what it was like to have a true friend who wouldn't shoot you in the head, tranquilizer dart or otherwise.

"I regained consciousness later that night," Medlock said quietly. "I washed up on the dark beach a few hundred yards north of Navy Pier. I suppose it's a double miracle that I didn't somehow drown and that the bullet hadn't caused any permanent damage. At that point, I had no options. I needed medical care, obviously, but going to any public hospital would have risked revealing my survival to the Agency. And so I did the unthinkable: I contacted a known enemy agency and offered them secrets in exchange for medical treatment and getting me out of the country for a time. And so that brings us here, to now, working to complete my ultimate mission. Which is *not* to destroy the world, as the Agency somehow foolishly thinks. Why would I want to destroy the world? Does anyone really ever want that? No, Carson, I want to *save* the world. One that allows an Agency like this to exist, one that considers covert organizations with zero trust the 'good guys.' We can never truly be safe in a world where those in charge don't trust us. The only way to save it is to destroy that agency."

I didn't know how to respond. It was all so much to take in, and all I could do was stand there and keep listening to the man I had thought was an insanely evil genius but was now starting to view as the most unlucky person I'd ever met.

"And you, Carson," Medlock said with a certainty that was impossible to ignore, "are now going to help me execute the last few stages of my master plan."

CHAPTER 49

WHEN BEING RIGHT ALL ALONG IS ODDLY UNSATISFYING

"**I** DON'T THINK I CAN," I SAID. "I MEAN, I GET EVERYTHING THAT has happened to you, I understand why you're so angry, why you want revenge. But . . . you tortured Olek. And you planned to release the Romero Virus—I overheard Jake and Phil talking about it. I will never, ever knowingly help out a man who once planned to do something like that. No matter the reason."

"But you don't have a choice," Medlock said.

"Why not?" Danielle asked for me.

"For one thing, Carson has already helped me execute

phase one, as I hinted at earlier," Medlock said, pulling a small device from his pocket. "Remember those 'secret plans' you confiscated from Ms. Pullman's computer? You know, the ones that contained the blueprints for that insane plan to blow up the Agency headquarters by drilling down and planting a bomb?"

I nodded slowly, already suspecting where this was headed.

"Well, there never was a plan to drill down to the headquarters from the school parking lot," Medlock said. "The plans were fake."

"So, you weren't plotting to blow up Agency HQ?" I asked.

"Oh, no, I'm definitely going to destroy their little den of lies," Medlock said. "Just not by drilling. I mean, that'd be absurd! Do you have any idea how deep down the Agency's base is and how hard it would be to drill that far with normal equipment right in broad daylight next to a school? I mean, come *on*!"

I did feel a little stupid for thinking that plan was feasible. But more than that, I was curious. If the plans were fake, then what was the point?

Danielle beat me to the question. "So what were the plans for, really?"

"Glad you asked!" Medlock said cheerily. "I knew that if I planted even a grain of evidence that Ms. Pullman might be working for me and that the whole heated parking lot project was a cover for a nefarious plot, the Agency wouldn't hesitate to dig deeper, to look into the plans and likely infiltrate her office. That's what they do best, spy on people. And so I planted the fake plans deep inside her hard drive, without her even knowing they were there. And then when you so conveniently brought the files down to Agency Headquarters and delivered them to Isadoris, he was actually unknowingly uploading a small virus of mine into the Agency mainframe."

"So, everything—from Dillon framing Gomez and getting Pullman hired as principal to the parking lot construction—was all just a setup to get me to hand deliver a computer virus to the Agency's mainframe?" I asked.

"You learn quickly," Medlock said. "That's why I still like you, Carson, even after all the trouble you've caused me."

"But sneaking into Pullman's office wasn't even a part of my mission," I said.

"Right, which is why I had one of my men show up and take some fake blueprints and an infected laptop into her office right in front of you," Medlock said. "I knew you wouldn't be able to resist going in of your own free will after that."

"So Ms. Pullman doesn't work for you at all?" I asked.

Medlock shrugged, grinning.

I wasn't sure if that meant yes or no, but my suspicions were that it meant she did not work for him, didn't even know he existed. Which was a relief. But that also meant that I had betrayed her trust and truly hurt her when I'd broken into her office. The expulsion wasn't some plot by a crafty enemy agent, it was simply an expulsion. I'd failed. That made everything I'd been through feel that much worse.

"So what does the computer virus do?" Danielle asked, her voice shaking.

"Well, it has given me control over the base's maintenance operational mainframe," Medlock says. "Of course, the firewalls on their most classified records and base security systems are way too advanced for any hacker I could possibly hope to hire. But the firewalls and security surrounding the base's daily operations, although very strong, were much easier to infiltrate. Especially when the virus is uploaded directly into the mainframe, thanks to you."

"I don't get it," I said. "You control base operations. . . . How could that be helpful? What are you going to do? Turn all the lights on and off? Power down the air-conditioning and make them all uncomfortably hot?"

Medlock surprised me by laughing. A real, genuine laugh.

"Sort of," he said. He held up the small device he'd been holding. "I mean, basically with one press of a button I can overload the fusion energy core and cause a nuclear meltdown that will incinerate the entre base. And, who knows, maybe even take out the whole town."

"What? Why would you do that?"

"Well, I don't *want* to do it," Medlock said. "I have no desire to destroy Minnow. But I will do it if necessary. That is, if you don't play ball and help me."

I stood there and stared at him, feeling so hopeless I wanted to scream and throw a temper tantrum like I used to do when I was four.

"How could you help him do this?" Danielle shouted at Dillon, who had been listening to our whole conversation with detached interest.

"You don't understand," he said calmly. "All Medlock's trying to do is get rid of this insane Agency and get his son back. You remember Jake, right? *Your* Agency kidnapped him! I mean, how can *you* stand by and let them do that?"

"It's not the same thing," Danielle said. "You don't understand what Jake tried to do."

"Oh no?" Dillon asked. "Why don't I? Oh, yeah, that's right, it's because my twin sister and my best friend lied to me for months. But I'm just supposed to believe what you say now?"

"Enough," Medlock said. He didn't shout, but there was a command in his voice that instantly silenced the bickering. "There will be time to hash this out later. The point is, yes, my intentions are simple. I want my son back. And I want to bring the Agency down. You see, they're about to complete a deal that will bring them one step closer to completely destroying the world as we know it. And we're going to stop them."

01000101010101010100110010101010101010101
010101010101010000010100101010100101010101
101010000100101001010101001010101010101
000010   001100101010101010101010
0010   001010101001010101010
101   10101001010101010101
100010101010101010101

CHAPTER 50

THE EXODUS PROGRAM

I WAS FURIOUS WITH MEDLOCK, AND DILLON, BUT I WAS IN NO position to argue at that moment. I figured I had to hear him out, see what exactly he was planning on doing before I made a decision that would get everyone I knew killed.

"What do you want us to do?" I asked.

"It's quite simple," Medlock said. "According to information my associates have gathered, the Agency is going to be making a significant purchase from a third party technology firm. All I need is for you to find out when and where this exchange is supposed to go down."

"What kind of purchase?" I asked. "And for what?"

"That doesn't concern you."

"Well, either way, I don't think I can," I said. "I just completely blew my assignment by helping Dillon escape. They'll never trust me now."

"Well, you'd better figure something out," Medlock said. "And don't try to tip them off to my plan. I now have access to the base's security cameras, and if I see any evacuation attempts, I'm pressing the button. The exchange is happening tomorrow, which means you have seven hours to find out the time and location. Dillon will help you get in touch with me once you have the information."

"What are they buying?" I asked.

"I'm not surprised they didn't tell you," Medlock said, pulling a phone out of his pocket and checking something on it. "But then again, maybe I'm not. You must have gotten some hints, though."

I remembered what Director Isadoris had hinted a few times, about so many agents working on a new initiative. This had to have something to do with that.

"It's a program the likes of which the world has never seen before," Medlock continued. "And the Agency's ultimate, terrible plot: the Exodus Program. It makes infiltrating any computer, any device, anything remotely connected to a network as easy as pressing a button. Bank funds, nuclear missile launch systems, the pictures stored on your mom's iPhone. Anything and everything is a mouse click away. It will essentially give them the power to know everything. To do anything. There will be no secrets from the Agency anymore. No privacy. No safety. This is a power *nobody* should *ever* have."

"Except for you?" I said.

"Me?" he scoffed. "Carson, I don't want to steal the program. I want to destroy it. You think the Agency will use it for good? The internet is the most dangerous piece of technology mankind has ever created. There is nothing good that can come of this, no matter who controls it. Deep down, you know that's true. If I can intercept the exchange, then not only can I destroy the program but I can also make them give me my son back. Two birds with one microchip."

I didn't know what to think anymore. I didn't believe for a second that Medlock would simply destroy the program. I also think I believed what he said about the Agency. It was hard to imagine them having a program that powerful and not using it to spy on average people.

They'd never shown any restraint in the past in over-stepping the normal boundaries of the law to carry out a mission. In time, this program would only make such actions even easier for them.

Then again, the program was probably better off with them than a guy like Medlock, no matter what he claimed. For now, though, I didn't have much choice. The Agency HQ getting blown up definitely wouldn't solve anything and so for now I'd have to play along.

"Okay," I said finally. "I'll try."

"Carson, you can't!" Danielle said, taking a step toward.

Medlock shot Danielle an annoyed glance. "Oh please, what else is he supposed to do? You want to see the base get destroyed? Then come on over here and press the button yourself." He held out the small device.

She looked at it and frowned. He had her and she knew it. You didn't get to be lifelong best friends with someone and not learn to read their expressions. She knew Medlock had us in a vise.

"Okay, then," he said, putting the device in his pocket and turning to leave. "You have seven . . . no, make that just under seven hours. You'd better hurry."

He stepped back into the shadows of the old Bonanza

kitchen and was gone. We all heard the back door open and close behind him a few moments later. Then it was just Dillon, Danielle, and me again. We looked at one another in the dark room uneasily.

In that moment I think we all knew nothing would ever quite be the same between us again.

0001010101010101001100101010101010101010
1010101010100001010010101010100010101010
0101000010010100101010010101010101010
0001010101010100011001 10101
0101011010100010010 0100
0101000010010100101 010
0001010101010101001 1 10

CHAPTER 51

RAT RIVERS
AND DIRT MALLS

THE THREE OF US RODE OUR BIKES UNEASILY TOWARD THE school. Well, Dillon and Danielle were on bikes, I was standing on the pegs on Dillon's back wheel. We hadn't said much before leaving Bonanza, just that we obviously needed to get into Agency HQ in order to try and gather the information that Medlock needed.

We pulled over a block away and ducked behind some trees near a bridge that passed over the Rat River. Technically its real name was the Souris River. But no one who lived around here actually called it that. It's a long story, one so boring I don't really even remember myself how it had come to pass.

"So," Dillon said, looking around with a blank expression on his face, "what are you guys going to do?"

Something burst inside me in that moment. Before I knew what I was doing, I was charging at my best friend, grabbing at his throat so I could squeeze the air out of his stupid windpipe. We both fell to the ground, with him flailing to get away from me. He pushed me off and stood up. I pulled at his winter jacket, but my hands slipped right off. He backed away from me as I stood. Danielle grabbed me and held me back.

"Stop it, Carson," she said. "That's not helping."

"How could you work for that guy?" I said to Dillon.

"How could you work for an Agency that shot their own employee in the head simply because he knew what they were doing?" Dillon fired back.

I opened my mouth to answer, but realized I didn't really have a good reply.

"That's why I didn't let them take you at the Dirt Mall," I finally said.

Now it was Dillon's turn to remain quiet.

"I know," he eventually mumbled. "Thanks for that, by the way."

I shrugged.

"I think we can all agree," Danielle said, "that whatever our individual motivations are, it doesn't matter. All I know is that our current situation sucks. And now we need to figure out how to fix it."

Nobody spoke for at least thirty seconds. We all just stood there and watched our foggy exhales dissipate into the November night air. I realized then just how late it was. It was almost 9:00 p.m. now surely. Which meant my parents had probably discovered that I was gone, and were terrified. They might have even called the cops. But being blackmailed by an evil genius to betray a secret government Agency had a way of making me feel like the local cops mattered about as much as a bushel of kale.

"This is getting out of control," Danielle said. "Can't you both see that?"

I nodded, but Dillon shook his head.

"Come on, Dillon," I said. "Can't you see that, no matter who wins, everyone loses? Yes, if we don't stop the Agency, this Exodus Program could mean the end of privacy as we know it. But if we help Medlock get his hands on the program—"

"What?" Dillon interrupted. "He'll get his son back? Medlock rants all the time about how much he hates the internet and cell phones and the way we're all connected, mostly due to how it gives organizations like the Agency and NSB a way to monitor what people are doing. He always says that he would just destroy the internet altogether if it were ever possible. So if he hated the internet so much, then why would he ever want a program powerful enough to take control of oh, wait, uh-oh . . ."

He trailed off. All three of us seemed to realize the same thing at the same time. Danielle was the first to say it aloud.

"Medlock wants to get the program so he can wipe out the internet entirely," she said.

"The Exodus could effectively do it," said Dillon.

"Can you imagine what would happen?" I said. "I mean, practically everything is connected to a single network. It would be the ultimate reset button that he's always talking about."

"But if he does that," Danielle said, "it's going to throw the entire world into chaos. People will get hurt. It will destroy life as we know it."

Dillon slumped down onto the ground, shaking his head.

"Everything he said always made so much sense to me," he said. "I can't believe I helped him this much. I truly thought he wanted to do the right thing."

"It's okay," I said, sitting next to him. "Look, a lot of stuff he wants to do makes sense to me, too. And it's not as if the Agency is much better."

"Stop your sulking!" Danielle said to us both. "Get up." We both stood up. "We need to do something about this, right? The question now is, what?"

I leaned against a tree and shoved my hands in my pockets as we all thought about possible solutions. That's when my hand wrapped around a business card still there from the last time I wore these pants.

I knew exactly what we needed to do.

0001010101010101010011001010101010101010101
101010101010100001010010101010010101010
010100001001010010101010010101010101010
0001   0011001010101010101010101
010   0010101010010101010100
01   CHAPTER 52   1010100101010101010
00   110010101010101010101

MORE SILENT
CONVERSATIONS

I REALLY HAD NO IDEA WHAT KIND OF RECEPTION I WAS GOING TO get. After all, I had taken out two fellow agents with tranquilizer darts, directly sabotaging several mission objectives. Part of me was even worried that they might let me in and then *retire* me, even if I was just a kid. Heck, I didn't even know if they were going to let us back into headquarters at all.

"Agent Zero," said a voice behind us as Danielle and I approached the shed. "We were beginning to think you'd deserted."

We spun around. Agents Nineteen and Blue stepped out from behind a few trees.

"No," I said. "But I do have some pretty important information about Medlock's plans."

"And we're just supposed to trust you?" Agent Nineteen said. His words weren't angry. The question sounded more curious.

"Yes," I said, "the same way I've always trusted you. And for the same reasons: because I know that you two, above all, want to do the right thing."

I honestly had a hard time saying that. I *wasn't* so sure about that anymore, to tell the truth. Could a guy who shot his former partner and best friend really ever do the right thing? But I had to sell the lie if I was going to carry out our plan.

"Carson," Agent Blue said, "you directly interfered—"

"Yeah, I know what I did," I said sharply. "And what I did was help out my best friend. That's all. I couldn't let you hurt him. I understand if I'm on the outs because of it. You can detain me, dismiss me, do whatever you want. But please, give me a chance to tell you and Director Isadoris what I've found out. Otherwise, we're all dead."

"It's true," Danielle piped in. "You need to hear us out."

Agent Blue and Agent Nineteen looked at each other.

They didn't say anything. They didn't need to. I'd seen them practically have entire conversations without so much as opening their mouths once. Then they looked back at us, but it was too dark to see their expressions.

"Okay," Agent Blue finally said. "But I'm sure you'll understand our need to handcuff you before we head down?"

"Of course," I said, holding out my arms to show I had nothing to hide. "It's what I would do."

CHAPTER 53

COUGH TALK

IT WAS AN ODD EXPERIENCE, BEING BROUGHT DOWN INTO Agency headquarters in handcuffs. They'd even cuffed Danielle, despite the fact that she hadn't been involved in what happened with Dillon. They didn't trust anyone, after all.

Agents Blue and Nineteen said nothing during the elevator ride down into the base and subsequent walk to one of the small concrete interrogation rooms. That's when they split up Danielle and me. This didn't surprise us. In fact, we'd planned for this before we'd even approached the maintenance shed.

As I sat there and waited in shackles, I wondered briefly if they would actually torture me. I hadn't seen them do anything like that, but I wouldn't put it past them.

Several minutes after they sat me down at the small plastic table, the lone door opened again and Agents Blue and Nineteen returned. They closed the door behind them and glanced up at the small dark bubble in the ceiling, which I knew housed a panoramic security camera. No doubt Isadoris was watching us.

As was Medlock.

He'd been very clear: Any signs of evacuation and he'd blow the base. Any signs of me telling them about his plans and he'd blow the base. All of our lives depended on what I said in the next few minutes.

"What did you need to tell us, Carson?" Agent Nineteen asked.

I buried my face in my shackled hands as if I were tired or frustrated, or both. I split apart my palms slightly so I could whisper to Agents Nineteen and Blue but not be heard by any of the recording devices that were surely in the room.

"Whatever you do," I said slowly, clearly, and softly, "do not react to anything I'm about to say. It's imperative. Cough if you understand."

There was a slight beat and then one of them cleared his throat. They obviously had no idea what was going on, but it was good to know they both still trusted me enough to follow my lead without blowing the whole operation right then and there. That was a good sign, I thought.

"You need to get us away from any security cameras," I said, again as slowly and clearly and quietly as was possible. I began shaking my shoulders and head as if I were crying or something instead of talking. "Our lives depend on it. You have to trust me."

There was another delay. And then a voice spoke. It was Agent Blue.

"Well?" he said. "Quit stalling. What did you want to tell us?"

I breathed out a low sigh of relief. They were playing along. So far, so good. But, this was still the early and easy part of our intricate, ridiculous, nearly impossible plan to save the day and fix this entire mess once and for all.

"I don't know where to begin," I said, finally raising

my head, making my face look as distraught as possible. "I think I might barf."

Agent Nineteen and Agent Blue stared at me warily. I wasn't sure if they were still acting the part or not. I had no idea what they'd do, or if there even was somewhere in this building out of sight of security cameras. I had come up with the barfing thing, hoping that the bathroom might be one of those places. Or at the very least to give them a believable reason to get me out of this room.

"Come on then," Agent Nineteen said.

They lifted me from the chair and led me out of the interrogation room and down the hall toward a bathroom. As we walked, Agent Blue coughed into his hand. At the end of his cough he faintly whispered something.

"When you get out, say you need to lie down," he said into his hand.

We got to the bathroom and Agent Nineteen opened the door for me. It was a single occupancy restroom, with just a small sink, toilet, and mirror. It was obvious from the way they'd acted that there were cameras in here. So I bent over the toilet and pretended to barf as best I could. Then I flushed, washed my hands, wiped my mouth, tried to look as sick as I could as I walked back into the hallway.

"I think I need to lie down," I moaned. "Are these really necessary?" I held up my shackled hands.

"I suppose not," Agent Blue said, before removing them.

"Can I lie down somewhere?" I asked again.

"Yeah, come on this way," Agent Nineteen said. "There's a couch in Director Isadoris's office. We can talk in there."

I nodded and followed them down the hallway. I could only assume this meant that Director Isadoris's office was the only place in the entire base that didn't have security cameras. Who watches the one guy in the country who, after tomorrow's purchase, would be able to watch anyone he wanted on the entire planet?

This thought made me even more determined, more sure that we were doing the right thing.

CHAPTER 54

STOP SAYING BOOM!

"**W**HAT'S THIS ALL ABOUT?" DIRECTOR ISADORIS PRACTI-
cally shouted as the three of us entered his office. "I told
you to conduct the entire interview in room three forty-
seven. I don't care if he's not feeling well."

"We're hoping he can explain," Agent Blue said placing a hand on my shoulder perhaps a little too roughly.
"Have a seat."

He pushed me down onto a couch adjacent to Director Isadoris's desk. The three of them loomed around me,

waiting for me to say something. I saw Agent Smiley and the other agent I'd tranquilized at the Dirt Mall earlier that day sitting at their usual table behind Director Isadoris's desk.

She glared at me with a look that could easily kill an elderly person or small child. I tried to ignore her glowering and instead focused on my thoughts before I started speaking. Isadoris was obviously furious, which meant I'd need to get right to the point.

"I asked them to take me somewhere there were no security cameras," I said, "because Medlock is watching your every move."

The news visibly rippled across the faces of three men looming over me. Agent Nineteen looked confused, Agent Blue frowned, and Director Isadoris looked downright outraged. Like he would tear off a puppy's head just to release the fury.

"How is that possible?" Director Isadoris asked through gritted teeth.

He looked like a man who was losing his grip on reality. It frightened me. And not just because he was the size of a four-door sedan. More and more I was beginning to realize that I might be looking at the most powerful man in the world. He certainly had more power than the president. After tomorrow's exchange, there'd be no question about it.

"The plans," I said. "The ones that you sent me to steal."

Director Isadoris cocked his head at me, only furthering his primal, animalistic appearance. "What?"

"The plans to blow up the base by drilling down from above," I said. "They're fake. The files on the USB drive and the laptops actually contained some sort of computer virus that Medlock has used to take control over many of the base's operational systems, including access to the security camera feeds."

"How do you know that?" Agent Nineteen asked.

"Because Medlock told me," I replied.

"It can't be . . ." Agent Blue muttered under his breath.

Director Isadoris slammed a fist onto his heavy wooden desk. We all jumped as it smashed right through the heavy oak surface, leaving a massive, splintered crater. Had I not just watched him punch a hole in his heavily lacquered wooden desk, I never would have believed it humanly possible.

He pulled up his fist and blood dripped from several large splinters that were poking out of his knuckles like a collection of small trophies.

"Agent Smiley," he said, calmly picking the splinters from his hand, "disable the base security cameras immediately."

"No, wait!" I whispered urgently.

Everybody froze. Agent Smiley's hand hovered over her computer's keyboard.

"If you do that, he'll know I told you," I said. "And then, well . . . boom."

"Boom?" Agent Blue said.

"What do you mean, *boom*?" Director Isadoris asked.

"Medlock will blow up this base," I said. "He said if he sees any signs of evacuation or that you know he's watching you, or that I told you any of this, that he'll blow up the base."

Agent Blue paced across the room. "There's a bomb here now? I thought you said the plans to blow up the base were just a Trojan horse, so to speak, for his virus?"

"Yeah," I said. "But Medlock told me he can cause the nuclear fusion core powering the base to melt down in a matter of minutes with a simple press of a button."

"Is that even possible?" Director Isadoris asked Agent Smiley.

She and the guy across from her exchanged a few

words that I didn't quite hear. Then Agent Smiley nodded slowly, her face still showing no emotions. Not even fear. "Theoretically, yes," she said.

Director Isadoris swore loudly. Then he walked around to the other side of his desk and sat down. He stared at me for such a long time, it felt like he was looking right through me.

"What does he want then?" Director Isadoris asked. "What's his endgame here? Why not just blow us up now? I'm sure that'd give him a thrill."

"He wants me to find out when and where you're making the buy," I said.

"What buy?" Director Isadoris said.

"The Exodus Program."

"How do you know about that?"

"How do you think?"

Director Isadoris hesitated. If anything, this only confirmed that it was true.

"Fine," he said. "How does *he* know about it?"

"I don't know."

Director Isadoris swore again. I was just glad he wasn't smashing holes in his massive desk again. It was too brutal a sight to witness multiple times at such proximity.

"Anyway," I said, "he wanted me to find out when and

where the deal was happening and bring the information back to him. He said he only wants to use it to blackmail you and get his son back. But I suspect, and I assume you'll agree, that he'd use it for much more than that if he actually got his hands on the tech. If I don't report back in a few hours, then . . . boom."

"Would you please stop saying 'boom' like that?" Director Isadoris said, rubbing his temples.

I shrugged, not sure what else to say instead. *Kill us all* sounded a lot worse in my opinion. As did *Blow us to smithereens*. Or even *Hit the switch*.

"So why did you tell us all of this, instead of carrying out his plan?" Agent Nineteen asked.

How could he ask me that?

"Of course I'm going to tell you!" I nearly shouted. "Why would I want to help out that psycho? I was *hoping* that by telling you, you would somehow know what to do. How to stop him. Besides, you'd never trust me with that information now, not after what I did at the Dirt Mall today."

"The what?" Agent Blue asked.

"At Arrowhead," I said, glancing at Agent Smiley and the other agent I'd shot.

"You aren't wrong," Director Isadoris said. "I don't

trust you any farther than I could throw you. Which, actually, would be pretty far, I guess . . . but that's not the point."

"Well, regardless, I'm still on your side," I said. "You do know what to do, right? How to stop him? He said if the information I give him isn't accurate, well . . . you know."

Director Isadoris looked at me evenly and then nodded.

"Maybe we do," he said. "But I still don't trust you enough to say anything more."

"Why?" I asked angrily. "Because I wouldn't stab my friend in his back? If anything, you should trust me *more* for that! Besides, you wouldn't know any of this if it weren't for what I did."

"That's assuming any of it's true at all," Director Isadoris said.

"Well, don't test it out or we'll all die," I said bleakly.

"Convenient, that," Director Isadoris said. "Regardless, I just don't think I can truly believe a word you're saying. Agent Nineteen, please detain this *civilian* and get him out of my sight."

0010101010101010101010101001100101010101010101010101010
010101010101000010100101010100101010100
101000010010100101010010101010101010101
0010101010101010011001...101010
1010110101000100101...1001
1010000100101001010...0101
0010101010101010100110...1010

CHAPTER 55

HYPOTHETICAL
BODIES AT OLD AUGUSTINE

STILL COULDN'T BELIEVE THIS WAS HAPPENING. DANIELLE AND I were being led down a dark concrete corridor somewhere inside the base. In handcuffs. And the worst part was that Agent Nineteen and Agent Blue, along with Agent Smiley, were the ones escorting us to . . . well, wherever it was we were headed.

Prison? Some gray site in Europe similar to wherever Jake was in custody? A concrete cell deep within the base? Our own graves?

I couldn't really rule anything out. But it didn't matter.

The end result would be unchanged: I had failed. I had failed in the very first few steps of our complicated plan to take down the Agency and Mule Medlock all at once. In order for our plan to work, I needed to get Isadoris to trust me and tell me where the exchange was going down. And so, yeah, it was probably a little foolish to have believed I could get that guy to ever trust anyone beside himself.

"You don't have to do this," I said suddenly. A last-ditch effort to save us all. "There's still time. Medlock is going to blow up the whole city!"

"Shut up," Agent Smiley said, jabbing me in the back painfully with a finger. "Traitor."

Danielle kept her head down, crying silently. The guilt was overwhelming. It was my fault she was here. It was my fault she'd gotten messed up in any of this in the first place.

And then suddenly an explosion dropped us all to our feet. Smoke filled the small hallway, and my ears were ringing from the deafening blast. I choked and coughed on the smoke, disoriented. Had Medlock just hit the button? Were we about to die? I had no clue what was going on.

But then someone was unlocking my handcuffs and pulling me to my feet.

"Run," a gruff voice shouted in my ear.

A hand shoved me forward. I began running. I couldn't see through the smoke but just kept running. I held my hands out to my sides to keep from slamming into the walls. Then someone was next to me. They grabbed my shirt and helped guide me to the left and through a doorway of some kind.

The door swung closed. We were somewhere dark and I couldn't see anything. I was shuffled into another room with a metal floor. Then, suddenly bright lights popped on and I shielded my eyes with my hands. Once my vision adjusted to the light, I realized I was inside a small metal elevator.

Agent Nineteen, Agent Blue, and Danielle were also there.

"What's going on?" I asked. "And what happened to Smiley?"

"She'll be fine, just a little bump on the head," Agent Nineteen said. "Take this elevator all the way to the top. There, you'll find a concrete tunnel with a ladder. You'll have to climb the rest of the way but it's not too far. Go home, both of you. Stay inside, stay with your families. Okay?"

"Why are you doing this?" I asked.

"Because what the director is asking of us isn't right," he said.

"We believe you guys," Agent Blue added. "He has no right to detain you both and send you away to a gray site."

I looked around the elevator. It definitely wasn't the one we normally used. This one seemed way less high-tech, it was more like a freight elevator.

"But won't you get in trouble for helping us?" I asked. "I mean, can't they see us right now? Plus, what about Medlock seeing this . . . it might make him . . ."

"No, there are no cameras in here," Agent Blue said. "It's an emergency protocol exit. The same one we're going to use to evacuate the base ourselves without Medlock knowing."

"Don't worry about us and the Agency," Agent Nineteen said. "We can handle ourselves with Isadoris, let us worry about that, it's not your problem anymore. He won't know we helped you escape."

I nodded. And then realized that if they were letting us go, there was still an outside chance that Danielle, Dillon, and I could complete our mission after all.

"Where and when is the exchange taking place?" I asked.

"I can't tell you that," Agent Nineteen said.

"You still don't trust me?" I asked.

"No, that's not it at all," Agent Nineteen said. "It's that I think you want to know because you want to go there and try something stupid. Well, don't. It will only end up getting you killed."

I sighed and looked away from his clear green eyes. Then I faced him again, determined to get what I needed at all costs.

"You turned your back on a partner once before," I said. "I know that now. Don't do it again. Please, just tell me—I won't go anywhere near it, I promise. I just need to know to make sure that Medlock hasn't figured it out somehow himself. I can give him incorrect intel."

My words visibly disturbed him. Agent Nineteen looked like he wanted to either break down and cry for an hour, backhand me for calling him out, or punish himself since the guilt clearly hadn't worn off yet.

"It's at old Augustine Church," Agent Nineteen said. "Right before sunrise, just under four hours away."

"Augustine Church?" I said.

"That's right," Agent Blue said. "What better place to do a covert exchange than in Middle of Nowhere, North Dakota, in November?"

Augustine Church was an old, abandoned church ten

or fifteen miles west of town. It was a local historical land-mark, being one of the oldest buildings in the state still standing. That said, nobody ever went out there, except for teenagers sometimes in the summer, who spent the night in the supposedly haunted building on a dare. It was the sort of place that would be the perfect dumping ground for bodies if Minnow, ND, ever had more than one murder per decade. Being out in the middle of nowhere meant it was essentially right in the middle of a mostly flat plain with very little to hide behind for miles. The truth was, that location might make it a lot harder to execute the last parts of my plan. But I couldn't worry about that now or it might give something away.

"Just stay out of the way," Agent Nineteen said. "I better not see you anywhere near the place. Now go on, get home, both of you."

He didn't wait for a reply as both he and Agent Blue stepped out of the elevator and then hit a button on the outside wall. The last thing I saw as the metal doors slowly slid closed, was Agent Nineteen reaching up toward his face to wipe the tears from his eyes.

```
100101010101010101100110010101010101010101010
010101010101000001010010101010010101010100
010100001001010010101010010101010101010101
0001010101010101001100                 101010
010101101010001001                     01001
010100001001010010                     0101
0010101010101001010
```

CHAPTER 56

A HANDHELD MEDLOCK

THE CLIMB UP THE METAL LADDER INSIDE THE CONCRETE TUNNEL felt extra long. Probably because I couldn't stop thinking about what it would feel like to be looking down the barrel of a gun held by Danielle. Which is essentially the equivalent of what had happened to Medlock all those years ago.

Danielle and I had said nothing on the relatively fast elevator ride to the underground sewer, or the climb the rest of the way up to a small street a few blocks from the school. We jogged back toward the school where Danielle had parked her bike.

There was a cop car parked up the hill in the school parking lot. The lights were off, but we could see two uniformed officers standing next to it, outside in the cold. It almost looked as if they were keeping watch for something . . . or someone.

"Think they're looking for me?" I asked as Danielle unchained her bike from a nearby tree. I was technically a missing kid after all—my parents hadn't seen me since that afternoon and had no clue where I was.

"Yeah, maybe," she said. "Come on, hop aboard."

I climbed onto the pegs of her bike and she rode away from the school toward Burdick Avenue. We crossed it without waiting for the light, since there wasn't much traffic after midnight. We parked our bikes behind the water treatment plant, nestled away in the trees on the riverbank. Dillon was there, waiting for us.

"So?" he asked as he handed me a grocery bag full of his old winter clothes.

"We got what we needed," I said as I put on his old winter coat and gloves.

"Good, let's go meet Medlock, then," Dillon said, turning toward Danielle. "Mom is freaking out right now. I keep texting her to calm down and that we're fine and will be home soon, but she's not having it. We're already grounded for three months."

"Big deal," Danielle said.

Dillon shrugged and then hopped on his bike.

"Follow me," he said.

Danielle and I followed Dillon, me on the back pegs of her bike. We rode along the riverbank, in the trees, away from any roads. I was sure that Dillon was afraid of a possible tail. And I supposed that made sense. Medlock would have been worried about it.

We ended up in Oak Park, which was so dark at night that I could barely see Dillon anymore, even though he was just ten feet ahead of us. I heard his bike braking, the tires skidding on the gravel bike path. Danielle slowed down, too.

A blue light appeared in front of me from what I thought was Dillon's phone. As I dismounted and got closer, however, I realized it wasn't a phone at all but another type of device with a small screen. That's when I realized we weren't going to meet up with Medlock face-to-face at all, a hunch confirmed a moment later when Medlock's face appeared on the handheld.

"What did you find out?" he asked.

"Here," Dillon handed me the small device.

I looked into Medlock's dark eyes. Even on the tiny screen they seemed to be too large and sharp to miss anything. It was uncanny how much they almost shined in spite of their dark color.

"Well?" he said impatiently. "Do I need to remind you about the button?"

"No," I said. "I mean, no you don't need to remind me. *Yes*, I got what you wanted."

"I'm glad to hear it," he said. "I got a little worried when you disappeared from the camera feeds for such a long time." He squinted suspiciously.

"Hmm . . . I didn't feel well so they took me to Isadoris's office to finish the interview."

Medlock scoffed. "Figures that Isadoris's office is the only one without a camera. Giving himself the privacy that he affords nobody else."

I didn't know how to answer that, or if he even expected an answer, so I just stayed quiet and looked into the small screen. Medlock stared back.

"Well, let's have it, then," he snarled.

"Oh, right. It's, uh, the exchange, I mean, is at sunrise. That's all he said, he didn't say a specific time. And it's happening out near old Augustine Church."

If that presented any problems for him, he didn't show it. In fact, he seemed relatively pleased, if the slight grin that appeared on his face was any indication.

"You're not lying to me?"

"If I am, then I just destroyed the base," I said. "And maybe the school, and who knows what else?"

"See?" Medlock said. "You learn fast. This could have been so much better had you worked for me from the start."

"So, what's your plan now?" I asked.

"Yeah, nice try," he said. "Give me back to Dillon, please."

I handed the device over. Dillon took it and gave me a momentary smile. Then he looked at the screen.

"Meet me at the gym," I heard Medlock say. "Come alone."

Dillon nodded and then disconnected the call and put the device back into his pocket.

"The gym?" Danielle asked.

"Code word," Dillon said, and left it at that.

We all just stood there in the cold dark night and squinted to see each other for a few moments.

"Well, you'd better go meet Medlock, then," I finally said. "I need to make a phone call and then get to work on the hardest phase of this whole mission. Danielle?"

"I'm going to head home so our mom doesn't call the cops on us, too," she said. "I'll retrieve those gadgets you got from Chum Bucket that I stashed for you."

"What about the exchange?" I asked.

"I'll still be there," she said. "I can sneak out of my house, too, you know."

"Okay, so let's rendezvous in three hours," I said. "Also, I'll need one of your cell phones since my dad smashed mine. So we can stay in touch."

Danielle pulled out her phone and handed it to me. Then they both nodded at me, reconfirmed our rendez-vous, and we all parted ways. Now it was time for the hardest part of my plan. In fact, I had no idea how I would accomplish what I needed to do next. Still, our plan was already in motion, and that meant I had to succeed or else dozens of innocent people would probably die.

There was no going back now.

CHAPTER 57

USING THE NEW
TO FIND THE OLD

TRACKING DOWN A PAY PHONE HAD BEEN A LOT HARDER THAN I'd expected. I'd never used one before. The only reason I knew they existed at all was old movies. But I still assumed there had to be one somewhere. Especially in a place like Minnow, ND, which always seemed to be at least a few years behind the rest of the country when it came to just about everything.

I eventually used Danielle's smartphone to find a pay phone. I couldn't actually use my smartphone for the call I needed to make because I knew that the Agency had the ability to track cell phone calls fairly easily. And I wouldn't put it past them to be tracking her calls right at that moment, even though they were currently busy with their own plans.

The nearest pay phone still in service was at a Hardee's just a mile away. I walked there and made a phone call. I half expected nobody to answer; after all, it was nearly 2:00 a.m. But I eventually got through and spoke to the exact person I needed to.

But that wasn't the hard part of my mission that night. The really hard part came after that. I once again used a simple Google search to find an address. It was close to the Hardee's, which was good, though it didn't give me as much time as I'd have liked to have to figure what I was going to say when I got there.

I took a few deep breaths as I ascended the front steps; the cold air bit my lungs. Then I approached the door and rang the doorbell. It was now 2:30 a.m.

And there I was ringing my principal's doorbell.

CHAPTER 58

THE ULTIMATE
TRUST TEST

I WASN'T SURE HOW LONG I WAS GOING TO HAVE TO STAND THERE and wait for someone to answer the door. And so I hit the doorbell at least a dozen times to ensure that *someone* would wake up and answer it. Turns out, even at that hour, you didn't have to wait that long to get yelled at after ringing someone's doorbell incessantly.

A light flickered on and then I saw part of a face peer out through a small window. The door swung open. A middle-aged man wearing only a bathrobe and boxer shorts scowled at me.

"I'm going to call the cops," he said.

"I need to speak to Ms. Pullman," I said, ignoring him.

"She's *sleeping*," he said through gritted teeth. "What . . . how . . ."

He seemed too angry and too tired to be able to put together rational questions. It was hard to blame him. Were it not for all the adrenaline from what I'd been through and was about to go through, I'd have been passed out by this point.

"It's important. *Please.*" I tried to look as desperate as I felt.

"John, who is it?" a voice said from inside the house.

I looked past the guy and saw Ms. Pullman standing in the hallway, also wearing a robe. Her eyes were squinting and her hair was frazzled. As if she'd just been rudely awakened in the middle of the night.

"*Carson*?" she said, clearly shocked when she spotted me.

"Hi, Ms. Pullman," I said. "I'm so sorry to bother you but it's important."

"What's wrong?" she asked, sounding more concerned than annoyed.

"It's, uh, hard to explain."

"Well, you had better hurry then," John said, "because

I don't want to miss the end of it when the police arrive."

He had a phone in his hand now.

"Wait, please, I just need to talk to Ms. Pullman for two minutes. Then you can call the cops."

John glanced at his wife. She shrugged and nodded. He looked back at me and rolled his eyes.

"Well, I have to work tomorrow," he declared, as if he deserved a medal for it. "So I'm going back to bed." He headed back toward his room.

We stood there and listened as he stalked away down the hallway. Their bedroom door slammed shut a few seconds later.

"He doesn't like to be woken at three in the morning," Ms. Pullman said. "Nor do I, for that matter."

"I'll get right to the point then," I said. "And this is going to sound insane. I get that. But you have to trust me. I mean, I know you probably shouldn't, I certainly haven't given you much reason to. But this time it's really, really—"

"I thought you said you were getting right to the point," she interrupted, leaning against the wall with her arms folded.

"Sorry," I mumbled. "Anyway, I need you to make sure the school is completely evacuated tomorrow morning.

No janitors, no teachers, nobody can be inside it or even near it at sunrise."

She stared at me for several moments. She seemed unable to comprehend my words at first. I didn't blame her.

"What?" she said eventually.

I took a deep breath to start explaining, but she didn't even let me start.

"Maybe John was right to want to call the cops right away," she said, moving toward the phone he had set on the edge of their dining room table.

"Fine, please, call the cops," I said. "In fact, I will call them for you." I pulled out Danielle's cell phone. "And I'll tell them whatever it takes to make sure the school is closed tomorrow."

"Carson." She furrowed her brow. "Be straight with me. What the heck is going on?"

"Right, okay," I said, realizing I was going about this in such a frantic way that she was probably starting to worry about my mental health. "I know that you think I'm a good kid deep down, and I really am. I mean well. I never wanted to betray you. It's such a ridiculous story and I don't expect you to ever trust me . . . but I'm a secret agent. A real one. And . . ."

I trailed off when I saw her face change. Now she clearly did think I was nuts.

"Do your parents know you're here?" she asked, picking up the phone.

"No," I admitted. "But that doesn't matter. I've never told anyone this before. In fact, I've been lying to just about everyone I know for the entire school year. But you have to believe me, or people might get hurt. Please, make sure the school is evacuated. I know there's no logical reason for you to do what I'm asking, no reason for you or anyone else to actually trust me anymore. But I'm asking you, because you're maybe the only person I've met this year who actually does."

My desperation must have shown on my face because the hand holding the phone lowered back to the table. She looked at me and I tried to meet her stare. And that's when I realized I was crying. I had no idea when I'd started or why, but, sure enough, there were salty streams running down my face.

I wiped at them, embarrassed. The stress of this was clearly starting to get to me. That was fine, though; hopefully this would all be over soon, once and for all.

"If I did decide to trust you," she began, "how do you expect me to do this? Principals only have so much power, Carson. I'm not the dictator of the school. More like a prime minister, if that."

I shrugged. "I don't know. I'm just a kid. That's why I'm here asking for your help."

"What's going to happen to my school, Carson?"

"I honestly don't know," I said. "Maybe nothing. Hopefully nothing. But maybe *something*. We just can't take that risk."

I couldn't believe she was actually considering helping me. Part of me, a significant portion, never actually believed I could pull this off. Deep down, I figured there was no way she'd ever trust me again. But, then again, deep down, maybe she really did think I was a good person. She had thought that at one point anyway. And that's what I'd been latching on to, since I saw it in her file.

"What on earth are you involved in?" she asked, even though I'd already tried to tell her the truth a few moments ago.

"You don't even want to know," I said this time, figuring that answer was truly better for both of us.

000101010101010101100110010101010101010101010
101010101010000010100101010100101010101100
010100001001010010101010010101010101010101
000101010101010100110011   101010
010101101010001001010   01001
010100001001010010101   0101
000101010101010101001110   1011

CHAPTER 59

JURASSIC PARK IS THE BEST MOVIE EVER

THERE I WAS, SITTING ON THE TOILET INSIDE THE FOURTH STALL from the door in Oak Park's public restroom, the last place I ever expected to find myself at 3:30 a.m. on a random Friday night, or early Saturday morning, technically. I wasn't actually using the bathroom; I'd just gotten tired of standing in the cold. Which is why I'd picked the lock and let myself in. That, and it was a pretty solid hiding place when the cops and your parents and who knows who else were out looking for you.

The idea of being a fugitive had always seemed cool

when I was a little kid, but I have to say that in reality it pretty much sucked. Especially in the winter. The feeling of having nowhere to go, nowhere safe to hide, was horrible. It almost squeezed any last positive thought I had left from my brain, like a giant melon juicer.

But we were near the end now. After we carried out our plan, I would simply turn myself in and face the consequences. And I wouldn't really even care what they were. Because if we succeeded, then Medlock would finally be gone, the Agency exposed, and all of this would finally be over. And if our plan didn't succeed, well, then we'd all be lucky to even see the next sunrise.

My mind was lingering on this morbid thought as I stared at the text message I'd sent to Dillon about a half hour before:

Jurassic Park is the best movie ever.

And at that moment, I heard the double honk just outside. That was my signal. The real question was: Where on earth had Dillon and Danielle gotten a car, and who the heck was driving it?

I stood up and crept toward the far wall, the only one with a window, but it was too high for me to see outside. I took a leap of faith and poked my head out the door.

Dillon and Danielle's mom's car was parked just

outside the bathroom in the parking lot. The headlights were off, so I could see my two best friends in the yellow glow of the streetlights nearby.

They'd actually stolen—or maybe borrowed is the better word—their mom's car. Things really were out of control now. I ran toward the car and dived into the backseat. Probably overkill, but you never can be too careful. There's no upside to lollygagging when you're a wanted man.

Danielle was driving. Dillon was in the passenger seat.

"Hey," Dillon said, turning around to face me with a grin.

"Glad to see you remembered the code," I said as Danielle carefully pulled out of the Oak Park parking lot, craning her neck to see over the large hood of their mom's old beater of a car.

"I'll never forget it," Dillon said. "It was my idea, remember?"

I nodded. The message I'd sent him was our code. Or, well, his code. He was the one who didn't trust text messaging. So he'd developed a secret coding system for us to use to transmit messages without saying what we actually meant. It was pretty simple really. There were only a few key phrases to the code, but changing any one of those words could mean a number of different things. Most of the code revolved around meeting secretly at various locations throughout Minnow, ND. That single text had meant for him to meet me at the Oak Park public restroom as soon as possible. Or so I'd hoped at the time. I didn't have the code system memorized as well as Dillon did.

We needed to use the code since it was quite possible the Agency was tracking my cell phone. I was an escaped detainee after all.

"You remember my theory on what really happens inside that park restroom, right?"

I somehow managed to smile back. "Of course. It's where all of the Oak Park squirrels meet secretly to plot their eventual invasion and takeover of Roosevelt Park."

Danielle scoffed as she started up her mom's car.

"That's right," Dillon said. "If you've never seen squirrels assemble to plot an invasion before, you're missing out."

I shook my head, and couldn't help but grin. It dawned on me how amazing it felt to have finally cleared the air between me and my best friend. It felt like everything was back to normal between us for the first time since I was handed that package and gotten wrapped up in international espionage in the first place.

"I think we should ditch our phones now," Danielle said. "Just in case."

"Definitely," Dillon agreed. "They can triangulate our positions using them."

We pulled over and dumped both our cell phones into a public trash can near the 4th Avenue bridge. Danielle bid farewell to her phone as if saying a last good-bye a sick grandparent. Dillon, on the other hand, was happy to finally get rid of his. He was probably the only kid in the whole universe who never wanted a cell phone to begin with—the only reason he had one is because his mom made him keep it for emergencies.

"Are the supplies in the trunk?" I asked once we were driving again.

"Oh yeah," Dillon said. "We had way, way more left-overs than we suspected. It's filled to capacity. And this is a 1996 Lincoln Town Car, which easily has the largest trunk of any midsize sedan in history."

"How could you possibly know that?" Danielle asked.

"Because," Dillon explained patiently, "I once had a working theory that certain cars were being marketed specifically to hit men. Greater trunk capacity equals more bodies. More bodies means more hits, which means more money. Right? It's simple math."

We all laughed. It died out quicker than usual, however as we neared the edge of town. Which meant we were getting closer and closer to the grand finale.

Hopefully just the finale of our plan, and not of our lives.

010101010101010101100110010101010101010101010101
101010101010000010100101010100101010100
0101000010010100101010010101010101010101
0001010101010101001100   101010
010101101010001001010   01001
0101000010010100101   010101
0010101010101010011   1010

CHAPTER 60

THE FIELDS OF FIRE

IT WAS STILL DARK OUTSIDE, EVEN AT 5:00 A.M. IT WOULD HAVE been pitch-black where we were, outside of town, a mile or so away from Augustine Church. That is, if not for all the fires.

They burned all around us, massive rolling flames that looked like small torches in the distance. Up close, the flames would have been hot enough to melt off our skin. These fires that dotted the vast plains around us looked even more eerie in the winter at night than in the summer. They were natural gas fires. Oil companies had moved into western North Dakota years ago to start fracking. Which is what they call the way they basically blow up the ground with explosives to get to the oil underneath the bedrock. Anyway, when they do that, a bunch of natural gas escapes. And so they light it on fire to controllably burn it off instead of just letting it pour into the atmosphere.

It's quite a thing to see at night. Miles and miles of darkness dotted by hundreds of massive flames, all underneath a sky blanketed with billions of stars. It should have been pretty, but instead it sort of gave me the creeps.

Fortunately, they weren't close enough to the county road we were on to even provide enough light to see where we were going. Which is precisely how we wanted it. The headlights were off and Danielle squinted over the steering wheel in an effort to stay on the snow-covered gravel road.

It helped that she was only going ten miles per hour. Any faster and we'd have been in a ditch a long time ago. Driving on these county back roads was dangerous enough by itself in the winter, let alone in the dark without headlights. These roads were used so rarely that by

January they were typically undrivable due to snow accumulation.

Keeping the headlights off was a necessary precaution. After all, the Agency was already expecting the exchange to get ambushed. So surely they'd have agents out here on advanced recon for signs of Medlock or his men.

Luckily, I knew these back roads well. My brother used to have a summer job scouting farm fields for crop diseases and he'd brought me along a few times. He'd have reams of old county road maps with him, and I learned them pretty well since he usually let me be the navigator. These were roads not found on any other map and so I was pretty sure we'd be able to sneak in undetected on foot after we silently parked the car in the dark a mile or so away from the church.

"Is this good, you think?" Danielle asked as she pulled the car over onto a flat section of the ditch.

"Yeah, I think so," I said, checking out our location on their mom's GPS. "It'll be a cold walk to the church, but we've got good boots and coats."

"Okay, let's get to work," Dillon said.

We all got out of the car and circled around to the

trunk. Danielle popped it open and I stared at the contents with wide eyes and the sudden feeling that what we were about to do was very, very stupid.

"Maybe this isn't such a good idea," I said.

"It was *your* idea," Danielle reminded me. "You said it's all surface burn, remember?"

I nodded nervously. "I just don't want anybody to get hurt."

"Neither do we," Dillon said, plopping two large plastic sleds from the backseat onto the ground. "Which is why we *need* to do this. Come on, no backing out now."

He was right. And so I started helping him and Danielle unload our cargo onto the two sleds. It didn't take as long as you'd think, considering just how much of it there was. Still, we were all breathing hard and sweating under our winter coats and hats by the time we finished.

"This will definitely do the trick." I panted, while looking down at the two three-person sleds packed to capacity with the payload.

"I hope so," Dillon said, picking up the rope to one of the sleds. He pulled it, testing the weight. It slid smoothly across the ground, but was still a struggle for him.

"Should we lighten the load some?" Danielle suggested.

"No, if we're going to do this, we need to go all out," I said. "No point in taking any chances."

"Yeah, it will be mostly flat ground," Dillon said. "Well, except for the last part anyway."

We all just stood there for a few moments and looked at the two sleds. None of us wanted to say it again, but I think we were all starting to get the idea in our heads that we were making a mistake. That was perhaps the dumbest plan, or prank, any of us had ever come up with.

But, like Dillon said, there was no turning back now.

Right?

CHAPTER 61

INTERCEPTOR, SIGHTSEER, AND THE PUSHMAN

NONE OF US SAID ANYTHING AS WE DRAGGED THE HEAVY sleds a half mile to the low hill in between where we'd parked the car and Augustine Church. There was a small row of trees that ran across the hill and we positioned the sleds in between them to keep them as much out of sight as possible.

Dillon gave Danielle and me each a walkie-talkie and then sat down between the two sleds and saluted us.

"See you guys on the other side," he said. "And stay frosty."

Danielle and I continued down the other side of the hill together. We each somehow resisted the urge to look back up at Dillon. I didn't want to think about what might happen to him if things all went wrong. Or to us, for that matter. But looking back wouldn't have accomplished anything since it would have been too dark to see him anyway.

Danielle and I stayed low and ran between the trees and boulders and abandoned farm shacks as we moved toward Augustine Church. We said nothing as we slowly picked our way to the top of another small hill. Of course, these were hardly hills by most people's standards. More like bumps in the landscape, as if the prairie had acne or something. But in North Dakota, even a small ant mound could be called a hill.

There was an old, crumbling farmhouse near us. Danielle crouched inside it with a riflescope she'd taken from her dad's cache of hunting gear. She peered at Augustine Church down the hill, several hundred yards away. It was still plenty dark, but the faintest hint of pink on the horizon indicated that the sun was on its way up. Which meant the exchange was nearing.

Danielle put the scope down and gave me a thumbs-up.

"Okay then," I said. "I'll see you afterward, right?"

She looked away, clearly struggling not to cry. She nodded without looking up again.

"Don't worry," I said. "I got this. This is what I do. I'm Codename Zero, right?"

Danielle didn't respond and so I didn't waste more time spouting off false confidence. But just as I got to the gaping hole in the western wall of the old house, Danielle finally spoke.

"Carson," she said. I turned around. "Stay frosty."

I gave her a single nod and then dashed outside.

At the bottom of the hill, I hit the deck and flattened down onto my stomach. From here on out, I'd need to be careful. There wasn't much cover between me and Augustine Church.

Still, the Agency was on the lookout for Medlock and probably a whole team of armed men, not one small twelve-year-old crawling across a snow-covered field in the pitch-black. So I actually did believe I had a chance.

It was even colder near the ground, but the adrenaline shooting through my body seemed to work like antifreeze in my veins. I was aware of the cold but didn't feel it. And so I kept crawling across the ground, staying behind the dead stubs of winter wheat stalks.

After several minutes my walkie-talkie crackled with activity.

"Interceptor, this is Sightseer, come in. Over," Danielle's voice said.

I pulled the transmitter from my pocket and hit the button.

"This is Interceptor. Over," I said.

"We have some activity northwest of your position," Danielle said. "Two Agency spotters with binoculars. Only proceed when I give you the go-ahead. Over."

"Copy that," I said.

Then a third voice crackled over the receiver.

"This is Pushman," Dillon said. "Anything near my position, Sightseer?"

"Pushman, you're supposed to say *over* at the end of the transmission. Over," Danielle said.

"Whatever. Over," Dillon said.

"Negative on anything near your position. Over," Danielle said. "Just stay low."

"You forgot to say *over* after the last part. Over," Dillon said.

I heard Danielle sigh into her receiver. Then silence.

I waited for Danielle to give me the go-ahead to proceed. It seemed to last for hours.

"Okay, Interceptor," Danielle finally said. "They're not looking your way. Proceed, but stay low. Over."

I began crawling again, faster this time. I'd need to cover as much ground as possible when I could. It was imperative that I got to the church before the people from the Agency who were making the buy, the people selling the technology, or Medlock arrived. My plan depended on it.

"Cease progress, Interceptor," Danielle said.

I stopped crawling and flattened myself to the ground. More waiting. I was breathing hard, not realizing until just then how much I'd been pushing myself. I wanted to peek up and see just how close I was getting, but knew better. I tried my best to slow my breathing, to remain as still as possible. My radio crackled to life again.

"Sightseer, this is Pushman," Dillon said. "I've got some possible activity on highway fifty-three. Over."

"Copy that," Danielle said. "I see it also. We've got two black sedans approaching from the southwest. They look to be slowing at the county road junction. Over."

I waited and listened.

"The two sedans just turned onto County Road Sixteen, headed this way," Danielle said. "I think it's the Agency buyers. Over."

A few minutes later, Danielle gave me the go-ahead to keep crawling. I did, keeping my eye on the area around the church. There were several good hiding spots nearby. A few trees, an old gazebo, a few outhouses, a row of snow-covered bushes, and even a massive pile of snow that had been plowed behind the church, perhaps by the Agency for this very meeting.

I was getting close enough to start plotting where I'd hunker down until the exchange, when Danielle told me to stop moving again.

"The two cars were definitely Agency," she said. "Agents Smiley and Nineteen and one unidentified agent are all here. And an unidentified fourth individual still inside one of the cars. Over."

I lay there waiting, trying to muffle my visible breath into my gloved hands. In the silence of the early morning, I heard faint talking. I couldn't make out who was speaking or what they were saying, but I heard them nonetheless. If they spotted me, would they shoot on sight, before even figuring out it was me? Or would they shoot anyway, even if they knew it was me? I tried to shake the morbid questions from my head. There was no time for that kind of thinking.

"A large SUV is approaching from the south," Danielle

said. I turned the volume on my receiver down. "Interceptor, if you want to get close, now's your chance. All eyes are on the newcomer."

I didn't even wait for her to say *over* before making my move. I quickly sprang into a crouching run and sprinted toward the back of the church, already knowing where I was going to hide. Staying low, I made my way toward the row of bushes next to the church and then dived right into them face-first. Of course I covered my face with my arms, assuming the bush had branches and everything. Several of them still managed to scratch my cheeks, but the winter sparseness of the huge shrub left plenty of room for me to basically perch inside it.

With all of my winter gear, I sort of figured the best place to hide was inside the snow-covered shrubs. I felt pretty secure and out of sight, oddly cozy even, crouching inside the huge bush. From this vantage point, I could certainly see the two Agency cars pretty clearly, even in the darkness of early dawn. I was perhaps only thirty yards away, obscured slightly by the corner of the old church.

"Interceptor, where are you? Over," Danielle asked.

"Inside the bushes. Over," I whispered into the receiver.

There was a long pause, and I was debating whether or not to risk repeating myself more loudly when she finally responded.

"Wow, took me a long time to spot you," she said. "Great hiding spot. Don't move. Over."

"Any sign of Medlock yet?" Dillon chimed in. "Over."

"Not yet. Over," Danielle said.

We waited and watched in silence from our three triangulated positions. The large gray SUV approached from the south, drawing closer by the second. It turned on to the county road and then eventually pulled up and stopped ten yards away from the Agency's sedans, even closer to me than I was hoping. I'd only been in this business a few months now, but in my experiences, I rarely caught breaks like this.

Once the car pulled up, the fourth person finally stepped out of the Agency's sedan. It was Director Isadoris himself.

Three people got out of the gray SUV. Two were large men in black suits, like bodyguards or something. The third person was a younger man with glasses that looked way too large for his face. He held a small metal case that was handcuffed to his right wrist.

The Exodus Program.

"That must be it, guys," Dillon said. "Should I release the kraken? Over."

"No, not yet," I whispered into my walkie-talkie. "I'll let you know when. Over."

"Okay, will do. Over," Dillon said.

"Pushman, do you have eyes on anyone aside from those at the church?" Danielle asked. "Why haven't we seen any sign of Medlock?"

I had been wondering the same thing. What was his plan? Perhaps he was waiting, and his plan was to intercept the program after the exchange. Which sort of made sense: Then there'd be fewer people to deal with. But then what did the Agency have in mind once he made his move? I guess it didn't matter, since I would be laying down my cards first hopefully, and then neither of their plans would even come into play.

The seller and his bodyguards approached the four agents. They shook hands and then Director Isadoris handed a briefcase to one of the bodyguards. The large woman popped it open and showed the contents to the seller.

"Now?" Dillon asked.

"Just wait!" I snapped. "Sorry, but you need to wait for just the right moment. Over."

There was no reply. The seller peered into the open briefcase, and even from a distance, I saw him smile. I didn't know how much money the Agency was paying for the ability to spy on the world, and I didn't want to know. It was probably over a billion dollars. Which was an impossible amount of money for me to even imagine. My parents made, like, eighty thousand a year combined. That alone seemed like a lot to me.

The bodyguard closed the case. The other one began helping the seller detach his own briefcase from his wrist. This was it. My heart was like a car spinning out of control on a patch of ice.

"Get ready, Pushman," I said into the walkie-talkie.

"Copy that," he said back.

Once the case was detached, he punched in a code on the front while one of the bodyguards held it.

"Now, Dillon, now!" I said.

I took as many deep breaths as I could possibly fit into the next thirty seconds.

The seller reached inside the open briefcase and removed something very small. This was it, my window. Why hadn't anything happened yet? Had Dillon not heard me? Had we been wrong about what we suspected would happen?

"Payload is being delivered," Dillon said, "if you're gonna go, do it now."

I took one last breath and then fired out of the bushes like a bullet. I had only taken a few steps in my sprint toward the exchange when an explosion nearly knocked me off my feet. I stumbled, but stayed up, and then next thing I knew there was screaming everywhere.

Not people, but bottle rockets. Which went along with a massive fireball blossoming just over a nearby hill.

CHAPTER 62

THE CONGRATULATIONS BOOM-BARROW

EVERY HEAD TURNED AWAY FROM ME TOWARD THE CHAOS. They instinctively watched as rockets streamed across the sky, exploding into showers of green and red lights. The main explosion itself was even more intense than I'd expected. It had only been two sleds full of fireworks pushed into a natural gas burn-off flame, after all.

We'd spent years saving up those fireworks. Every Fourth of July we all hung out at nearby Cherry Lake and launched fireworks for hours. We always bought huge variety packs and then stashed away the extras. Over time, we began supplementing the stash with post–Fourth of July discount sales. After six years, we'd amassed a huge stockpile of fireworks. Our plan had been to load them all into a giant wheelbarrow and then set it on fire during our eighth-grade graduation ceremony. We were going to call it the Congratulations Boom-Barrow. But this seemed like an even more important use for them.

The point was this: It was a lot of fireworks. And it served its purpose. Every agent, the seller, and both bodyguards were looking away from me. Which meant I needed to keep moving. I couldn't pause, even for a second, to watch the incredible fireball surrounded by thousands of multicolored fireworks going off.

Instead, I quickly fired a few leftover smoke disks from my hidden wrist launcher that I had recovered from Chum Bucket's supply closet. I'd aimed them right at the exchange point. I'd need to make a clean getaway, after all.

I already had in the special contact lenses that I'd also found among his stash. They had night vision and anti-fog vision, which would let me see the program, even if the smoke was thick. As I approached, there it was, still clutched in the seller's hand.

All of them were crouching and disoriented, trying to

see through the impossibly thick smoke in the pale, red morning light. I sprinted right between the two body-guards and went into a baseball slide. The seller was hunched on the ground, likely trying to get away from the thick smoke and ducking from the errant and wild fireworks explosions. I slid right by him, reached out, and easily plucked the program from his hand as I did so.

And just like that, I was holding a small USB drive.

"The program!" I heard the seller shout. "I've lost the program!"

I turned to retreat toward the church when a hand grabbed my arm. It gripped it so hard that my hand went numb and the USB drive fell out and into the snow.

I looked up. It was one of the seller's massive body-guards. He scowled at me through the smoke, even though I doubted he could see me without antifog contact lenses. But it didn't matter; his grip was like a cyborg's. I struggled, but already I saw him drawing a gun with his other hand.

But then a leg came flying in out of nowhere. The heel from a black dress shoe connected squarely with the bodyguard's jaw. He released me immediately and fell to the ground.

"Get the drive and go!" Agent Nineteen said, as he

followed through on his kick.

He didn't have time to stand there and chat with me, as he spun around and then dived for the bodyguard, who was already reaching out to grab the gun he'd dropped. I didn't wait around to see if he got it back or not. Instead, I hit the deck and searched on my hands and knees for the USB drive.

I found it, snatched it up, and then sprinted back toward the old church and its many hiding spots.

A few seconds later, I heard gunfire. Lots of it. I had no idea if they were shooting at me or at one another or just into the air. It sounded as if it was coming from everywhere. There was shouting, gunfire, and the sound of more fireworks explosions.

I kept my head down and sprinted as I fired more smoke disks all around me. It was so smoky now that without my special contacts I'd probably have crashed right into the side of the old church and gotten a concussion at minimum, and more likely been knocked unconscious. But they somehow cleared the smoke from my vision just enough to give me time to react when the church came into view. I veered right and dived head first through a giant hole in the side of the ancient building.

After quickly scrambling to my feet, I ran down the

center aisle, between rows of ancient pews. The back door was gone, which left a wide-open exit for me to continue my retreat. I headed toward it, still running as quickly as my tired legs would go.

But I had to hit the brakes suddenly as a large figure filled the doorway, blocking my path. I wasn't able to stop in time, and stumbled on the slick cold floor. The figure stepped aside and allowed me to basically fall onto my face in the snow just outside the old church.

I rolled over and looked up.

Medlock stood over me, grinning. He pointed toward the USB drive still clutched in my right hand.

"Carson," he said smugly. "Once again, you've proven yourself to be so very useful."

CHAPTER 63

SOMEONE SAID BOOM

I HEARD HIS WORDS CLEARLY EVEN THROUGH THE GUNFIRE AND shouting that continued all around us. He stared down at me with that infuriating grin on his face. Once again he thought he'd outsmarted me. Used me to help him get exactly what he wanted.

But this time, he had actually played right into *my* hands.

So I smiled back.

"I'm glad you found me among the chaos," I said, "since this is exactly what I wanted to happen."

356

His smile twitched but didn't go away. He removed the small device with the button from his pocket and held it up.

"Remember this?" he said. "Hand over the program, or I press the button. Agency headquarters will be no more."

"I was hoping you'd say that," I said.

Without waiting for any kind of reply, I calmly removed six large cherry bombs with shortened fuses from my pocket. They were taped together into a giant megacherry bomb. I sandwiched the USB drive between them quickly, more deftly than I'd suspected my shaking fingers could have moved.

"What are you doing?" Medlock asked, his smile finally gone. "I'll press the button!"

I pulled out a small lighter and lit the shortened fuses, tossing the megabomb to my left almost immediately. Before it even hit the ground there was a relatively small pop. Had there not been a raging gun battle happening on the other side of the church, the whole thing probably would have been more dramatic. But as it was, the force was still strong enough to blow the USB drive into dozens of small pieces.

"No!" Medlock yelled. He pressed a button on his

device. "You just destroyed the Agency, my little friend. It may take a few minutes for the reactor to overheat, but the explosion is inevitable now. The process is irreversible."

"Good," I said, and I meant it.

Medlock tossed aside the device and pulled out a handgun. He pointed it at my face and suddenly my joy at having the plan go about as well as could be hoped for evaporated in an instant.

"Now I will finally get to destroy you," he said.

I closed my eyes and waited for the dark.

0001010101010101010100110010101010101010101
1010101010100001010010101010010101010
0101000010010100101010010101010101010
0001010101010101010011001   10101
0101011010100010010   0100
010100001001010010   010
0001010101010101001101   1010

CHAPTER 64

THE FOURTH PARTY ARRIVES

I FIGURED I'D BE DEAD BEFORE I EVEN HEARD THE GUNSHOT. Which is why it surprised me when a sudden crack rang out. It surprised me even more when I was able to open my eyes a few seconds later. Was he really that bad a shot? Had he missed me entirely?

But then I saw that Medlock was no longer holding his gun. Instead, he was clutching a bloody hand to his chest, cradling it like a fresh puppy. The smoking remnants of his pistol lay on the ground between us.

That's when I became aware of the sounds of a

helicopter above me. A chopper was descending about twenty yards away. Hanging out of the open side door was NSB Agent Loften. He was holding a rifle with a scope, which he set aside as the chopper landed.

He and several other agents rushed over. Agent Loften helped me to my feet, while the other two began restraining Medlock, who seemed to be in a sort of shocked daze.

"Right on time," I said.

"It was quite a challenge convincing my superiors to trust me on this," Agent Loften said. "I can still hardly believe it myself. If it weren't for the missing evidence, and the fact that your old principal really didn't seem like any sort of evil mastermind, I probably would have hung up on you. But something about your school didn't sit right with me; I hadn't liked it from the moment I got there. I'm glad you still had my card and thought to call me."

That's when I noticed that the gunfire had stopped. The sounds of more helicopters and cars were all around us. Sirens blared, and men were screaming at people to drop their weapons and get down on the ground. Since we were on the other side of the church, I couldn't see what was actually happening, but I knew those were the sounds of the NSB apprehending everyone else involved.

I didn't know what they'd do with the people from the Agency; the Agency's existence was classified even from the NSB, so it would probably take a long time for them to sort it all out. A pang of guilt stabbed at my guts. But it had to be done. I knew that more now than ever before.

"Where's the Exodus Program?" Agent Loften asked.

"Destroyed," I said, pointing at the fragments of USB drive at his feet.

He frowned and then waved one of his fellow agents over.

"Bag it," he said, pointing at the pieces. He turned back to me. "Come on, I'll give you a ride back to town."

I followed Agent Loften back toward his helicopter. The other two agents were escorting Medlock, one on each side. The damage to his hand from Loften's shot was apparently too severe to handcuff him. Not that it mattered—he looked truly defeated, his head was down and he shuffled his feet along reluctantly but without much fight.

I looked back toward the exchange point again. Director Isadoris was on his knees, handcuffed and getting his Miranda rights read to him. He looked at me. And if eyeballs could fire bullets, my brains would have been all over Agent Loften's jacket.

Director Isadoris looked back at the agent reading him his rights and began shouting something about how he would be sorry and he outranked everyone there and they were making a big mistake and all that sort of thing.

Next to him, Agent Nineteen was also handcuffed, but he wasn't struggling or shouting or anything. He was actually smiling. Smirking at seeing Director Isadoris acting like such a lunatic. Then he looked right at me and nodded.

I nodded back.

Dillon and Danielle were near the helicopter, talking to a pair of NSB agents. When they saw I was okay, they smiled and waved. I smiled and waved back.

That's when the ground began to shake. It rumbled so violently that everybody fell. The earth spun as I tumbled to the ground.

And I realized the truth: Agency HQ had just been completely incinerated.

```
0001010101010101001100101010101010101
010101010101000010100101010100101010101
010100001001010010101001010101010101010
0001010101010101001100                10101
010101101010001001                    0100
010100001001010010                    010
0010101010101010011                    101
```

CHAPTER 65

WHEN A TWO PERCENT CHANCE OF SURVIVAL SOUNDS PROMISING

THE NEXT THING I REALIZED, I WAS PROPPED UP ON MY ELBOWS, the world still spinning. My vision blurred and I noticed that most everyone else was still on the ground, unconscious. My first thought was the utter horror at realizing just how violent the explosion must have been to have shaken the ground all the way out here. I was suddenly having visions of an eight-city-block crater in the middle of Minnow, a hole in the earth that had swallowed hundreds of homes and thousands of people. And it was my fault. What had I been thinking?

But that's when I noticed that one person was on his feet, running toward the helicopter. It was Medlock, his two NSB escorts still on the ground in a daze. I watched in horror as he reached the chopper, leaned over and grabbed Dillon's body and then climbed inside the cockpit, taking him along.

Every part of me screamed at me to stay down. The violence of the earthquake had rattled every joint and organ in my body. But the sight of Medlock getting away with my best friend washed all that away.

I was on my feet before I even realized what was happening, sprinting toward the helicopter as it began rising off the ground. I got there and put everything I had into a massive running leap.

Somehow, I just managed to hook an arm on one of the chopper's landing skids. The helicopter rose off the ground with me dangling from it. I told myself not to look down, and for once, I listened. Instead, I just focused on pulling myself inside the back of the helicopter. But I couldn't budge. I locked my right hand around my left wrist, hugging the landing skid.

I had no idea how high we actually were now, but the cold wind whipping across my face told me we were definitely moving fast. And so if I let go, I'd surely be as good as dead.

That's when I felt a pair of hands grab my arm. I looked up and saw Danielle's face close to my own. She nodded at me and then pulled me up inside the helicopter.

Once inside, she held a finger to her lips and ducked behind the bulkhead where the pilot's seat was. I followed, crouching next to her behind the divider.

"I saw him grab Dillon and so I hopped aboard," she said.

The noise of the helicopter was so loud that we could talk without fear of being heard up front. In fact, we could barely even hear each other, even though we were shouting, and our faces were only a foot apart.

"Me, too," I shouted. "What's the plan?"

Danielle shrugged. "I just jumped on. Thought we'd figure that part out later."

"Well, we have to do something," I said.

I leaned back slightly and looked up front. I saw Dillon slumped in the passenger seat. Blood matted his forehead. He must have hit his head when he fell during the earthquake. The good news was that I saw his chest rising and falling, so he was still alive.

When I turned back, I saw that Danielle was gone. I spun around and then saw her holding a huge wrench, creeping her way up toward the cockpit. I lunged forward to stop her, to remind her that if she knocked out Medlock, none of us knew how to pilot a helicopter. But she was already aware of that, because instead of hitting him with the huge wrench, she merely threatened him.

"Take us back down or I'll smash your face!" she screamed.

Medlock turned, looking startled for only a moment. Then he actually smiled.

"I should have known that I couldn't get away from you," he said. "Even up here!"

Then he quickly pitched the helicopter to the side. Danielle stumbled and had to drop the wrench to keep from falling out of the helicopter through the open side door. I also slid across the floor but grabbed a pouch on the back of the passenger seat.

Medlock leveled the chopper again and then pointed a finger back at Danielle.

"Don't move again, or I will crash this thing!" he yelled. "Don't think I won't. I'd rather be dead than in prison."

He clearly had no idea I was also onboard. Danielle

nodded at Medlock and then sat down, her arm wrapped around a safety handle to keep from falling out. She glanced at me quickly, a signal that it was up to me now.

I crawled slowly over to the wrench. I wrapped my hand around the hard metal. There were three choices facing me:

1. Pick this thing up and just knock out Medlock without warning, leaving one of us to fly the helicopter. Probability of fatal crash: 97.4 percent.
2. Try to threaten Medlock again, testing his promise about crashing it on purpose. Probability of fatal crash: 99.3 percent.
3. Just stay low and out of sight and go along for the ride. Probability of death at the hands of Medlock after landing somewhere where his henchmen were waiting: 100 percent.

Clearly, surviving this would be a miracle. But, even still, there was the one option which was slightly better than the rest.

And so I stood up and swung the wrench toward the cockpit in one swift motion. It was a lot heavier than I expected and suddenly I was worried that it might actually kill Medlock. As much as I hated the guy, I didn't want to kill him. Part of me still felt kind of bad for him—it sounded like he was an okay guy before the Agency drove him to madness.

But it was too late, the wrench too heavy to pull back now. It connected with the back of Medlock's skull with a solid *crack*. He slumped forward and then I looked at Danielle and our eyes met and we both knew we were screwed.

Neither of us had any idea how to fly a helicopter!

CHAPTER 66

NOBODY WANTS
TO DIE IN THE RAT RIVER

THE HELICOPTER DIDN'T ENTER INTO A FREE-FALLING TAILSPIN death dive right away. Instead it just sort of lurched and shuddered.

I clambered up front, next to Dillon. Danielle hovered between us and the pilot's seat. She didn't lecture me for knocking out the only pilot. Instead, she calmly grabbed the yoke and tried to hold it steady.

But we could still feel the helicopter begin to descend rather rapidly.

"What do we do?" I shouted.

"I don't know!" Danielle shouted back.

And that's when Dillon woke up and spoke.

"Grab the collective!" he shouted.

"I think he has a concussion!" I yelled over the whirring blades. "He's talking crazy!"

"No, I'm not, grab the collective," he repeated, sitting up.

"What's that?" Danielle asked.

"It's a handle on the left side of the pilot's seat," he shouted. "It controls the throttle and the lift. We're losing altitude because Medlock's hand must be pressing it down!"

I climbed over Medlock's body to find the collective.

"Since when do you know how to fly a helicopter?" Danielle asked her brother.

"Well, I don't technically," he said. "But I read a helicopter manual once, since I thought it contained a coded message about where to find Forrest Fenn's buried treasure."

"Who's what now?" Danielle asked.

"Guys, it doesn't matter!" I shouted. "I can't reach the collective."

I leaned back and grabbed Medlock's shirt. Danielle and I pulled him into the back, while Dillon slipped over into the pilot's seat without needing to be told. We tied Medlock to a nylon net bolted to the wall of the helicopter, to make sure he wouldn't fall out. He had blood on the back of his skull and I truly hoped I hadn't killed him.

Danielle and I joined Dillon up front again. The helicopter felt steadier, but we were still descending, and wobbling like a toddler's first steps.

"Guys, I don't think I can actually land this!" Dillon said. "I've never flown one before. I mean, I theoretically know how to use the pedals, and collective, and yoke, but that's about it . . ."

He trailed off as he saw what Danielle and I had just noticed ourselves. We were flying over the school. Except . . . there was no school. Where Erik Hill Middle School used to be was now just a massive hole in the earth, filled with rubble and concrete and debris. The school had completely caved into the ground at least a hundred feet.

But I was relieved to at least see that the destruction was limited to just the school grounds.

A sudden warning chime brought our attention back to the dire situation at hand. I'd nearly forgotten that we were in the middle of crashing a helicopter.

"I can't . . . I don't know what I'm doing!" Dillon

shouted as he continued to struggle with the controls.

"We feel pretty steady," Danielle said hopefully. "We're not, like, spinning wildly or plunging toward the ground in a fireball."

"Yeah, well, just the same I promise it will be a bumpy landing!" Dillon said.

"There!" I pointed. "Aim for the wide bend in the Rat River. If we're going to crash, better to do it on water, right?"

Dillon nodded and did his best to steer us toward the quickly approaching river. Seemingly every year, some guy fell through the thin ice and drowned in the Rat River. And every time it happened thousands of people like me called them idiots for walking on a frozen river too early in the winter. Which is why nobody ever wanted to die in the Rat River.

And now here we were, willingly try to crash into the icy river. But, at least this way the water would hopefully put out any fires so we wouldn't burn to death if we somehow survived the impact.

"You can do this, Dillon!" Danielle said as we got closer and closer to the river. "You can do this!"

"I think I'm doing it!" Dillon said suddenly. Then panic spread across his face. "But if I land us safely, we're still going to smash through the ice! If I'd known I was such a good pilot, I never would have agreed to land here!"

But it turned out Dillon had nothing to worry about. Because he wasn't that good of a helicopter pilot. He wasn't a helicopter pilot at all. That much was very clear when we were ten feet from the frozen surface of the water. It rushed up toward us in a fraction of a second and then we crashed into the river with a sickening and deafening crunch of metal and glass.

And then all I remember is pain, icy cold water running around me, numbing my body and pushing me into darkness.

0000101010101010101001100101010101010101
0101010101010000101001010101001010101010
1010100001001010010101010010101010101010
000010 001100101010101010101
0010 0010101010010101010100
101 010101001010101010101
000 1001010101010101010101

CHAPTER 67

WHAT PUTTING THE PAL IN PRINCIPAL REALLY MEANS

I WOKE WITH SOMEONE'S ARMS WRAPPED AROUND MY CHEST. I was being dragged out of the water and onto a snowy bed of ice that felt a lot warmer than it should have. The person dragged me across the ice and then flopped me up onto the shore. I assumed it was Danielle at first, but then I looked over and saw her blue lips trembling next to me.

She looked over and smiled. Her mouth was full of blood and she was missing one of her two front teeth. I hoped she wasn't dying, but I was too cold to say anything.

I looked to my right and saw Dillon on the other side of me. He was sitting up, his arms wrapped around his legs, shivering.

If they were there, then who saved me? Was it Medlock?

Then I saw Ms. Pullman's face hovering above me. She smiled and tapped my face lightly.

"Carson?" she said. "Carson, stay awake!"

"W-w-wh-wh-what a-a-r-r-r-e y-you d-d-oing he-h-here?" I managed to mumble through my chattering teeth.

"I came to the school to make sure it was evacuated," she said. "Then it collapsed into itself. A short time later I saw your helicopter crash in the river. Don't worry, the ambulance is on the way. What's going on, Carson?"

She was shivering, too. She'd clearly had to get into the river herself to pull us from the helicopter's wreckage. I closed my eyes, wanting to rest. I just felt like I needed rest. A hand slapped me.

"Stay awake, Carson!" Ms. Pullman yelled. "Come on, talk to me."

"Th-th-ere's . . ." I started, but then paused. Did I really want to do this? But then I realized I had to, I couldn't just let him die. "Th-there's an-n-n-other-r m-m-an in the ch-ch-chopper. But be care-f-f-fu-l-l-l, h-h-he's the b-b-b-ad guy."

Ms. Pullman nodded and didn't even hesitate as she disappeared from my view. I craned my neck enough to look up. She was running across the ice toward a twisted mess of metal and glass that looked more like a pile of scrap metal than a helicopter. It was a true miracle any of us had survived the impact.

I put my head back down. My neck and head and body hurt far too badly to watch her climb back into that freezing water on an evil psychopath's behalf. I closed my eyes again.

Another slap woke me up.

"Carson, stay awake!" Ms. Pullman said.

I was covered in blankets now. As were Dillon and Danielle who were both conscious and sitting next to each other, talking softly. A few people from nearby houses must have spotted us and brought out blankets. I saw several people nearby, looking into the street, likely watching for the ambulance.

"Thank you for saving me," I said.

"Carson . . ." Ms. Pullman said, as if she were about to tell me it's what anyone would have done. But then the rest of the words caught in her throat and tears pushed at her eyelids. Instead of saying anything more, she gave my hand a squeeze and then stood up and walked over toward an ambulance that was just now coming down the street. An NSB sedan and two cop cars were right behind it.

A low moan called out a name to my right.

"Jake," the voice said. "Jake, I did it for you. I just wanted my son back."

Medlock was lying next to me, also covered in blankets. He looked over, his face bloody. We made eye contact and all I saw in them were sadness and heartache.

"Where's my boy?" he asked. "Where did they take Jake?"

"I don't know," I said. "But Agent Nineteen wouldn't let anything happen to him. I know that's hard for you to believe but it's true. Whatever happened to you guys in the past is gone. He's different now, and I promise he didn't let the Agency harm Jake. You'll see him again."

Medlock blinked. He breathed in and out deeply, laboring to get out more words. But he couldn't. And so instead he reached out a bloody hand that was missing a few fingers. It was gross, but I wasn't about to leave a possibly dying man hanging.

So I reached out and grabbed Medlock's hand. It was

cold, even in spite of the warm blood flowing out of it. And then Medlock actually smiled at me.

And that's the last thing I remembered before blacking out again. Lying there next to my two best friends on the riverbank in the snow, holding the freezing cold and bloody hand of my archnemesis, Mule Medlock.

CHAPTER 68

AGENT ZERO IS DEAD

THE FALLOUT FROM THAT DAY WAS INSANITY. IT'S HARD TO EVEN explain what happened to everyone. But I'll do my best based on what little I know.

Principal Gomez was cleared of all charges against him. I heard he ended up retired somewhere down south. I wish that old jerk the best. Seriously.

As for the school, well, it didn't fare so well. The way Agency HQ was constructed prevented any leakage of radioactive material after its implosion, but it still caused the school above it to basically cave in completely. Classes eventually resumed later that year inside the town's civic center until a new school could be constructed. Nobody died in the blast, and Ms. Pullman and I have yet to discuss what happened that early morning before she found us in the crashed helicopter.

In the meantime, she was hailed by the media as a hero for issuing an evacuation order that morning, preventing the deaths of several janitors and extracurricular weekend school groups. Oh, and also for pulling three kids and an unidentified man from the burning wreckage sinking in the freezing Rat River. She is still the school's principal, the best one it's ever had. And she's my hero, too.

You're probably wondering about Jake Tyson-Gulley, too. He was finally returned to his mom's custody. He has yet to return to school and supposedly is seeing a therapist three times a week. He refuses to reveal to anybody where he was all that time. But he seems largely okay. I just hope Jake doesn't hold any sort of grudge against me. . . .

Dillon and Danielle are still my best friends, and the two coolest kids I know. After everything that happened, I think we can safely say that will never change.

And Medlock, well . . . I don't know much about

where he ended up. But I do know he survived and the NSB detained him and is holding him in a maximum-security federal prison specializing in terrorists. But his existence is no longer a classified secret, and he's not going to "disappear," to put it the way the Agency would have. Agent Loften has assured me that his chances of escape are as close to zero as you can get, but at least he won't be forgotten. After everything that happened, I think it's important that people remember. I don't know if he ever saw his son again, but part of me hopes so. I did make the man a promise after all, and despite who he is, I hope it didn't make me a liar.

The collapse of Agency headquarters, although never publicly tied to the Agency, exposed them within government circles. Which, in essence, forced the government's hand, and the Agency was finally disbanded several months later by the president. When their existence became public, there was a lot of outrage, a lot of peaceful protests and such over just how much the United States government was hiding from its citizens. Supposedly Director Isadoris was transferred to some boring, low-level desk job at the NSB, which was more than he deserved, if you ask me. He must have struck some kind of deal, but I don't know the details.

And as for the last two people you're probably wondering about, well, I saw them only one more time. It was a few weeks after that crazy morning when the world seemed to collapse on itself. A car showed up at my house and two men came to our door. One of them was Agent Loften. He said he needed to take me downtown to tie up a few loose ends. My parents reluctantly agreed. Basically, anything short of an actual NSB agent saying he needed to see me for purposes of national security couldn't get me out of my room at that time. I was *that* grounded.

Anyway, Agent Loften drove me to some weird unmarked brick building on the edge of town.

"Uh, am I being assassinated?" I asked as we parked around back.

"What?" he asked. Then he laughed. "No! Why would you even think that?"

I wanted to reply, "Because it's something the Agency would probably do." But instead I just shrugged.

"Your presence was requested," Agent Loften said.

"By who?"

"Two old friends who wanted to say good-bye."

Nothing more was said and a short time later, I found myself sitting in a small room at a small table across from

Agent Nineteen and Agent Blue. They both looked okay. Better than I'd seen them in a long time, actually.

I couldn't meet their stares at first. They had saved me, even after I had betrayed them. I had broken almost every cardinal rule of being an agent, and put their lives at risk, and they still worked to save mine, twice. How could I ever face them again?

"Carson, we forgive you," Agent Nineteen said right away.

"I'm sorry," I said.

"He just said we forgive you already," Agent Blue snapped.

"Sorry," I mumbled.

"Look at us," Agent Nineteen said.

I looked up. He smiled at me. So did Agent Blue.

"You did what you had to do," Agent Nineteen said. "What you needed to do. We get that. Things with the Agency had gone too far, and we couldn't see it. You could."

I nodded. "Thank you."

"It's a miracle you didn't get us all killed, though," Agent Blue added.

I shrugged as Agent Nineteen elbowed him gently in the ribs.

"What's going to happen to you guys?" I asked.

"I'm being transferred to the Utah branch of the NSB," Agent Blue said. "Yippee."

I ignored his sarcasm and looked at Agent Nineteen.

"I'll be with the CIA," Agent Nineteen said. "But maybe it's best if I don't say where. You know how it is."

"Yeah," I said with a laugh. "I guess I do."

"We just wanted you to know before we go," Agent Nineteen said, "that you really were one of the best agents I've ever worked with. Well, one of the best and worst. I mean, your instincts and natural talent are admirable. But in order to do this job correctly, you sometimes have to choose between the mission and your friends. I don't think you can really ever make that choice."

I nodded, because he was probably right.

"What he's trying to say is," Agent Blue said, "we respect you. And there are no hard feelings. You made the choice we couldn't. We should have trusted you more, all of us. We realize that now."

"Thank you," I said, trying to fight back the tears.

"One more thing." Agent Nineteen stopped, looked over my shoulder for more than a few seconds before continuing. "The story Medlock told you is true. I was young then, a fool. I thought I was doing the right thing by following orders, and I've been following those same orders every day since, trying to justify what I did. But doing the right thing isn't about blindly following orders. It's about finding people you trust, and staying true to them. It was time someone showed me that. Anyway, best of luck to you, Agent Zero."

"Please," I said. "Call me Carson."

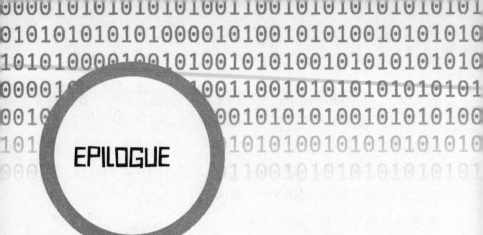

SIX MONTHS LATER

MILITARY SCHOOL SUCKS.

So does Nebraska. In fact, it's almost as bad as North Dakota.

That said, at least I don't have to wake up every day worried about some evil genius plotting to destroy the world or anything. And I'm not getting lied to on a regular basis. Nor am I lying to my friends all the time anymore. Military school is pretty simple that way. Which is kind of appealing.

Every day is the same thing. You get up at the crack

of dawn. Run four miles. Shower. Eat breakfast. Go to classes all day. After school you either practice with a sports team or work out more with your unit. Then it's study time. Then dinner. Then a few hours of free time. Then lights-out. Rinse and repeat.

Weekends are nice. We have more free time then. Sometimes Dillon and Danielle come down to visit. On most weekends I actually like to go to a nearby park to write, if you can believe that. That's where I am right now, writing all of this down.

"Excuse me," a voice says, as a shadow drifts across my page.

I look up. A man in a tracksuit is standing over me. He looks like he's out for a run except that he isn't sweating or breathing hard.

"Yeah?" I say.

"Are you Carson Fender?"

"Maybe."

"My name is Scarecrow and I've been watching you for some time," the man says. "We have been watching you."

"Oh man," is all I can think to say.

"The work you did last year makes you uniquely suited to a certain job," he says. "I work for an organization so

classified that it technically doesn't even exist. We call ourselves the Entity. Our main goal is to monitor all other government and nonaffiliated agencies for security breaches and ethical protocols. We're basically the world's lone, universal undercover police force. We're like the cops of the cops."

I sit there and wait for what I know is coming next.

"We need your help," he says. "Are you up for it?"